ASCENT FROM ASH

SILVER TALONS GUILD: BOOK TWO

C.L. CARNER

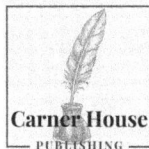

Carner House
PUBLISHING

CARNER HOUSE PUBLISHING

FOREWORD

Although the first book in this series started as a young adult fantasy, the characters have grown up and are now taking over kingdoms. With royalty; comes the duty to marry and continue the royal line. For my family members who support me and read my books, I feel the need to tell you in advance that parts of this book were heavily influenced by the memories of reading the collection of Harlequin Romance novels that Grandma gave me in high school and of course, the BookTok community and their recommendations. This book is intended for ages 18+ and contains; adult language, sexual situations, violence, pregnancy, and one scene between dragons that involves SA by coercion, but I promise, in the end, the bad guy gets what he deserves.

PROLOGUE

THE HISTORY OF ASH

A generation before the kingdom of ASH was known as such, it was known by another name. It was called Adesh. Like many of the kingdoms across the sea, Adesh was named for its Queen, Anu Adesh. She had been born into the role of Monarch. Her father died before she was born, and shortly after her birth, the same fever took her mother too. For many years, the Regent sat the throne in Anu's stead, until she came of age.

On the fourteenth anniversary of her birth, Anu was crowned Queen and sat upon the throne for the very first time. For seven years, the kingdom struggled and commoners had to choose between paying their taxes or feeding their families. Angry villagers stormed the castle gates daily, those who made it past the stationary guards, were often caught by sentries in the castle gardens trying to steal whatever they could carry.

Queen Anu ordered her men to expand the dungeon to make room for the thieves who would dare steal from the royal gardens. The miner's families received a month's compensation for the miner's absence in advance and then they started to dig. The hammering of pickaxes and the chipping and cracking of stone echoed through the castle for days, until they were well beneath the old stone floor.

The miners discovered coal, and sparkling white diamonds in the depths of the dungeon, and when the Queen's captain of the guard saw what they had found he ordered them to keep digging and extracting the diamonds. The miners had no concept of day or night, they lost track of how long they had been digging. Their families came to the Queen often to ask when the men would be able to come home, and her response was always the same. Queen Anu would put two gold pieces in their hand and say; "soon." The truth of it was, there were too few of them. To get the work done faster, Anu needed more men.

She asked the nearby kingdom of Ledora to send help. In return, she promised to send each miner back with his weight in gold- after she sold the diamonds, of course. The King of Ledora happily sent willing miners to earn their riches, but one day the wall of the mine collapsed, and water came rushing in. The ceiling caved in and buried most of them alive. Those who weren't buried, drowned.

The townspeople heard the commotion and the rumbling from underground. They gathered around the castle awaiting news and hoping to see their loved ones emerge. When they found out that the miners were lost in the collapse and would not be returning, they went mad. Mobs of people stormed the castle. When news traveled back to Ledora, the King sent a group of his soldiers to demand the payment promised, each man returned *with* his weight in gold. The king felt it was the very least Queen Anu could do for the many families that were now grieving because of her greed.

William Lazar, a local sugar cane farmer, and rum runner, led the group of Adeshi men inside the castle; they found the queen and delivered swift justice as the mobs outside burned the kingdom to the ground in protest. William ascended the steps to the throne and sat upon it.

"Adesh will henceforth be known as The Kingdom of Ash, to remind us all of how we suffer under a tyrant's hand. I will do my duty to the realm and build a kingdom from the ashes like no one has ever seen!" The soldiers in the throne room all took a knee and bowed to their new king.

"All hail, King William, of Ash!"

Three years into his reign, at the urging of the King's Counsel, William took a wife and had three children; Theo, Natalia, and Anca. His wife, Queen Clarice, passed due to fever shortly after their youngest was born.

As king, William grew the sugar cane fields and expanded the rum-making warehouses. Soon, the kingdom of Ash was the leading producer of rum in the world. King William was well-loved by the people of Ash because he always paid them fairly, took care of the families of his workers, and took the kingdom from squalor to riches. Despite his popularity, the king was unhappy. He longed to sail the seas again. The memories of his time with the rum runners in the years before he took the throne were second only to the memories of his children being born. He vowed to prepare Theo to take his crown, and when he stepped down, then he would retire to the sea.

In an effort to restore peace between Ash and Ledora, King William wrote to the Ledoran king and offered a betrothal of his eldest daughter, Natalia to Prince Haki, who would take the Ledoran throne after his father.

The King of Ledora saw this offer as a great insult and he refused to wed his son, Prince of Ledora to the second in line for the throne of Ash. In the years following this failed betrothal, many men and women came to court. There was a banquet, and a ball every full moon. Theo met a raven-haired beauty named Luciana and became enchanted. They courted for a few years before they married. Luciana was the youngest of four children. She had three brothers in line for the throne in her own kingdom, and there were whispers in the beginning that it was for this very reason she set her sights on Theo.

Anca, the youngest, and by far the bravest of King William's children, disappeared one day. It was rumored that she disguised herself as a boy and left with the rum runners, although that was never confirmed. William was overcome with grief. His interest in ruling diminished more every day.

Natalia married a noble that she met at court from Immernacht, a kingdom far east. After they wed, she went with him back to his kingdom as wives were expected to do. William knew that his time had come. He held a coronation for Theo and named him King of Ash. Two weeks later, William was at sea once more.

Shortly after King Theo announced that his wife was to give birth to their first child, he became ill. During the time King Theo spent bedridden, a dragon attacked the kingdom and burned the sugar cane fields to the ground. It had been the first sighting in a decade, and it had been a black dragon at that. No one knew much about them, the black dragons were rarely spotted, even in the days before the age of Kings when dragons were everywhere. No one knew if it was because there were fewer of them, or if they were just smarter than the others; smart enough to avoid humans most of the time.

Theo tried to get news to the rum runners and his father, but word came back that their ship had been destroyed by a monstrous sea creature in Blackwater Bay. Theo grew weaker every day, and his dear, pregnant wife Luciana sat at his bedside quietly praying to the gods for his recovery. The sickness took him in the night; the next morning, Luciana was crowned Queen. With the rum runners out of business, and the sugar cane fields now barren, Luciana began taxing for imports and taxing the businesses within the kingdom.

No one liked giving up that which they had earned, especially when it was barely enough to feed their families as it was without the sugar cane income. Families who could afford it bought passage to other kingdoms and only those who were too poor to leave remained in Ash.

By the time her daughter was born, Luciana was finished being abandoned. She never bonded with her child. Akiri was nourished by the wet nurses and looked after by the castle staff. Akiri learned magic, and how to crew a ship, but she never learned what love was, not even from her mother.

I

AKIRI

T he clicking of Akiri's heels on the stone floor echoed through the council chamber as she paced back and forth across the room. Six men sat at the long rectangular table, three on each side. They looked at her expectantly.

"How many gladiators have signed up for the tournament?" She asked.

"Forty, Your Grace." The answer came from a thin weasel-faced man who sat in the middle seat on the left side of the table.

"What is the entry fee?" She asked.

"One hundred gold pieces."

"How about we require an entry fee for each event instead of the whole tournament? We can lower the entry fee to fifty gold, but then it will be fifty for the joust, fifty for beast taming, another fifty for hand-to-hand combat, and yet another fifty for weapons combat. Assuming the knight or gladiator wanted to participate in all the events, that would be two hundred gold pieces each."

"Then would the prize be increased as well?" the weasel-faced man, Timothy Ackerman inquired.

"Instead of one prize, each event could have its own purse. The winner will get thirty percent of the pool." Akiri shrugged her shoulders and widened her eyes as if to ask them what they thought of the idea. They mulled it over for a moment or two then they each began nodding in agreement.

"Now that the tourney is sorted out, My Queen, we must discuss diplomacy." The man seated next to Akiri on the right side of the table stood up.

"Okay, what have you today, Ser William?" Akiri asked.

"You have a proposal from a Ser Archibald Wentworth of Braidwood. Next, another proposal, this time from a man who claims to be immortal. He has offered his gift of immortality for your hand."

Akiri nodded and rolled her eyes. "He wishes to be king, and even if he *is* immortal, that just means that we would be stuck with the same king, and queen forever. I wake up some days not sure if I want to do this job at all, let alone *forever.* What else do you have?"

"Your lair is almost complete. According to all the tomes we have requested from Ravenhall, you will be able to produce a clutch of eggs soon, they will only produce dragons if..." The man cleared his throat and gave Akiri an uneasy look. "If they are fertilized, Your Grace." He quickly looked away from her."

"I only know of one male dragon, and there is no way he would help me produce a clutch, he is the son of King Haki of Ledora. The other two dragons were female, and I am pretty sure they killed the black dragon. How are we going to find another male dragon?" Akiri asked.

"Perhaps we do not need another *dragon.* My Queen." The man bowed to her and then took his seat once more.

"Does anyone else have anything to add?" Akiri asked. The silence was the only thing that followed, so Akiri adjourned the meeting. As she rolled Ser William's words over in her mind, her head became heavy, she felt the need for fresh air. Akiri didn't wait for the men to get out of their seats. She pushed past the table and rushed out the back door and across the western courtyard to the newly constructed arena. Akiri stopped and felt the wind on her face as she closed her eyes and after removing her robes, she began to shift into her dragon form. It was easier now, It used to hurt, but now it felt like a good stretch. Akiri's large green talons dug into the sand as she prepared to run the length of the jousting arena. The sidelines became a blur as her feet moved faster, propelling her forward. A cloud of dust expanded out from beneath her wings as she took flight. The air was cool on her face and little droplets of condensation from the clouds clung to her whole body as she ascended into the sky. She always flew above the clouds, trying to remain out of sight. She read of dragon hunters in the ancient texts and feared that she would one day be hunted too.

Akiri flew across the kingdom, and to the western sea. When there was no land nearby, Akiri dipped down to the edge of the water, dragging her feet lightly across the surface. When she ascended again, she rolled to one side, and then the other, and then went upside-down as she rolled into a flip, dancing in the sky to a tune that only she could hear.

Akiri thought about the council meeting and Ser William's words. What would she even do with a clutch of dragon eggs if she had them? She knew that they could teach the dragons to defend the kingdom, but beyond that, she had no idea who would be responsible for raising them, or more importantly, feeding them. Would the dragons share the ability to shift into human form, or would they only be dragons? Akiri couldn't stop thinking about all the questions, flying was supposed to help her clear her mind, but she found that it was not working in her current situation. Akiri's counsel brought up the subject of her marriage quite often as of late. She knew that it was a royal's duty to marry and have children so that the kingdom would always have a ruler, but Akiri never wanted children when she was younger and the thought of being a mother used to make her feel ill, but dragons sounded nice. She wondered if she were cut out to rule the kingdom after all.

When Akiri landed back in the jousting arena she saw someone in the stands. A frail-looking figure wearing all black. The person's hood was drawn, obscuring their face in the darkness. As Akiri picked up her robe and hastily pulled it on, she hurried further toward the arena's exit. Akiri saw the figure turn to follow her, so she quickened her pace.

Akiri broke into a sprint and ran from the arena to the castle doors, then up the grand staircase, and down the left-side corridor to her chamber. She only let out a sigh of relief when she closed and barred the heavy oak door behind her.

Akiri leaned her back against the door with her eyes closed until her breathing slowed; but the second she opened her eyes, the figure was standing right in front of her. She could see the face clearly now, smooth pale skin, no hair, and no holes where the eyes should be; only skin. It was the seer, the oracle that her mother had sent with her to Choddrath. Akiri felt the air leave her lungs as she tried to scream.

The woman pointed her long bony finger and pressed it right in the middle of Akiri's forehead. Everything around her went black and she felt herself falling into nothingness, a large black void where no life existed. *Is this what it feels like to die?* Akiri wondered.

2

SOPHIE

An ominous dark cloud loomed above Highland Tower. Sophie drew in the power of the wind and swirled her right hand clockwise, pulling the clouds down into a funnel with her mind. A bolt of lightning, followed by a deafening boom of thunder broke her concentration and the cloud bounced back into its former shape.

"You have to maintain, no matter the distraction, don't lose your focus," Ryul instructed. "Try again, this time, I want you to make the cyclone touch down."

Sophie took a deep breath and turned back toward the storm cloud. She fixed her gaze on the bottom of it and pictured in her mind what she wanted to happen. Sophie swirled her right hand again and as if her fingers were holding onto the bottom of the cloud, it started to mimic the motion of her hand. The lightning struck again, this time, Sophie anticipated the boom that followed and kept her eyes intently on the cloud.

As Sophie swirled her hand and pulled the cloud down into a point again the cyclone got larger. It was now spinning enough that she didn't need to keep moving her hand in a circle, but she had to pull it down. She focused, she saw it in her mind, she saw exactly what she wanted to happen, but she just couldn't get it to work. She almost had it, but she was getting tired and wasn't sure how much longer she would be able to keep going.

"Sophie!" She heard Gabe's voice call out from the side of the tower. She turned to look, forgetting all about her work, but it was not Gabe she saw. It was the Wizard Ryul.

"Your enemies will use any tactic they can to destroy your spells, they will use not only the voices of your loved ones, but sometimes they will take those you care about most and bend you to their will. It is best to have no attachments. We can be done for the day, rest up and we will start again in the morning." Ryul turned and went back inside the tower, the dark cloud departed with him as it evaporated back into the sky.

Sophie went to the edge of the cliff and watched the waterfall cascade down the rocky form. She sat at a picnic table under a tall poplar tree. It wasn't like the forest, or the weeping willow where she and Gabe spent much of their childhood, and the waterfall was nothing like the stream in which Gabe always tried to get her to wade.

ASCENT FROM ASH

Since Sophie's first day at the tower, the full moon had come and gone three times already. It was the end of summer when she'd arrived and now it was harvest. Sophie would be going home after harvest to spend Solstice with her family, and then she would come back to the tower to continue training. Sophie almost changed her mind and decided not to go after she and Gabe kissed, but being a wizard was her dream, and there was no one telling her she couldn't do it. Part of that was because she was a dragon shifter, and the other part was because her father was still in charge of the eastern guild, The Silver Talons Guild.

The Red Order, those who were loyalists to the red dragon, set up a temple in Alasia so they could be close to Sophie, their queen. Some of the men were not happy when Sophie changed their mission. Men who craved power for themselves were shunned from the order and left without a home to wander the world. Those who stayed were tasked with doing good deeds and helping those in need. Sophie was determined that her reign would not be remembered as a reign of terror.

The sun began to set and a cool sea breeze brought out goose flesh on Sophie's arms. She hugged herself, rubbing her hands up and down her arms to warm them as she walked back to the tower. Her room was warm; there was a low, crackling fire in the hearth. Sophie walked over to it and warmed herself as she watched the flames dance. Ryul must have started the fire right after he came inside. He was not what she had expected. When first they met, he had been younger in appearance than her father. Now he looked more like a great, maybe even great-great-grandfather. He used glamour when he had surprise visitors because he didn't want to appear broken or frail. He was neither of those things when his magic was strong, but proving it used more energy than he cared to put into it on any given day. Sophie helped him in the evenings when his magic waned for the day and had come to see him as her grandfather. Sophie never knew her real grandparents, so Ryul was the closest she would ever have.

When it was time for dinner, Sophie helped Ryul to the table and poured him some water. She looked at the table, which was bare, except for two plates, two cups, and a pitcher of water. Sophie closed her eyes and pointed to a spot on the table. She thought of a whole chicken, and imagined it in her mind; the crispy golden skin covered in fresh herbs and the aroma of a perfectly roasted bird. Next, she thought of freshly baked rolls with fresh butter from the dairy farm in Blackwater. Sophie imagined a large garden salad with mixed greens, carrots, tomatoes, peppers, and a light ginger dressing. Finally, Sophie pictured the fruit pastries from her mother's sweet shop. When she opened her eyes, the very feast that she imagined lay before them on the table. Ryul smiled at her.

"Well done Sophie, conjuration is a difficult thing to master," Ryul clapped his hands together as he looked at the feast Sophie's magic had given them. They filled their plates and ate until they were full. When they finished, Sophie waved her hand over the top of the table and as she moved her hand, the surface of the table cleared as if it had all been an illusion.

"You are learning so quickly. I am so proud to have such a wonderful student. I can feel the elves of Aranor calling me home. It will soon be time for you to take my place. Tomorrow will be for copying spells, copy as many as you can so you can continue to learn even after I am gone." Ryul placed a wrinkled hand on top of Sophie's.

A tear slid from Sophie's eye as she placed her other hand on top of his. "We do not need to talk of such things now, you still have time, I know it." She stood up and began helping him to his feet. She walked him to the rune circle at the base of the stairs and she pictured the wizard's room in her mind. A moment later they were standing in the matching circle in his room at the top of the tower.

She helped him to bed. He would change his robes in the morning when his energy was restored, she was certain. Sophie bid him goodnight and quietly retreated to her room downstairs.

3

DOMINIC

E lectricity coursed through the body of the golden dragon as it flew through the sky. The people of Ledora knew that one day the golden dragon would return, and now that it had finally happened, the streets were filled with Ledoran men, women, and children, who gathered to see Prince Dominic fly.

Dominic dipped down low and made a quick glide over the crowd before soaring back up into the clouds. He could hear them cheering below. Dominic roared and unleashed his true breath weapon into the air. The loud popping sound of a large electrical spark rang out as lightning streaked from Dominic's mouth across the sky. The only thunder that followed was thunderous applause from the crowd below.

King Haki watched his son, The Golden Dragon of Ledora, with pride from the balcony of the King's Keep. When Dominic was finished with his flight, he landed on the beach south of the castle. He looked out at the old wooden boardwalk and the docks where the flagship of the royal fleet used to drop anchor. The beach always reminded Dominic of the day that the Crown Jewel, Zahara, capsized in the storm. Luckily, most of the crew was rescued and returned to Ledora aboard another ship.

Dominic knew that his father had worried when the surviving crew returned home without him. Dominic didn't realize how long he had been gone. It seemed like only days, but in reality, he had been gone for several months before he returned to Ledora.

First, King Haki hugged his son, then, he scolded him, and finally hugged him again, this time not letting go for what seemed like hours. The Prince's expedition nearly left the king without an heir and left the throne in danger of being challenged. Because of this, King Haki was more insistent than ever for Dominic to choose a wife.

The days since Dominic's return were busy, every waking hour had been scheduled much like it was before. After waking and eating breakfast, Dominic began the day with studies of lore, not only dragon lore, but also the histories and stories from all around the world. After lore, he studied Draconic, the ancient language of dragons. After that, he practiced casting, and then he had lunch. The afternoons were spent flying and fighting in dragon form. Before dinner, Dominic sat on his mother's throne while King Haki listened to the concerns of the Ledoran people. The King allowed Dominic to handle some things, to prepare him for the decisions he would face as king someday.

After granting an audience to the subjects, King Haki turned to Dominic. "My son, at week's end, we have planned a royal ball, we have invited all of the noble ladies from Ledora, as well as Queen Sophie, and Kamara. I know that you have expressed your desire to choose a match in your own time, but-" The King's voice dropped off and he closed his eyes and took a deep breath before continuing, and Dominic could tell that whatever he had to say was difficult for him.

"I'm not well. I have been sick since before you left. I didn't tell you, because I didn't want you to worry, but my illness is progressing and the shaman believes that I will join our ancestors soon. I should like to meet your wife, and maybe my grandchild before that happens." He placed a hand on Dominic's shoulder and when Dominic looked up from the floor, his face was wet with tears.

"Father, I am so sorry. I didn't know." Dominic choked back sobs as he threw his arms around his father.

"I know, son. Just, promise me you will be open to your options."

Dominic nodded. "I will, father."

Dominic spent the rest of the evening thinking about what the king had told him. He wasn't ready to be king, he wasn't ready to get married, or have children, but most of all, he wasn't ready to lose his father. Emotions came in waves and Dominic fought back the tears for as long as he could, and when he felt unable to hold his emotions together any longer, he ran to the beach and the dragon within him took over. With a loud mournful screech, Dominic took flight. The golden dragon blended into the sunset as he did a barrel roll and changed direction to fly North. There was only one person he wanted to see.

He flew up high into the sky, above the clouds to obscure him from the view of people on the islands below. Dominic knew about the islands below from his days on the flagship of Ledora, Zahara, which was named after his mother. Pirates ruled a cluster of islands in this area and normal sailors dared not to stop there if they had a choice, for they would surely sail out a lot lighter than they came in, and that was IF they were lucky.

The next island he saw below him, Dominic had to fly around rather than over. The island of Immernacht was always covered by a dark cloud. He didn't know why it was always storming there, but in Ledora, Dominic heard a lot of whispers about an evil there that despised the sun and fed on the blood of others. He gave Immernacht a wide berth and then finally, after hours of flying, he reached The Cliffside Coast that rose to the right of Torzana and looked over the Southern forest of Blackwater.

He landed at the edge of the forest and resumed his human form. He hurried through the trees, to the beautiful silver temple, the Temple of Ophay. It was late at night and he didn't know if Kamara would be awake, but the temple was always open to those who were friendly and warded against evil thanks to Sophie and the wizard Ryul.

Dominic walked inside and down a corridor on the left. He found the room that he often stayed in when he visited and saw that Kamara had made up his bed, and she left a clean tunic and pair of trousers hanging in the closet. Dominic walked to the chest of drawers and opened the top drawer.

She thought of everything. Dominic thought with a smile as he pulled undergarments from the drawer and put them on. There were two very unfortunate things about being able to turn into a dragon, the transformation always destroyed your clothes; unless you thought to remove them first, and in dragon form, you had no pockets, so even if you did remove your clothes, you couldn't take them with you unless you carried them in your mouth. Then again, showing up places completely naked could be amusing.

Dominic tiptoed down the corridor to Kamara's room and opened her door softly. He tiptoed to her bedside, knelt beside her, and brushed his fingers up and down her cheek. She stirred at his gentle caress.

"Kamara," he whispered. She brushed her hair out of her face as she drew a deep breath.

"Dominic?" Kamara whispered without opening her eyes.

"Yes, It's me."

Kamara lifted the silk sheet and down-filled comforter, then patted the bed in front of her. She moved back toward the wall so Dominic could crawl into the bed in front of her. As he laid down with his back to her, Kamara covered him with the bedding and put her arm

23

around his middle. He felt so safe with her arms around him like she could take away all the hurt he'd ever felt with the softest touch.

Dominic didn't remember closing his eyes, but when he woke up, despite there being no windows in the room where they had slept, he could tell that it was morning. Kamara was already up and Dominic had no idea how she got out of bed without him noticing. He hurried back to his room and dressed in the tunic and trousers Kamara had left for him.

He found Kamara in the breakfast nook; she was reading a book as she absentmindedly stirred her morning tea. Kamara looked up from her book when she noticed him standing in the archway watching her.

"The water in the kettle is still hot if you would like some tea?" she asked.

Dominic nodded and took a jar of tea leaves from the shelf and poured a mug of hot water from the kettle. He placed the tea into a square of folded cheesecloth and tied it off with a string. He took his mug to the table and sat down across from Kamara.

"How was your flight?" She asked as she placed her book face down on the table to save her page.

"It was fine, it gave me time to cry it out before I got here," he admitted.

"Cry? What's bothering you?" Kamara's eyebrows turned up at the inside corner and Dominic could see that her concern was genuine.

"My father is ill, he told me yesterday, he might have a couple of years left." Dominic removed the tea bag from his mug and squeezed the rest of the liquid out before discarding it. Dominic thought if he met her gaze at that moment, he might cry, so instead, he sipped his tea, which was still much too hot.

"I am so sorry about your father. I got his invitation to the ball just two days past. It said that you intend to choose a wife so that the Kingdom of Ledora will continue the royal line. I didn't know that these plans were so urgent." She placed her hand on his. Dominic couldn't hide his thoughts from her. She sensed his apprehension about choosing a wife and ruling a kingdom without his father's wisdom.

"If I have to choose a wife, I want to choose someone who means a great deal to me. Someone I know will be caring and kind. Kamara, I can't think of anyone else I want to spend my life with; when I got the news from my father, I only longed to be comforted by you. I can feel my feelings without fear of judgment when I am with you. Kamara, will you please, come to the royal ball so I can ask you this officially?" He moved from the table and bent down to one knee. "Kamara, you are my best friend; I want to spend the rest of my life with your guidance and love. Will you please do me the honor of accepting me as your husband?"

Kamara looked at him in shock, and tears welled up in her eyes. She nodded her head, unable to make words come out. She accepted with her whole heart.

4

AKIRI

The black void swallowed her whole. She could feel herself falling through the nothingness until she hit the solid ground with a THUD! Akiri sat up and looked around for the woman, the exit, or even a weapon she could use. There was nothing there but darkness. Then a flash of light attracted her attention. Akiri whirled around to see a massive black dragon breathing its fiery breath across the Kingdom of Ash. She heard the screams as the subjects fled their homes and ran out into the open, into a trap. The dragon breathed a wall of fire down every cobblestone street, engulfing the houses and livelihoods of her people. When the entire city was on fire, the dragon turned its attention to the castle. The city looked older and Akiri wondered if the seer was showing her the past.

The lights went out again. *Am I inside the seer's mind? Is this her vision?* Akiri's mind raced as whispers swirled around her.

"Ash will fall again, you cannot trust your council; one of them will betray you," The whispers warned.

"Who is this betrayer?" Akiri asked as she looked in every direction for the source of the whispers.

"I can't see who, it's best to not trust anyone."

Akiri was suddenly surrounded by a flash of white light as bright as the day star. When everything went dark again, Akiri opened her eyes; she was in her bed. She looked around her room for the woman, but there was no sign of her. *Was it all a dream?* Akiri wondered.

It was dark outside and the breeze carried the smell of wood fire stoves, which was pleasant, but also the not-so-pleasant smell of the muckrakers cleaning the latrines, or the armorers tanning their leather. Akiri walked to the window and closed it. There was a small fire in her hearth and it had enough flame left to light some incense.

Akiri noticed a letter on her writing desk that hadn't been there yesterday; it was stamped with the golden seal of Ledora. She opened it and took out the elegant invitation card inside.

Akiri thought about the last time she saw the King of Ledora, she had blown a hole in his throne room doors, tried to melt His Majesty with an acid ball, and stormed out of his kingdom on a mission to kill his only child and take the orb of power all for herself. When she thought about it now, it all seemed so juvenile, yet as sick as the gladiators when they fight to the death. She was so angry, at people she had never met, and for reasons that were only implanted in her mind by her mother. She regretted everything, but it was too late to take anything back.

She set the invitation on the table beside her bed as a visual reminder to take it to the council meeting first thing in the morning. Akiri tried to sleep, and she might have- for a little while at least. She tossed and turned all night, and kept seeing the black dragon burning the kingdom and the face of that old woman in her dreams.

When the first light beamed through her bedroom window, Akiri dragged herself out of bed. Her shoulder blades ached and her neck was stiff. She walked over to the looking glass beside her wardrobe and turned her backside to the mirror. A dark purple bruise covered her left hip and her normally porcelain complexion was red- dened across her buttocks and lower back. She winced in pain as she touched the bruise to feel the tenderness. She definitely had not been dreaming when she fell.

Akiri dressed and brushed her long black hair, put on her crown, and grabbed the Invitation from Ledora. A cool rush of air made Akiri shiver as she made her way to the council chamber.

"One of them will betray you. Trust no one." The seer's words echoed in her mind as she saw the six men gath- ered around the table. They stood as she walked past them to her seat at the head of the table and they didn't sit down until she did.

"Before we begin, I received this invitation in my bed chamber. Do any of you know who delivered it there?" Akiri asked.

The men looked from one to the other, all agreeing that none of them knew anything about the invitation.

"What is it for, My Queen?" Ser William asked. He was a heavy-set man with only a horseshoe of gray hair around his head. He was a former Knight and had served on the city guard for many years. Akiri slid the invitation over to him and watched his expression as he read it.

"The last time I saw the King, I tried to kill him. If it had not been for his anti-magic barrier, I might have succeeded. Now he is inviting me to a royal ball? It doesn't make sense. As my Master of Diplomacy, Ser William, tell me, should I go, or does this seem like a trap?"

"Your Grace, You have the power to turn into a mighty dragon at will. It would not be in their best interest to try to lead you into a trap. There is no doubt in my mind that they want to make peace so that they will not have you as an enemy."

"If he has an anti-magic field, that could prevent Queen Akiri from shifting into her dragon form, they could imprison her-or worse." The young captain of the city guard, Nohan Arach, interrupted. "I don't think it is a safe idea for Her Majesty to attend."

Akiri gave him a serious look. "What if this Prince wants to choose another dragon for a wife, and THAT is why they have invited me. Perhaps they crave power, and having two powerful dragons is better than one.

In that case, Don't you think it would be a good move, diplomatically, of course, to merge our kingdoms and our Draconic line?" Nohan looked as if Akiri had just beaten him in combat. He hung his head and as he did, he muttered; "Yes, Your Grace."

"Now, the tournament is days away, and the arena is nearly set up, how are the accommodations coming?" Akiri asked the castle Steward, Roland Koffery.

"The chambers are all ready and the kitchen staff has already begun preparations for the opening feast."

"Very well, Thank you, Mr. Koffery." Next, Akiri looked to the weasel-faced man, Timothy Ackerman. Before she could speak, the voice inside her head whispered again, *One of them will betray you, don't trust anyone.* Akiri shook the thoughts away and continued.

"How is our budget for the tournament?" Mr. Ackerman looked at his ledger, the numbers were orderly and detailed, outlining how the crown spent every copper.

"Our budget looks good. The fees for the contests will cover the cost of the tournament; we should come out a few thousand gold pieces ahead when all is said and done." Mr. Ackerman said.

Next, Akiri looked at the leader of the builder's guild. "Are the new stables ready for our guests?"

"Yes, Your Grace, the construction was completed two days ago and the stalls will be stocked and ready to go this afternoon before guests start arriving."

"I assume if there were any threats or concerns for the security of the castle or your Queen, you would have already acted, right, Ser Stewart?" Horace Stewart silently nodded to his queen. "Okay, then this concludes today's meeting, Mr. Koffery, if you would, please, tell my chambermaids that I would like to have a bath drawn," Akiri said as she stood up. The council members stood as well and waited for their queen to exit the council chamber.

As Akiri walked down the hall, she heard the voice of the woman in her head again. *One of them will betray you*, the voice whispered. Akiri turned back to look at the door. Horace Stewart and the guard who stood outside the chamber door were only a few feet away from her as they usually were, protecting her yet still giving her space. The other men filed out of the room and scattered in all directions to attend to their other duties.

"Ser Stewart, may I ask you something?" Akiri looked at the man in his silver half-plate armor and green cloak.

"Yes, My Queen."

"You are sworn to me, by the oath of your life to the sword, yes?"

"Yes, My Queen." Akiri moved in close to the Captain of the Queen's Guard and whispered her next words.

"If one of the men on my council would betray me, who would you think it would be?"

"Your Grace, I could not say, but if you like, I have eyes and ears all over the city ready at my command, would you have me utilize them?"

"Yes, please. I received a grave warning from the seer and we must be vigilant, she said someone on my counsel would betray me."

"The seer? She was presumed dead after you returned without her and the ship."

"She is not dead, I can tell you that for certain. It does seem very strange that she would want to warn me of anything. I was not very kind to her when she sailed with me to Choddrath."

"Perhaps the betrayer is her, and sowing these seeds of mistrust within your counsel is her way of isolating you from your protectors. I will send word to all of my informants and see what they can find out."

"Thank you." Akiri turned around and walked toward her chamber. When she entered, her guards stood at the door. Akiri set the invitation back on the writing desk where she found it. She undressed and headed for the bath. The water was still steaming. Akiri dipped a toe in to make sure it wasn't too hot and then eased herself into the water. She felt her muscles release and all the tension in her lower back and shoulders slowly eased. She closed her eyes.

When Akiri opened her eyes, the water was cold. She stepped out of the bath and grabbed her robe. She quickly tied it around her and tiptoed across the stone floor, leaving small puddles of water beneath her feet as she moved from her bed chamber to the hall. Everyone was gone. The castle was quiet. There was no light coming in through the windows, and no lanterns to light. Akiri held the stone banister as she descended the stairs. When she reached the bottom, she looked at her hand; it was covered in a layer of thick, gray dust from the railing.

The room began to spin and everything became a blur. When the world stopped moving around her, Akiri could see that she was in her lair. An underground cave that had been built for her dragon form. The council wanted her to lay eggs to produce more dragons to protect the kingdom. Akiri wondered if it was really to protect the Kingdom, or if it was to have more power than the other kingdoms or cities. From the back of the lair, Akiri heard a small snuffling sound. She walked back to the nest in the back of her lair and she saw the tiniest baby dragon.

It wasn't green like her, it was as dark as the night sky, and it looked up at her with such big bluish-green eyes. She knelt beside the dragon and put her hands out in front of it. With little hesitation, the tiny dragon crawled into her hands. It snuggled against the warmth of her skin and curled into a ball. It trusted her like a child trusts a mother. Akiri watched the dragon sleep in her palms, admiring each bump of its skin. She felt connected to it. This was her child, her dragon.

Akiri knew it was a dream-she knew it, but she didn't want to wake up. This new, indescribable feeling overwhelmed her. She had never been so happy. The little creature in her hand started to fade, and the lair around her began to disappear. "No! I'm not ready!" She screamed, but the dream melted away and she startled awake in her cold bathwater.

Akiri knew what it was- that feeling- It was love. She would do anything to feel it again. That meant she would have to produce a clutch, she wanted to raise a dragon.

5

SOPHIE

Ryul did not come down for breakfast. He also did not send Sophie any telepathic messages. By lunch, Sophie began to worry. The teleportation circle was not working. Ryul usually erased or changed one of the runes at night so that no one could teleport in without his permission so this didn't particularly bother her, but the fact that he had been so silent and had not eaten caused her to worry. She took a tray of lunch up the stairs. She forgot how many there were, two hundred to get to the library alone, then probably another hundred steps to get to the top, where Ryul's room was.

Sophie knocked quietly and waited for any sound from the other side. When she heard none, Sophie opened the door slowly and peeked in. The hinges on the door creaked loudly, giving her away. *No point in trying to be stealthy now*, Sophie thought. She went over to the desk to set down the tray of food. The room was dark and smelled musty. She went to the window, parted the heavy curtains, and then opened it to bring in some fresh air.

Sophie called for Ryul as she walked around his room. He had already made his bed, and he was nowhere to be found. Then she saw it- the letter addressed to her. It was there on the nightstand beside his bed.

Sophie-

I wish I could have stayed to teach you more, but I am afraid my illness is getting worse. Although the lives of my ancestors are long, we are not immortal. I have gone to the elven city of Ravenhall to be with what is left of my family. I wanted to spare you seeing me like this. You have a special gift and have already learned so much. You are ready to take the torch and lead the way. You are the last red dragon, Queen of the Red Order, and you are becoming a powerful wizard. I have left you the tower and all of its contents. The wards and protections will expire upon my death, so practice what we have been working on and set up your own defenses. Most of all, Don't be like me, enjoy your family and friends and live life to the fullest.

All my best,

-Ryul

Sophie wiped the tears from her eyes as she put the letter down on the bed. She had known it was coming, he had told her as much, but she didn't think that it would be the next day. Sophie couldn't tell if she was sad or angry. Maybe she was feeling all the feelings at once. Sophie left the tray of food where it was and ran from the room. She left the tower and started to run. Right before she got to the edge of the cliff, her wings emerged. The rest of her dragon form followed and in one swift movement she was no longer a girl, she was a dragon, flying over Blackwater Bay toward her home, her family, and Gabe.

It only took her a few minutes to fly across the bay, but she didn't want to land in Torzana, it was too far south. She turned and flew north toward the arena her father had built for dragon training. When her talons touched the ground below, she ran with her momentum from the flight and slowed herself with each step until she was finally able to come to a complete stop. She changed into her human form, and then cast a quick illusion spell to make it appear she had on clothes. *This will work well enough until I get home,* she thought.

From the arena behind the Silver Talons Guild Hall, Sophie walked around the western side of the building and through the west side of Blackwater. Her family's home was not extravagant, rather, it was as plain as all the other houses in the town. It was larger and more spacious than some of them though, as befitting a guild-master's station. Sophie opened the door and called for her mother. Samantha was in the kitchen hanging herbs to dry. A few bunches of sage and several bunches of Rosemary remained on the counter as Samantha hung the last bunch of lavender.

"Hi Sophie, it's so good to see you, how's training going?" Samantha asked as she opened her arms for her daughter.

Her tears flowed freely in the comfort of her mother's arms. Samantha didn't force her to talk, she just held her tightly. It had been so long since Sophie had been home, Samantha would hold her forever if she could.

"Ryul left. He's dying. He said that he wished that he could have trained me longer, but-" She buried her face in he mother's shoulder.

"Shh, I'm here, my sweet, my little Sophie Sweet." Samantha brushed her hand up and down her daughter's back as she held her close. Sophie Sweet was the nickname her mother called her when she was little. It always made her feel safe and happy.

Sophie pulled away slowly and smiled just a little before she walked over to the counter and began helping to hang the herbs. They tied the thin string around five or six stems to make a bunch, then hung them upside down from the flower drying rack above the counter. When The herbs were finished, Sophie thought of Gabe.

"Mama, I'm going to stop by and see Gabe." Samantha smiled and nodded to her daughter. Sophie went to her room to change into some real clothes, her spell would only last an hour and it was nearing the hour mark. Her room was just as she had left it, not a thing was out of place. On her desk, three of the five feathers that she had plucked from a sleeping raven, called to her like a muse. She picked up the longest of the three and she suddenly felt the urge to write. She thought of Gabe and then grabbed a piece of parchment. For this spell, she didn't need ink. She had practiced this with Ryul many times during her training. Sophie wrote:

Meet me at the willow tree. -S

The words showed up on the parchment lightly, as if she had written them with water. Then they disappeared. If it worked, Gabe would be at the tree by the time she got there. Sophie dressed quickly, putting on a pair of her most comfortable trousers and a tunic. All the other girls wore dresses, but Sophie preferred not to. If she did, she always wore trousers underneath. She did not dress like a man, her deep green tunic was fitted to her- tapered at the waist, and her black trousers were more like tights with pockets, but thicker and they did not go past her ankle. She paired the outfit with brown leather sandals, which she found she liked more than boots because they didn't make her feet hot.

Sophie pulled her bouncy red curls into a bunch, separated them into three strands, and then braided it to one side. When she was finished, the braid reached her waist. Her hair had grown a lot in the last year and Sophie often had to braid it to keep it from interfering with her spells.

The thought of seeing Gabe made Sophie nervous. She didn't know why. She walked across town slowly, trying not to let her eagerness and nerves show. The Blackwater market was bustling with shoppers going from cart to cart for vegetables, fruits, jewelry, eggs, and various cooked foods. It smelled like roasted meat and exotic spices and herbs all at once. Sophie hurried past, trying not to make herself too hungry. She hadn't brought any coin with her.

When she got to the forest, she took the same path she always took, only now, it was overgrown and untrodden. It made her wonder if her spell had worked, but as soon as she made it past the first set of trees, the willow came into view, and Gabe too. He was a man now, not the boy she remembered him being not even a year ago. His shoulders had broadened; he looked stronger, more muscular. His face now had hair on it, not much, just stubble, but it made him seem older. She stood there, watching him for a moment, noticing all the vast differences a year could make. She could feel her chest fluttering and a stirring feeling as she stood there gazing at him. She regretted that she had left before they talked about their kiss.

Sophie would have stood there frozen for even longer, but he looked up and saw her. She moved out of the thicket and into the clearing under the willow. She expected him to run to her, but he didn't. He smiled, but there was pain behind it. She walked up to embrace him, but anxiety made her pause. She could see the moisture in Gabe's eyes.

"I'm sorry I-" Sophie began.

"No, Soph, it's okay, I know why you went to the tower, it's just that..." His voice caught in his throat and he looked as if he were going to cry.

"My father passed," Gabe said.

"I'm so sorry. I didn't know." Sophie tried to reach out to caress his cheek, but Gabe backed away.

"My mom drank her feelings every night down at the Loose Anchor, she gambled away every last copper we had and when the coin ran out, she gave up the deed to the house. I couldn't let them take my mother's home and kick her out to the cobblestones like a rat, but let's face it, Soph, scribes don't get paid well enough to cover that kind of debt." Gabe wiped a tear from his face. Sophie had no idea what he was about to say next, but she knew it was painful for him. "I'm sorry, Sophie... I accepted a position with the guild to pay off my mother's debt. The house is free and clear, and the deed belongs to me so no one can ever take it from her, but I am leaving on assignment in two days' time.

"They're sending you on a mission alone without a team?" Sophie asked, confused. "They wouldn't, my father wouldn't-" Sophie began to tear up.

"Not exactly. It's a top-secret assignment, so I can't tell you more right now. I just want to tell you that I will always love you, but you have to move on," Gabe said.

"You say that like you're not coming back." Sophie couldn't hide the fear in her voice.

"I'm sorry," Gabe said again. It looked like he might cry too, but he turned away from Sophie before she could see his tears. Sophie stood sobbing under the willow where she and Gabe had so many memories. Under the willow where they played as children, read stories from around the world as teens, played in the creek, and collected components for Sophie's spells. It was there under the willow where they shared their first kiss, and

now, it was there under the willow, where Gabe broke
Sophie's heart.

6

AKIRI

The sun was bright and hot. Akiri regretted her wardrobe choice not even one match into the tournament. The first event was the joust. Watching men run at each other with sticks, trying to knock each other off their horses was quite boring to her, but she was the Queen of Ash, so she had to at least feign interest in the tournament.

After the joust, was archery, then hand-to-hand combat, then weapons combat, and finally, the last competition of the day, the magic casting tournament. Akiri was never so glad to take off a corset in her life. Even though she had a layer of cloth beneath her corset, it still clung to her. The whale bones inside the garment left indentations on her skin, and even though she was no longer wearing it, the hourglass shape remained. She admired the curves in her chamber's looking glass. She had the curves of a woman now, she was no longer a child.

Akiri cleaned herself up and dressed quickly in her flying robes, a garment she could easily take off before shifting, and put back on after resuming her human form. Akiri had called for a council meeting after the tournament. This was usual to discuss budget and other things, but that was not the reason for this meeting.

The men were gathered around the table and all stood up as she entered. She motioned for them all to sit down and walked quickly to her seat.

"I called you here because I have urgent news. I have taken your advice, and I have chosen a husband. We will meet at Prince Dominic's Royal ball and travel back here together and I want to be married within a week. I think a clutch of eggs, and an heir or two were both sound suggestions. I will need you, Mr. Koffery, and Mr. Ackerman, to set up, and decorate for a royal wedding. I want a private ceremony, but gather the entire kingdom in the front courtyard for our first public appearance and King and Queen."

"Yes, My Queen," they said in unison.

"Mr. Ackerman, did we come out ahead from the tournament?"

"Yes, Your Grace, we are several platinum richer after the settlements."

"Good, apply that extra coin to the wedding. Meeting adjourned."

Akiri ran as quickly as she could from the castle and to her lair. Her stomach cramped on the lower right side, and the pain radiated through her into her back. She experienced cramps like these every month, they usually hit a day or two before her month's blood. This time it was different, she knew. They felt stronger and lasted longer. Akiri took off her robe and shifted into her dragon form. She curled onto her nest and winced through the pain. Her moans of distress sounded much louder in dragon form, but her larger size helped distribute the pain so that it was not so concentrated.

She spent the whole night in the lair, curled in her nest. In the morning, she felt more energetic and the pain wasn't as strong as it had been the night before. She took a flight, and then returned to the lair for her robe. Her betrothed would arrive in a couple more days, and she had to prepare. Akiri soaked in a tub of milk and lavender to soften her skin and make her smell fragrant. It was just her luck that her month's blood would come soon- just as her future husband was to arrive. She didn't know if others could tell, but her Draconic blood heightened her senses and she thought during this time of the month, she had a very distinct smell, like old coppers that have been rolling around in the trousers of millions of people, or like the smell of the miners after a day in the iron mines.

After her bath, she put on a pair of snug-fitted undergarments and lined them with a folded absorbent cloth. Next, she put on a pair of sheepskin bloomers to prevent leaking during the night. While she dressed, her chamber maids turned down her bed and put a warming pan under her sheets at the foot. They also had a blanket warming by the fire to cover Akiri after she crawled into bed. The warm blanket eased her muscles as the ladies tucked her in. She didn't even hear them creep out of the room before she drifted off comfortably to sleep.

The next day, Akiri did not feel like going to the council chambers, so she had her maids set up seven chairs around the hearth in her room. They assured her that preparations for her intended's arrival were on track and that they had put coins into the pocket of every local shop owner in the kingdom as per her wishes. Of course, they were all interested to know which suitor she had chosen, but Akiri liked feeling in control of her choices and gave nothing away. She did not need a council of men telling her who to marry. She was Queen and could make a match for herself.

After the meeting, Akiri asked for some warm tea and a pain relief tonic. The maids brought it to her and warmed her blanket again. She thought about the kingdom under her mother's rule, and how much happier the subjects were now since the crown was no longer imposing harsh collections on their businesses. The tournament and gladiator arena not only provided income for the kingdom but entertainment to the subjects.

She was making a difference, and soon, she would secure her line of succession and have a family of dragons to guard their homeland.

7

GABE

L eon Rend sat behind his mahogany desk. The fur-
nishings in his office were all matching in a carved
wood décor. Gabe fidgeted in his chair, across the desk
from Leon. The guildmaster's face was stone. Gabe was
waiting for him to say something about Sophie. He was
sure he had heard by now that Gabe had told her that he
was leaving.

"We need to talk about your assignment, Gabe," Leon
said. Gabe felt a twinge of hope in his chest. He hoped
that Commander Rend was calling the whole thing off.

"When you get there, and it's done, I will need you to
be able to get messages back here secretly. What I am
about to teach you, cannot leave this room. We need a
telepathic link to each other, but it cannot be an item,
just in case you are stripped of your possessions and
searched for magical items, so we need to create a link in
a more dangerous way, but it is undetectable. The only

way someone would know is if they are reading your mind while you send the message, so you have to make sure you are alone when you transmit your thoughts." Leon said.

Gabe was not sure what he meant by all of this, but he knew that there would be no getting out of this assignment.

"Sir, I had hoped we might talk about Sophie, is she okay?" Gabe asked.

"You didn't tell her about the mission did you?" Leon asked as his stone expression turned to alarm.

"Only that I was leaving, not what I was leaving to do," Gabe told him.

"Good, the less she knows the better. She will be fine, in my teens, I suffered more than a few broken hearts and still ended up a happily married man, I am sure Sophie will be no different.

The thought of Sophie married to someone other than him, gave Gabe a crushing sensation in his chest. He could not hide his pained expression from Leon's perceptive gaze.

"I know this is hard for you too. I know you love my daughter. I am sorry, If we had a better option, know that I would have given you my blessing to marry Sophie." Leon paused and his face softened toward Gabe. "It doesn't have to be forever, but we really need a young man on the inside, and it might take a long time to earn their trust and gather the intel." Gabe nodded.

"So, how do we form the telepathic link?" Gabe asked.

"With this." Leon pulled out a small container. The inside of the box was lined with ice, it had to be a spell, there was no other way to get ice in summer, except in the Icy Channel north of Northport, and it would be melted by the time it reached Blackwater. Gabe looked at the two pieces of gray matter inside that seemed to be pulsing with electricity and beating like a heart.

"What is it?" Gabe asked.

"This is the neural pathway of a mensmonstrum," Leon said as he picked up a piece and slid the box over to Gabe.

"Wait- those things are *real?* I thought those were an old fable told by parents to get their children to be honest."

"No, they are very real. They live in a world deep beneath ours, where no sunlight ever shines, and only evil thrives. If we share this piece of elder brain, it will create a neural link between us and our minds will be able to send messages to each other whenever we want. This is a closely guarded secret, not many people know about this ability. Luckily, our necromancer is infinitely wise and forever advancing that knowledge of our bodies, as well as those of our enemies. This link will only last a few weeks or so, long enough for you to carry out phase one and report. Well, no time like the present." Leon popped the fleshy tissue into his mouth and swallowed it whole.

"I thought you said this was dangerous?" Gabe asked as he ate his piece apprehensively.

"It can be, sometimes the host brain tries to reject the neural link and they will hear whispers forever, or sounds that pain them physically as well as mentally-it can drive a person mad," Leon said. "It could take up to a day to complete the fusion into our minds, but let me know if you hear whispers, or screeching, anything like that, okay?" Leon stood up and rounded the desk to Gabe as he stood.

"I will, Sir," Gabe said.

That night, Gabe had trouble sleeping. A million thoughts ran through his mind, but the thought that was the most recurring, was the sight of Sophie as he turned away from her. That image was sure to haunt him until he returned if he ever got to return. Gabe rolled over and cried into his pillow until he fell asleep. In the morning, he heard Leon's unexpected voice in his mind.

"This is a test, Gabe can you hear me?"

"Yes," Gabe answered aloud.

"Don't speak your answer, imagine me standing there in front of you and just think what you want to say."

"Oh, okay, like this?" Gabe thought.

"Yes exactly," Leon said.

"Can you hear my thoughts all the time?" Gabe asked.

"No, only when you mean for me to hear," Leon replied.

Gabe really hoped that were true. He didn't want anyone to know the anguish he felt at the thought of leaving Sophie behind. It would only make what he had to do that much more difficult.

8

DOMINIC

K amara and Dominic flew to Ledora together. Dominic did not want to break the news to his father until the ball. He was sure that guests were already arriving, so Kamara's presence would not necessarily give them away. Before they left The Temple of Ophay, Dominic made a special bag that he could carry in his dragon form so that they could bring a change of clothes with them. They dressed on the beach. The moon was nearly full, tomorrow night it would be. If Dominic believed such things, he might have warned that having a royal ball on the night of a full moon would be a bad idea.

Before they left the beach, Dominic embraced Kamara and pressed his lips to hers. The moonlight danced on her skin as the tiny hairs on her neck, and her arms stood on end. She wrapped her arms around his neck and kissed him back, deeply.

"We should split up, if we walk in together, they will suspect something. My father took a lot of time to plan the ball, and I would like for him to think that it was through his effort we were matched," Dominic said.

"I understand. I will go into the city to go shopping for a new dress before I come to the castle, May I have my coin pouch please?" Kamara gave him a sly smile as he dug into his bag to pull out the last item in it.

"Thanks. I will see you soon." She blew him a kiss as she walked toward the golden city.

"Prince Dominic, there you are!" The King's jovial voice rang out through the foyer of the castle. He was standing with two elegantly dressed, older women. "I want to introduce you to a couple of our guests. This is Lady Harlow, of Ellsworth, and Lady Delacroix of Immernacht, they have both brought their daughters to meet you at the ball tomorrow night." King Haki stepped back to let the ladies engage with the prince.

"It's so lovely to meet you both," Dominic said as he suavely swept each woman's hand to his lips and placed a gentle, courteous kiss just above the knuckle of their middle finger.

"King Haki, you said he was handsome, but I am afraid you did not do him justice." Lady Harlow said.

"My lady, you are too kind." Dominic put on his best diplomatic voice. "I am terribly sorry, but I just got back from my travels and I am afraid I need to freshen up. I look forward to seeing you and meeting your daughters tomorrow night." The ladies bowed to him as he left and went up the stairs to his chamber. He did not bother calling for the castle staff, Dominic waved his hands around a cauldron on the floor beside the hearth. Blue wisps of light encircled the pot, swirling as his hands moved. The cauldron began to fill with water. When it was full, he lifted it and hung it on the iron tripod inside the fireplace. He produced a bolt of flame that shot from his hand and engulfed the logs beneath the black iron pot.

Dominic walked to the balcony of his room. It over-looked the courtyard and he could see more guests as they arrived. He hoped that he would see Kamara, but he heard the low rolling sound of a boiling cauldron. Dominic used a spell to levitate the cauldron to the tub and pour the water into it, and then he used another incantation to double the amount of hot water in his bath. He draped his arm over the side of the tub and ran his fingers across the surface of the water, his fingers turned bluc and steam rose from the bath until Dominic pulled his hand away from the water.

When the temperature was just right, Dominic stepped into the bath and washed his body with a cloth. He washed his braids too, they were growing out and would need to be re-done, but he knew he would not have time before the ball. When he finished his bath, Dominic massaged mineral oil onto his skin, paying close attention to his hands, elbows, and knees. The festivities would begin at breakfast and continue throughout the day, so he needed to get some sleep. As soon as his head rested on his pillow, Dominic was in a deep, dreamless, slumber.

9

SOPHIE

An early summer breeze blew through the window and rustled the papers on Sophie's desk. She rushed over to the scene and placed a book on top of the invitation to secure it in place while she packed. Sophie looked at her bed and Leon's old leather backpack, the one that she carried with her to Choddrath only a year ago. She had piles of clothing folded and laid out across the bed, not everything was going to fit into the backpack, so she would have to make some choices. If she left within the next hour or two, Sophie would be in Ledora by late afternoon and would have plenty of time to shop for a new ball gown.

She grabbed her coin pouch and put it into the bag first, then her spell book. Next, she added a stack of sleeping clothes and a stack of plain day clothes. Sophie crossed the room and grabbed her hair comb, a box of hair pins, and her lavender pomade. She started to cross the room but turned back when she was halfway. She added a bottle of perfume to her already full hands and crossed back to the bed. She dropped everything into her bag and closed up the backpack.

Okay, coin purse, spell book, sleep clothes, day clothes, hair things, perfume... It seems like I'm forgetting something. Sophie thought. She looked around the room, but couldn't think of anything she'd forgotten. Sophie undressed and cast the illusion spell to make herself appear dressed.

Downstairs, her mother was in the kitchen baking pastries for her sweet shop. Samantha smiled and offered one to Sophie.

"Thanks, Mama," Sophie said as she took a bite. "I'm heading out to Ledora today for Prince Dominic's ball."

"I'm so happy you decided to go anyway. I know you would have invited Gabe if things had been different. I hope that you will still be friends when he comes home," Samantha said.

"We'll see, mama. I love you." Sophie kissed her mother's cheek and waved as she walked toward the door.

"I love you too, Sophie. Be careful!" Samantha called.

Sophie walked quickly to the arena. She was sure that Gabe already left, but just in case she was wrong, she hurried to avoid running into him. She laid her backpack on the ground in front of her when she got to the middle of the arena, took a few steps back from it, and stretched as her body grew and transformed into a red dragon. She gently hooked a tooth under one of the straps of her backpack, so she could use her talons to get a running start.

The beating of her wings kicked up the dust covering the arena floor and left a cloud beneath her as she lifted from the ground and up toward the clouds. She ascended until she could see nothing but the sky. She felt so free above the clouds, like nothing mattered, not her broken heart, not Ryul joining his ancestors, not her father sending Gabe away, and least of all, where she was going to choose to live when she returned. Lapis Highland was hers now, and she did still have a group of red dragon enthusiasts who called her Queen and were loyal to her. Lapis Highland could be her own kingdom, but her family was in Blackwater.

Sophie flew for hours to get to Ledora, the sunlight made it difficult for her to see but her calculations were correct, it was late afternoon when she touched down on the eastern beach of Ledora. Sophie noticed the tracks of two other dragons on that beach. *That's strange, the green dragon would surely land on the western beach given the location of Ash.* Sophie thought. Sophie never even learned the name of the green dragon. She hadn't thought much about her at all since the day her father told the guild council that she declined the invitation to join the Dragon Alliance. Sophie wasn't even sure what they were calling themselves these days, Dragon Council, assembly, committee, union... nothing much had changed; only one new law had been made, and it was proposed by Leon- killing a dragon was now punishable by death.

Sophie changed on the beach and walked toward the castle. She wanted to find her room and drop off her bag before going shopping. As she approached the gates in front of the castle, two heavily armored guards blocked her path.

"State your business," one said.

"I'm here to attend the royal ball," Sophie told them.

"Present your invitation." Sophie took off her pack and reached inside, feeling for the stiff parchment on which the invitation was written. She dug to the bottom of the bag before her mind thought back to the window and the breeze that almost blew the invite away. She saw it plainly under the book on her desk.

"I accidentally left it," Sophie said. "But, I am Queen Sophie, of Lapis Highland and Blackwater."

"Come back when you have an invitation or an escort."

"It will take me hours to fly home and back!" Sophie protested. They looked surprised when she said "fly" and they shared a glance, but stood firm.

"An invitation, or an escort, Miss Sophie."

She huffed at them as she walked away. *Great,* she thought. Instead, Sophie walked toward the city. She could find a dress and then go through her spell book to see if she could get a message to Prince Dominic.

The Golden City was beautiful. Tall white archways trimmed in gold marked the entrance to every street. The city guards wore golden half-plate and white cloaks trimmed in gold embroidery. The buildings were all pristine, not a single broken shutter or stone out of place. Instead of the clapboard houses they had in Blackwater, these buildings were all made from white clay. The trim sparkled with a golden shimmer, and each door bore the symbol of the golden sun with a dragon silhouette.

Sophie wandered around, looking at all the shops and taverns in amazement. Ledora made Blackwater seem like a remote village. Sophie walked into the first dress shop she saw. The inside was lavishly decorated with a formal sitting area, beautiful antique looking glasses, several changing areas, and plenty of staff to help patrons get into their formal wear. There were rows and rows of dresses that hung from horizontal poles. At the front of each row, a mannequin modeled a dress that could be found on the corresponding rack. The dresses came in all sizes and each one was just a little different in style but the racks were sorted by color. Sophie had never shopped in a place like this, she rarely wore dresses, and when she did, they were made for her by the guild seamstress.

"Looking for a gown to wear to the ball?" A woman's voice interrupted Sophie's thoughts and she looked up at her from the dresses.

"Yes Ma'am, but I'm afraid I don't know what size to get."

"I can help you with that, dear," she said. "My name is Adelaide, but you can call me Addie, and what's yours, dear?" Addie asked.

"Sophie Rend," she replied.

"Oh, Sophie, what a beautiful name, and what beautiful red hair you have. I think I know just the dress for you, but we will have to get your measurements first."

Addie walked over to the counter and grabbed a ribbon with strange markings on it that looked like the sticks the builders used to measure materials. Addie wrapped the ribbon around Sophie's waist, and then her chest, hips, the length of her torso from her belly button to the curve of her waist and then from her breast bone to her belly button, and finally, the length of her arm. She wrote the measurements on a piece of paper and then led Sophie to one of the privacy screens.

"This is Margaret, and Henrietta, they will help you dress. Do you need an underbodice?"

"I'm sorry a what?" Sophie asked.

"It's okay, dear, I will bring you one, go ahead and undress."

Sophie did as instructed and Addie started bringing pieces of clothing to Margaret. The first was a white cotton tube with drawstrings on both ends. Margaret instructed Sophie to put her arms up and then slipped the fabric over her head. She pulled the first drawstring so that the garment was snug beneath Sophie's breasts and tied it in the back. Then she tightened the bottom, which went down to Sophie's hip.

Then Addie handed Henrietta a cream-colored corset with metal clasps on the front of it. Henrietta fitted it around Sophie's waist and lined up the hourglass shape of the corset with the natural curve of Sophie's waist and then she hooked the busk. Margaret had Sophie put her hands on the wall as she began tightening Sophie's corset, alternating pulling the X's from the bottom to the top, until she came to the middle. Sophie was surprised at how comfortable the corset was, she was prepared to feel pain, or to have trouble breathing, but she found that the corset took the pressure off of her lower back and improved her posture-which at times, could be pretty atrocious.

Next, they dressed her in a petticoat with sewn-in hip pads. Then came the dress. It was a beautiful dark green silk dress with a golden pattern on the bodice and skirt which Addie called d*amask*, except for the triangle that started at a point in the middle and fanned out to the outsides of her feet. That section of the dress was a shimmering emerald green. The sleeves fanned out at the elbow and were layered in the green damask and black to match the front of the dress. Sophie had never felt so beautiful. When she saw her reflection, she did not see a girl who longed to be a wizard or the mighty dragon, she saw a woman suited for life at court. Sophie expected to hate it, but she didn't.

"What do you think?" Addie asked her.

"I love it. How much is it?"

"Everything you have on is a total of one hundred gold dragons," Addie replied.

"Oh." Sophie pulled some gold out of her coin pouch. "All I have are these." She said. Sophie hadn't even thought that perhaps Ledora used their own money, Everywhere she had been previously all used the same gold, but she was across the ocean now.

"Okay, let me weigh it." Addie put a piece of Sophie's gold into the bowl of a scale and put a piece of Ledoran gold on the other side. The side with the Ledoran gold was slightly heavier. Addie added another of Sophie's gold and it tipped the scale the other way.

"Throw in twenty more of these, and we have a deal because I like you," Addie said.

"Sophie counted out one hundred and eighteen more gold and added it to the other two on the counter.

"You will be sure to win the Prince's heart in that dress," Addie commented.

"No, but I-" Sophie began to tell her that she wasn't here to win Dominic's heart but stopped short.

"Sophie?" A familiar voice startled her and she turned toward the doorway.

"Kamara!" Sophie exclaimed.

"You look amazing!" Kamara gushed. "Is this what you're wearing tonight?"

"Yes, I was thinking about changing back into my day clothes but I'm not sure how I would get back into this dress," Sophie admitted.

"We can get ready together! Addie, would you please have this dress sent to the castle with mine?" Kamara asked.

"It would be my pleasure, Ms. Kamara," Addie said.

Sophie excused herself to go back behind the dressing screen to change. Margaret and Henrietta helped her remove all of the pieces of her ball gown. They hung and packed the pieces neatly together and marked the cover with Sophie's name.

When Sophie was dressed she stepped out from behind the screen to see Kamara was still waiting for her.

"I thought maybe you would want to walk back together," Kamara stated.

"I do need an escort. I forgot my invitation at home." Sophie explained.

"No problem, I can get us in." Kamara pulled out her invitation.

When they got back to the castle, Kamara had no trouble getting the guards to let her in.

"When did you get here?" Sophie asked.

"I arrived yesterday," she said. Sophie remembered the dragon tracks from the beach.

"Did you land on the eastern beach?"

"Yeah, why do you ask?"

"I saw two sets of dragon prints on the beach when I landed, I thought maybe you were here, but I wondered who the other set belonged to."

"Shh, I have much to tell you, but let's get up to my chamber first." Kamara smiled as she thought about whatever it was she wanted to tell her, and Sophie couldn't tell for sure, but she thought that Kamara was blushing.

The inside of the castle was more beautiful than the outside. The floor was made of dark gray marble and had a path of white tiles, edged with gold down the center of the hallways and leading to the throne. Beautiful archways much like the ones in the city lined both the eastern and western sides of the throne room. On their way to Kamara's chamber, they ran into Prince Dominic.

They curtsied and greeted the Prince according to the customs of the court.

"Please, we are friends," Dominic said as he motioned for them to stand. "Sophie, it's so good to see you, where is Gabe? I thought he would be here with you?" Dominic asked.

Sophie's smile faded and she looked forlorn. "He left for assignment with the guild," Sophie explained.

"Ah well, next time then?" Dominic asked.

"Sure, next time," she said.

"There will be no shortage of noble young men here tonight, I would say fill your dance card with as many of them as possible and save one for me," Dominic said. He gave both Sophie and Kamara a quick embrace. Sophie noticed that Kamara's hug lingered a little more than hers did.

When Dominic walked away the two women hurried to Kamara's chamber like school girls ready to gossip.

"So, you first, it seemed like you were sad when Dominic brought up Gabe, did something happen?" Kamara asked.

"He told me he was leaving on assignment with the guild and that I needed to move on." Sophie's eyes welled with tears. "It took me all that time to finally admit that there was anything more than friendship between us, then I left to train with Ryul. I took for granted that Gabe would always be there, and now, I think I have lost him."

Kamara sat down next to Sophie on the large canopy bed. She reached out and wiped the tears from Sophie's cheek.

"I'm so sorry, Sophie. I know how much he cared about you, I don't understand why he would just leave like that." Kamara put her arm around Sophie's shoulder.

"Whatever, what about you? You said you had so much to tell me earlier."

"Well, it's about the other set of tracks you saw on the beach. They were Dominic's," Kamara said.

"What were you two doing out there?" Sophie asked. "Wait- were you..."

"Shh!" Kamara covered Sophie's mouth with her hand. "He came to visit me at the temple. We flew back together."

"Are you guys together?" Sophie asked. Before Kamara could answer the question there was a knock on her chamber door.

"I have a delivery for Kamara and Sophie from Adelaide's." Kamara opened the door and took the dresses from the servant. She thanked him and hurried back to the bed to lay out their dresses.

"It's time for us to get ready!" Kamara squealed excitedly. Sophie couldn't tell if the change in subject was deliberate, or a well-timed coincidence, but Kamara was already taking the pieces of their dresses from their packages.

Sophie helped Kamara with her corset, and then she did the same for her. When they were dressed, they did each other's hair and sprayed a little of Sophie's perfume on the inside of their wrists. The perfume was a symbol of status, not everyone could afford the fragrances, for each was hand-made by a perfumer. This skill was not a common one, so supply was very short and the demand was high. Perfumes were expensive, and only royalty could usually afford them. Sophie's had been a gift from Leon and she used it very sparingly.

"Are you ready? You look gorgeous!" Sophie said, admiring the gold ball gown that Kamara chose.

"I'm ready, you?" Sophie nodded. "Don't think about *him* tonight. Enjoy yourself," Kamara said as she took Sophie by the hand.

IO

AKIRI

Queen Akiri admired her form in the looking glass,
Her black lace dress hugged every curve of her
body and her porcelain skin peeked through in the most
strategic places. There was no way her new intended
would not fall to his knees at the sight of her. Her crown
was the final touch. It was made of silver and onyx to
match the juxtaposition of her skin and dress.

A knock on the door startled her and she jumped.
"Enter." She called.

"My Queen, Your intended has just arrived and is getting ready in the west wing. He would like to accompany
you to the ballroom and requests permission to come to
your chamber beforehand."

"Permission granted," Akiri said.

Akiri was feeling nervous. She hoped she was making
the right choice. There were so many suitors, ones who
she knew, and some she did not. Most of them craved

wealth or power. Akiri chose the only one who seemed different. He did not desire the throne or seem to crave the powers of magic or dragons. He would make the perfect husband if all those things were true about him.

It wasn't long before he was at her door. Akiri took a deep breath before she opened it. She was pleased with what she saw. The young man before her bowed deeply, respecting her position as queen.

"Please, Rise. It is so lovely to meet you." She said.

"Likewise, My Queen." The words rolled off his lips so effortlessly and Akiri could already see the devotion in his eyes. He looked at her from head to toe. "You look beautiful, My Queen." Akiri smiled and a slight pink rose in her cheeks. *Did he just make me blush?* Akiri thought.

"Shall we?" He offered Akiri the crook of his arm and she slid her arm through it, resting her hand on his forearm.

When they got to the end of the hallway, a castle guard sent them in separate directions.

"We are going to announce the new royal couples, ladies in this hallway, gentlemen in the other, when we call your names you will meet at the top of the stairs for your first public appearance together." He said.

Akiri and her betrothed glanced at each other and nodded before going to their waiting areas.

The dancing would not begin until they were all down the stairs, but Akiri could hear the sounds of people mingling on the floor below. She looked over the edge of the balcony at the beautiful white marble floor and the gold trim around the archways. This castle was much brighter than hers and seemed happier. Maybe it was because Prince Dominic still had a loving father, and all Akiri had was her council.

Akiri thought about what would happen when they got back to Ash. They would wed, of course, then immediately try for their first heir. She didn't want to wait. She watched the people below as they talked to each other, masking their flaws and making themselves appear perfect to each other in hopes of impressing those around them. She saw it, especially in the men, a kind of peacocking that Akiri found insufferable. She waited anxiously to hear her name and descend the stairs with her future husband.

II

SOPHIE

K amara and Sophie were mingling with the other girls when the royal announcer blew a quick tune on his instrument to get everyone's attention.

"Introducing, the newest royal engagements of the season; Princess Juliette and her betrothed, Sir Andrew Lee." Sophie watched the top of the stairs as a girl came from the right hallway and met up with a man from the left hallway. They paused together at the top of the stairs before descending into the ballroom. "Next, Prince Stephan, and his betrothed, Miss Angela Flores." Sophie poured another glass of punch from the large bowl and took a handful of grapes, after each announcement, the ballroom erupted with applause. Sophie popped a grape into her mouth.

"Queen Akiri Of Ash and her betrothed, Gabriel Taylor." Sophie gasped and the grape rolled into her throat, she started coughing as Queen Akiri came into view.

It can't be, no... it can't. Sophie thought as Kamara hit her on the back until she coughed up the grape. She tuned out everything around her. She thought she heard Kamara's voice asking if she was okay, but it faded away until all she could hear was her heartbeat. Sophie watched the top of the stairs and sure enough, it was Gabe. *Her* Gabe, here, with Akiri. Not just *with* Akiri, but *engaged to* Akiri. Sophie turned to face the table and gulped down her punch. She thought about escaping, but just as she turned to look for the nearest exit, the first dance began. She had already promised her first three dances. The first gentleman approached her, bowed, and extended his hand politely.

"Are you okay?" He asked her as she placed her hands where they needed to be.

"I just had a bit of a shock is all. I'm sorry." Sophie said as she tried to shake off her feelings of anger and rejection.

"What is your name?" He asked.

"Sophie."

"That's a beautiful name. I am Bastian." He whirled her around the dance floor. He was watching her eyes intently and followed her gaze to Gabe and Akiri.

"I see, was he an old flame?" The question startled Sophie, she hadn't realized that she was staring.

"Days old," Sophie admitted bitterly.

"I am so sorry that your heart has been broken, but if I may be so bold to say, it is *his* loss, truly." Bastian smiled at Sophie.

"Thank you for saying so, you're too kind." Sophie tried to enjoy Bastian's company, but she hadn't even had time to process the shock before the dance began, and then, it was over much too soon.

Bastian bowed to Sophie again. "I would love to dance again later if you wish, or we could take a walk onto the terrace and just get to know each other. Until then, Sophie." He bowed to her deeply and then disappeared into the crowd.

Sophie looked at her card. She did not see the man who had signed his name under the second dance. Kamara was dancing with someone already, and she had lost sight of Gabe and Akiri, which was probably for the best.

"May I have this dance?" She turned to see Dominic extending his hand to her. He held her close to him as they began their dance.

"I'm sorry, Sophie. I had no idea. I never would have asked you about him had I known."

"It's okay, I didn't know either. It was a total shock to see him here." A tear slid down Sophie's cheek as she stole a glance at Gabe dancing with Akiri. Dominic wiped her tears away.

"I have an idea," Dominic said as he guided them closer to Gabe and Akiri. "Put on your brave face Sophie, and try to look like you're into me, just a little." Dominic chuckled as he slid his hand up Sophie's back and dipped her, when she rose to face him again his lips were less than an inch from hers, she could feel his warm breath on her lips as he caressed her cheek and then trailed that breath down her neck and to her cleavage as he leaned her back in his arms once more. Sophie could feel Gabe's gaze on them, but she didn't even look his way. She was staring at the Prince who so willingly chose to show Gabe what he was missing and make Sophie feel beautiful and desired.

Before the dance was over, Dominic felt a tap on his shoulder. His smile indicated that he expected this to happen. He turned to look at Gabe.

"May I cut in?" Gabe asked.

"I am sorry, I do not wish to give up my time with Sophie. Perhaps you can find her later." Dominic said as he moved his forehead to touch Sophie's again. He looked into her eyes and held Sophie's full attention. Gabe huffed as he walked away. When the dance ended, Dominic bowed to Sophie again. "Let me know if you need a rescue later," he winked at Sophie as he allowed her next dance partner to offer his hand.

After the third dance, there was an intermission for the band, and a chance for the dancers to get a drink. Sophie grabbed two chalices of wine from a passing tray and hastily drank both.

"Hey, Sophie!" Kamara called. "That was quite a dance huh?" She smiled at her friend.

"Yes, He's a wonderful dancer, the closeness, I assure you was just to spite Gabe," Sophie told her, afraid that she would get the wrong idea about her and the Prince.

"I know, it's fine. Honestly, I thought it was kind of..." Kamara raised her eyebrows and Sophie grinned as she let out a gasp of shock.

"Kamara!" She scolded playfully.

"What? Can you blame me? Look at you both!"

"Excuse me, would you like to dance with me next?" A man asked as he offered his hand to Kamara.

"I would be delighted." She said. She handed him her dance card and he wrote his name on the line beside the number four.

"I will meet you over by the refreshments. I think I need another drink." Kamara told him. He bowed to her slightly and walked away.

"I could use another drink too," Sophie said.

As Sophie sipped her punch, Bastian approached her again. He smiled at her as he poured himself a glass. Bastian was dressed in a white suit with a blue tunic underneath and his wardrobe went strikingly well with his shoulder-length blond hair.

"Sophie, It would honor me greatly to dance with you again," he said.

"It would be my pleasure," she replied, handing him her ballspende. He signed it and then continued mingling. Before intermission was over, both Sophie and Kamara only had one open dance left on their cards. Every time Sophie danced, she scanned the floor for Gabe and Akiri. She wished that she could just forget about him and enjoy the company of others, but she felt so betrayed.

Of all the men she danced with, Bastian was her favorite. Not because he was the best dancer, that was definitely Dominic, but because he was interested in getting to know her and didn't only talk about himself like a lot of the men did that night.

In between dances, Sophie pounded back glasses of wine, until eventually, she was numb to the world around her. Most of her senses were dulled by the alcohol, but the sensation she felt at another's touch was heightened. She loved the way Bastian's hands held her as they danced, and she loved the way he glided his fingertips up and down her arms. She wasn't sure how it happened, but she found herself kissing him. Bastian was surprised by this but eagerly kissed her back and they moved slowly out of the crowd until Sophie's back was against the wall. Things were getting heated until Gabe tapped Bastian on the shoulder and asked to cut in.

Bastian was too disoriented from their heavy public display of affection to refuse, still trying to sort out just how they had ended up in that situation, he moved aside and allowed Gabe to sweep Sophie back to the dance floor.

"What are you doing?" Gabe asked angrily.

"What do you mean? I'm enjoying myself like you should be doing." Sophie said.

"First that dance with Prince Dominic, and now this. Are you trying to punish me?" Gabe gestured to Bastian who had retreated to the refreshment table.

"At least I didn't show up engaged." Sophie could not hide the bitterness in her voice.

"I know how it looks. It's not what you think."

"So, you're not engaged then?" Sophie demanded. When Gabe did not confirm, Sophie nodded at him.

"That's what I thought." She tried to pull away from him but he held her hand and twirled her back in so his lips were next to her ear.

"I never stopped loving you. My engagement is business, not pleasure. Do you really think this is what I wanted?"

"How am I supposed to know what you want any more, Gabe?"

"It will always be you." Gabe finished the dance with a bow and quickly left the dance floor.

Sophie watched helplessly as Akiri found him and wrapped her arms around his waist. She whispered something to him and they disappeared from the ballroom.

The ringing of a bell caught her attention and the King spoke.

"My son, Prince Dominic, has chosen his future bride!" Cheering and applause broke out across the grand room. When Prince Dominic joined him on the stage, many of the girls he had danced with throughout the evening screamed at the sight of him, hoping that he was about to call one of their names.

"Lady Kamara of Ophay, would you join me please?" Dominic waited for her to come up onto the throne platform with him. He took her hand and got down on one knee.

"You are the light in my darkness, and more beautiful than all the stars in the night sky, will you please make me the happiest man alive and give me the honor of being your husband?"

"Yes," she whispered through tears as he slid a beautiful opal ring onto her finger.

Dominic stood and kissed her. The crowd cheered again but not in the excited way they had before.

"Now, the final dance is for the future King and his future Queen!" King Haki announced. The ballroom floor cleared as Dominic and Kamara walked down the steps and onto the dance floor. They looked at each other like they were the only two people in the room. Sophie wanted that too someday. She downed another glass of wine as they took the floor. They danced alone on the dance floor for the first minute of the song, until others were allowed to join in.

Bastian appeared with a soft smile and held out his hand to Sophie. She never noticed how his blue eyes sparkled until now. She took his hand and followed him into the dancing crowd.

12

KAMARA

W hen the ball was finally over, Dominic and Kamara disappeared from the crowd and made
their way to the beach. Soon, they were in the sky, the
two dragons raced through the clouds. Dominic sent a
flash of lightning from his mouth across the endless night
sky. Kamara's breath blew cold and each droplet formed
into crystals and she made it snow. Each snowflake
turned to rain before it reached the ground below so
to the rest of Ledora it looked as if a thunderstorm had
rolled in.

The dragons tangled themselves together as they
danced through the sky. It was almost morning when
they reached the temple of Ophay. Kamara's home was
their own private getaway; the best place for a newly engaged couple to celebrate. Very few people knew
about the temple, those in Blackwater, and of course,
Dominic's father.

Kamara led Dominic to the back of the temple and out into the forest behind it. They didn't bother getting dressed, where they were, no one would see them. When the trees ended, Dominic saw what it was Kamara wanted him to see. The tall, flat mountain that stood before them now had a large opening in it that led into an enormous cavern. They walked inside the entrance and took in the natural splendor.

"I only wanted a small lair, and when the builders opened the entrance to this, they were done. It was perfect and made by the Goddess, Mother of the Land. It's like it was meant to be". Turquoise hot springs bubbled softly and surrounded a large deep pool that reflected the speleothems that hung from the rocks above like icicles made of stone.

"Wow, this place is incredible," Dominic said as he looked around. He noticed a large nest toward the back of the cavern.

"What's this for?" He asked walking back toward the large bed of moss and twigs.

"It's for our eggs. I have done a lot of research while here. Dragon couples have the highest chance of producing viable dragon eggs. Dragon and human couples have a lower chance, but it isn't impossible. Dragon couples can also have human children who will become dragonshifters themselves at the end of their seventeenth year as we did. Dragons who mate with humans also have less of a chance of their child being a shifter, but their children can be just as powerful, like Sophie."

"So, you've been thinking of having kids already huh?" Dominic smiled a mischievous grin at Kamara and raised and lowered his eyebrows in quick repetition as he grabbed her around the waist and pulled her close to him. She smiled back and playfully pushed him. He kissed her passionately. It made his knees weak and every part of his skin tingled with excitement. Dominic stepped down into one of the bubbling pools and reached for Kamara's hand to help her down into the hot spring too.

He guided her to his lap and she kissed him as they both felt every sensation all at once. They spent hours in the cavern and when they could no longer evade sleep, they went back inside the temple to a new room that Kamara had asked the builders to construct as an engagement gift. The room was a chamber fit for a King and Queen, complete with windows and a four-poster canopy bed with heavy curtains that blocked out the light.

"I know we will be spending most of our time in Ledora, but I thought we could keep the temple as a home away from home, somewhere we can visit when the pressures of court become too much."

"It's perfect. We don't have to live in Ledora; not until I have to assume the throne. We could live here until that time comes. We could raise our children here, away from court and the weight of responsibility. Here they will be safe. I will see to it. We can invite some staff and security here and turn this place into our little village, just for us."

"That sounds amazing," Kamara said.

Dominic and Kamara fell asleep and snuggled together in the middle of the enormous bed. Kamara's mind was filled with dreams of their life together, their children, and the dragons they would become.

The next morning, Dominic and Kamara made the trek through the forest to Blackwater. They spoke to the guildmaster, Leon Rend, about contracting help from the guild to make improvements on the temple, and about buying some horses. Leon sent them to the stable master with a letter of importance. Sometimes the wait list for a horse was long, mares carry their foal for almost a full year and only give birth to one. It takes three years before a horse is of breeding age, and two years before most breeders will sell.

Kamara gave the letter to the stable master and he led them to the horses.

"I only 'ave two colts right now, they're two and a half years old, or thereabout. If you're lookin' to breed 'em, you can come back next spring and this gal here will be ready t' go."

"That's okay, Sir. We'll take the two Colts, we are going to ride them ourselves, or hitch them to a cart when needed."

"Okie Dokie then." The man said and he started preparing the horses. Kamara paid him and they took the horses with a lead and a feed bag. Next, they went to the saddle maker. She measured their horses and wrote everything down.

"Give me about a week and I will have them done for you," she said. Kamara and Dominic noticed the several saddles that she and her three apprentices were already working on and simply nodded to her.

"Thank you very much," Kamara said as they left.

"Anything else you want to do while in town?" Dominic asked Kamara. She thought about it, and suddenly, her face lit up.

"We should stop by and visit Juniper and Laughlin," Kamara said.

They led their horses through the eastern forest. Kamara took in her favorite sights and sounds, green foliage guiding winding pathways through the trees; trees that were older than time itself, and birds singing in the canopy above. It all brought Kamara great joy.

When Laughlin and Juniper's cabin finally came into view, Dominic hitched the horses to a nearby tree so that he and Kamara could go to the door together. As they took the first step onto the porch a loud bark from inside the house startled them. Kamara jumped because she hadn't expected Dusk to bark. Dominic knocked and they waited for someone inside to answer. They heard a shuffling through the door and then finally, Laughlin opened the door.

"Hey, how are you guys? Long time no see." Laughlin said as he moved aside and gestured for them to come inside.

"Is Juniper here? We were hoping to share our news with both of you." Kamara looked around and then at Laughlin.

"Uh, no, she went out to gather herbs and said she needed the fresh air. She should be back soon though if you want to wait, I'll put on some tea." Laughlin said grabbing his kettle from the wood stove. He filled it up from his kitchen sink.

"How did you do that?" Kamara asked.

"I made a special rain collection system. Come, I'll show you." He led them out the patio door and showed them a barrel that he had mounted to the side of his house.

"Inside the bottom of this barrel, I have layered different materials that are used for filtration, I covered the top of the filter with a thin white cloth. I attached this bit of hose, it's a new bendable material, which makes my life easier. When I lift this handle, the pressure on the hose releases, allowing the water to flow, and when I push it down like this, it puts pressure on the hose and stops the flow of water."

"Wow, that's nice! We need a setup like that for our place." Dominic said to Kamara.

"Oh, is that your news? You're moving in together?" Laughlin asked. "We have news too, but I need to let Juni tell you herself."

"It's a little more than moving in together," Kamara told him.

Just then the kettle started whistling and Laughlin rushed over to pull it off of the wood stove and pour the hot liquid into teacups. Just as they took their seats around the table, Juniper came in. Right away, Kamara and Dominic could see what news Juniper had to tell them. She had a perfectly round and swollen belly.

"Juniper! Are you..." Kamara began. Juniper nodded and grinned from ear to ear. She hugged her friends tightly and they took turns putting their hands on her belly to see if they could feel the life that was growing inside of her.

"I am so happy for you guys!"

"Me too," Dominic said.

"What was your news?" Laughlin asked.

"We are engaged, and talking about making the temple of Ophay our home until we are needed in Ledora to rule."

"That's wonderful! When is the wedding?" Juniper asked.

"We didn't talk about that yet," Kamara said as she looked at Dominic.

"Soon, I hope," Dominic said, he looked at Kamara with starry eyes. She smiled and leaned over to rest her head on his shoulder.

"Good news all around. This deserves a celebration, a housewarming, and an engagement party. I can plan it, Kamara, handle the guest list, and Dominic, you, and Laughlin can handle decorating. We will meet you at the temple tomorrow morning to get started." Juniper couldn't hide her excitement.

"We should be getting the horses home, but that sounds great! See you tomorrow." Kamara hugged Juniper again and congratulated them several more times before they made it out the door.

They rode the horses bareback on the return trip to the temple. Dominic cast a dome of protection over the horses to protect them from the elements until they could build a barn. Dominic put up both of his hands with his palms facing the horses. He moved around them in a circle as blue runes rose from the ground and spread like lightning across the dome. When he was finished, Kamara could only see a faint blue shimmering veil over the horses.

"I'm going to name mine Phoenix. How about you?" Kamara looked over at Dominic.

"I'm not sure, I'm going to sleep on it. Maybe you could think of a name for mine tonight." Dominic said.

That night their dreams brought them images of their life in the new kingdom of Ophay, and their children growing up happy and healthy with friends from the neighboring town of Blackwater.

13

GABE

"How are we getting back to Ash?" Gabe asked.

"We're going to fly, of course." Akiri smiled. "Don't worry, I had a special harness made to strap a rider to my back." Akiri could see that Gabe was still anxious.

"So, what was going on between you and the red dragon?" Akiri asked as she packed her things.

"Huh?" Gabe looked up. "What do you mean?"

"The girl you danced with last night with curly red hair. I know that you traveled to Choddrath together, but you seemed worried about her last night, so I was wondering if you used to court her?"

"Not exactly. We grew up together, that's all, we were friends," Gabe said.

"Were? Does that mean you aren't anymore?"

"We had an argument a few days ago and we just hadn't talked since, I didn't want to leave without apologizing is all," he told her.

When they got to the western beach, Akiri showed Gabe the harness she had made. It was a large saddle with armored sleeves for the rider's legs. The straps were adjustable so that his legs would be anchored to the harness.

"When I take shape, you have to buckle the harness around me. Make sure the belts are tight." Akiri went under the saddle, which looked more like a cave compared to Akiri's slender human form. She started to grow and her shining green scales shimmered in the moonlight as Akiri disappeared and the green dragon took her place. Gabe watched in amazement as her body grew into the underside of the saddle perfectly. When the leather was snug around her body, Gabe pulled the belts tight and buckled them.

A large saddle bag hung from each side of the leather saddle and they had packed their clothes in them. Beside the saddle bag on the dragon's right side was a ladder to climb up into the seat. Gabe strapped his legs into the leather sleeves that buckled just above his knees. The backrest had a leather belt to wear across his chest as well and by the time he was all strapped in, he felt surprisingly safe.

When Akiri started to run, the momentum pushed Gabe's body back against the saddle and when she lifted off the ground, Gabe closed his eyes. His heart was pounding so fast and his palms were sweaty. He didn't know how high off the ground they were, but he was sure if he opened his eyes to look he would pass out. He gripped the reigns tightly just for something to hold onto.

When Akiri was finally gliding smoothly in a straight line, Gabe found the courage to open his eyes. Stretching on forever, as far as his eyes could see, the night sky glittered with millions of stars. His heart started pounding faster as he dared to look down. He was thankful for the clouds, which obscured the truth of how high up they actually were.

Flying wasn't as bad as Gabe had expected. Before the end, he thought he might even like it, but as they neared The Kingdom of Ash, Akiri began pointing her nose down and Gabe's stomach dropped. He felt like he might be sick as they descended. The wind pounded into his face, stinging like thousands of tiny needles poking his skin and he found it hard to breathe. Gabe leaned forward and positioned his face behind Akiri's head.

They landed in the arena and Akiri waited for Gabe to unbuckle and dismount before she returned to human form and walked out from underneath the saddle. She grabbed a dress out of the saddle bag and slipped it on, and then detached the saddle bag and threw the strap over her shoulder like a soldier's duffel bag. She went to the other side, unhooked the other bag, and gave it to Gabe to carry.

"Come on, I'll show you to your chamber. I have a council meeting and I am sure they will all want to meet you before the wedding tomorrow night, but you can rest tonight and I will let them know that you will accompany me to the council tomorrow." Akiri was no longer the girl he had spent the night dancing with, she was now Queen Akiri, a monarch with duties, and responsibilities. Gabe thought about his mission here, so far he had nothing to report. He was listening for plans and plots against the Dragons Guild, which was the new governing body of the northern continent. Akiri's refusal to join the guild was viewed as a seed of mistrust. The Silver Talons Guild, mostly Leon, wanted to know more about the Queen of Ash. He specifically wanted to know what her plans were, and how she was using her dragon powers, and he wanted Gabe to make friends with someone on her council.

Gabe wasn't ready to get married-especially to someone he met only hours ago, but if he didn't go through with it he would blow his cover which might mean death and if he did go through with it, he would lose Sophie forever. He wasn't sure which was worse.

The outside of the castle was dark; a collection of black, towering, spires silhouetted the full moon. The decorations for the wedding made it look festive and welcoming though. Lilies of every color and bright blue roses brightened the walk to the castle doors. Strings of small oil lanterns illuminated the flower gardens and walkways. It made the dark castle seem almost inviting.

The interior of the castle was as dark and drab as the outside. Black iron sconces held torches and illuminated the hallways in the soft flickering light. The shadows moved like ghosts that followed them down the hall. Akiri opened the door to a large bedchamber. Despite the look of the rest of the castle, this room was brighter. The bedding was royal blue with black velvet buttons sewn into the comforter where the material gathered together to make it look like a royal cushion. An abstract painting above the hearth looked like a stained glass window. The top of the canvas was even curved into a semi-circle to enhance the illusion of a window. Had it been on the wall, and not the fireplace, Gabe might have mistaken it for a real stained glass window. A large Chandelier with unlit candles hung from the center of the ceiling and made the room look elegant. The fire in the hearth was new, the three logs would last the night at least.

"You can have the servants draw you a bath if you like. This will eventually be our room, but until you're comfortable and we know each other a little better, I will stay in my old room just down the hall." Akiri smiled as she turned to go to her council meeting.

Akiri was not what Gabe expected at all. He had not paid much attention to her when they met on Chod-drath, he had been too preoccupied with trying to save Sophie. He expected her to be cruel, much like all the stories he heard about her mother, the late Queen Luciana, but so far, she seemed kind. Gabe wondered if it was just to make him feel comfortable until the wedding. They didn't have much time to get to know each other. She was in a hurry to be married for some reason, and it wasn't about wealth, because Gabe didn't have any of that.

Gabe changed into sleeping clothes. He couldn't wait to snuggle between the sheets. He had never slept in a bed so fancy. The sheets were as smooth as silk but as soft and warm as his cotton stockings. A knock on the door startled him.

"Yes?" Gabe answered. Two servants came in, they were both boys and Gabe thought they looked much younger than himself. He guessed them to have seen the thirteenth anniversary of their birth, but not more than that. Gabe stayed under the covers in his half-dressed state as they busied themselves about the room. They picked up the clothes he had just taken off and put them into a basket for washing. One of the boys had red hair, Gabe caught himself thinking about Sophie and what her sons might look like when that time came.

"Would you like a bed warmer, Sir?" The dark-haired boy asked. Gabe nodded and the boy grabbed a metal pan with a long handle. He watched the boy scoop hot coals from the bottom of the hearth to fill the pan. The lid had holes in it to vent the heat and he fitted it over the bottom lip of the pan perfectly. The boy lifted the comforter and the sheets at the foot of the bed and slid the warmer in. Gabe hadn't realized before how cold his toes had been, but the warming pan made them feel toasty; the warmth spread throughout his body and made him shiver as the last bit of cold left him.

Gabe was more comfortable than he had ever been before, but still, he could not fall asleep.

14

AKIRI

T he council members were all sitting in their seats waiting for Akiri to come in. When they tried to stand as she entered she motioned for them not to bother. She was tired from her flight after all, and she only needed to give a quick update.

"Prince Dominic chose Kamara, the silver dragon. There were no other events of significance except that I met my betrothed and we traveled back together as planned. Thank you for making yourselves scarce as requested for our return."

"My Queen, this is most unorthodox. You are going to trust this man to rule at your side and you have known him for a day." The captain of the city guard objected.

"I have not met any of the other men who requested my hand either, so are you upset that I am engaged and the six of you did not get to choose my future husband or are you upset that you yourself weren't considered?"

Akiri looked at each of them and when no one said another word, she continued. "Well? If anyone has anything to say about their queen's decision, it's best to get it out now." Some of the men looked down at the table, and others shifted in their chairs, but none of them spoke another word.

"Okay, good. Meeting adjourned, be back here in the morning for introductions, and please have a chair placed at that end of the table for your future king." Akiri gestured to the spot directly across from her.

"Yes, My Queen." was all Akiri heard as she left the room as quickly as she had entered it. She went back to her room. It was the room she had been in since childhood. She could have moved to the Queen's quarters when she was crowned, but all of her memories were there in that room. Her mother had not been the sentimental type though, so Akiri never really had toys to play with or even human friends. She had made friends with a rat once. She remembered that she had named her Rally the Rat. She used to sneak food to her room after dinner and she always left a few crumbs beside the crack in the wall where she saw her scurry one day.

Rally would only come out at night when Akiri was quiet. She couldn't move or it would scare Rally away. Akiri left crumbs for the rat every night, leading her further and further away from her hole, until one day, Rally was close enough for her to reach out and try to touch her. As soon as she started to lift her hand though, Rally ran away and darted back into the crack in the wall. Akiri was determined though, she kept leaving breadcrumb trails and leading Rally closer and closer until one day, she took the crumbs right from Akiri's hand. She petted the rat's head with her fingertip. Rally nuzzled it for a moment and then happily scurried back into the hole in the wall.

Most of her childhood memories were lonely. The only time Akiri's mother paid any attention to her at all was when Akiri was in trouble. The maids and her tutors were nice enough, but when their job was done, they left and Akiri was alone again. She hoped that now, with Gabe she could fill that emptiness and never feel alone again.

Sleep evaded her. Tomorrow, she would be married. She tossed and turned until finally, she gave up. She got up and put on a long robe. The torches in the hall were no longer lit so she grabbed one and lit it in the fireplace. She carried it with her through the darkened halls and made her way to the kitchen. She placed the torch in the sconce just above the breakfast nook in the corner and then opened the store room for wine and ale. She did not need the torch in there, she knew exactly where her favorite wine was. Akiri grabbed a bottle and turned around to see Gabe standing in the doorway.

"You couldn't sleep either?" He asked. Akiri shook her head. She had planned to drink that bottle of wine herself and force sleep to come, but now that Gabe was here, she felt it might be rude not to offer him some. She grabbed two silver chalices and they walked over to the table. She poured the fragrant red wine into both cups and slid one across the table to Gabe.

"Thank you."

"You're welcome. Are you nervous about tomorrow?" Akiri asked.

"I would be lying if I said I wasn't," Gabe admitted. "What about you, are you nervous?"

"Extremely." She drank down her cup of wine and poured another.

"How about while we drink, we get to know each other? That might make both of us feel better." Gabe suggested.

"Sure. You go first, ask me anything." Akiri told him. Gabe looked at her and thought about what to ask her. He took a long drink of his wine as he studied her facial features and expression.

"What is your biggest fear?" He asked, finally.

"Oh, we're jumping right into the deep stuff. Okay, um... I guess the thing I am most afraid of is never knowing what love feels like." She didn't look at him, instead, Akiri took a drink before asking him a question. "What are your parents like?"

"When I was little, things were great, My dad was a jack of all trades, and my mom was a seamstress. I didn't grow up wealthy, but we weren't poor either. When my dad got injured and could no longer swing a hammer, or a sword, he got angry and started drinking. My mom drank to deal with him, and then it spiraled downward from there. My dad passed away, and my mom drank and gambled away any coin she had left. It was then I knew I would have to take care of myself." Akiri could see the pain in his eyes as he thought about his parents. "What were your parents like?" he asked.

"I don't remember my father. Mother never talked about him much either. Mother was cruel and only wanted what was best for her. She never cared about me."

"I'm sorry, I know that must have been a lonely life to grow up with a mother like that," Gabe said as he reached across the table to place his hand on top of Akiri's.

"Yeah. Okay, next question, Have you ever been in love?" Akiri asked. Gabe knew if he lied, his face would betray him, and honesty was important in a marriage, so he answered with the truth.

"Yes." He said no more, but Akiri studied his face.

"Are you still in love?" She asked.

"That's not fair, you don't get to go again, it's my turn." Gabe smiled at her and pretended to scold her, wagging his finger back and forth with a "tsk tsk" as she looked at him surprised.

"Let's see here, I have to make my next question good." He thought for a moment and it seemed longer than a moment to Akiri before he spoke. "When you think of the future of this Kingdom, what do you see?" He looked at her intently. She sipped her wine and a drop of the red liquid spilled out of the corner of her mouth and rolled to her chin. She wiped it away with the back of her hand. The answer to that question was easy, she had been dreaming about it since she was a little girl.

"I see a Queen and King with many heirs living happily and doing everything they can to help the kingdom and all of its residents flourish."

"That's quite an answer. I like it."

"My turn. The same question; are you in love right now?" Gabe had hoped she would forget that inquiry, but now he had to answer.

"Yes," he admitted. Akiri poured the last of the bottle of wine into their cups and they both drank it down.

"The red dragon?" Akiri asked. She knew it was Gabe's turn to ask a question, but she couldn't help it, the words came out involuntarily.

"Her name is Sophie, but yes. I fell in love with her, but she didn't choose me, so I decided to move on with my life far away from Blackwater, which is why I sent my proposal to you. I am glad you accepted and in time I could see myself falling in love with you too. We will help each other fill the loneliness in our hearts."

Akiri saw the pain in his eyes that mirrored her own, she knew that they were the same; craving love they never received. She couldn't resist any longer. Akiri laced her fingers through Gabe's and stood up and moved toward him. Gabe admired her beauty, and how even in her dressing robe, she radiated royalty from her core. She guided his hands to her waist and lightly grazed his neck with her fingertips. Gabe followed her lead as she moved her face toward his and pulled him closer. Her kiss was hungry and needful and Gabe could feel himself losing control of his lust. She walked backward slowly, pulling him with her until her backside was against the table. She sat on the edge of it and wrapped her legs around him as they both unleashed years of repressed passion. The ties of Akiri's robe loosened and the shoulder fell to one side, exposing her breast to him. Gabe groaned and pressed his body against hers as they kissed. She could feel his bulge pressed against her inner thigh and she wanted nothing more at that moment than for him to ravage her right there on the kitchen table. She pushed her hands up the front of his tunic and felt his smooth abdomen and twirled her fingers in the patch of hair on his chest. Her fingers trailed back down to the strings of his trousers, she pulled one of the strings and felt the knot pop as his trousers loosened. She was about to claim her prize when they heard a startling sound.

"Ahem."

Akiri gasped and frantically adjusted her robe to cover herself as she saw Roland Koffery, the castle steward, standing in the doorway.

"My apologies Your Majesty, I heard a commotion and came to investigate." Mister Koffery averted his gaze until Akiri was decent.

"It's alright, Mister Koffery, This is Gabriel Taylor of Blackwater, my intended."

"It is a pleasure to meet you, sir. I look forward to the wedding, which is another reason I was on my way to the kitchen, I have to prep dinner for after the ceremony tomorrow."

"We'll get out of your way. Akiri grabbed the chalices and another bottle of wine from the store room. "Care for a nightcap?"

Gabe nodded as he tied his trouser strings and followed from the kitchen. When they got to her room, she poured them each a glass of wine. Akiri raised her glass.

"To the start of a marriage filled with adventure." Akiri's cheeks were bright pink as she smiled and touched her cup to Gabe's. Mister Koffery might have ruined the mood, but Gabe found that he still craved satisfaction; the feel of her skin against his. He wondered what it was about her that had that effect on him. He was certain that his chance with Sophie was gone, so moving on was really what was best for everyone. Akiri was beautiful, there was no denying that, and it seemed that they had a connection that was deeper than duty. He was there to do a job, but he saw no reason why he shouldn't enjoy it.

"Thank you for an enjoyable late night, but I should try to get some sleep now," Akiri said as she stood up from the chair beside the fireplace. "I will see you in the morning at the council meeting, but then not until the wedding. I hear it's terrible luck." She winked and kissed him on the cheek before walking him to the door.

Gabe watched her with a longing gaze as she closed her bedroom door and left him out in the hallway. He wandered back to his room and collapsed onto his bed with a groan. The soft cushion of the comforter enveloped him and he felt like he was laying on a cloud. He slept deeply for a few more hours until the servants came knocking.

15

SOPHIE

Morning light roused Sophie from a deep sleep. She was still in Ledora, but this was not her bed, and she was not wearing any clothes. She turned her head to see Bastian still asleep beside her. Sophie let out a deep sigh as she slowly slid out of bed. She didn't want to wake Bastian and have the awkward *'it's not you, it's me. I'm not ready for anything serious,'* conversation. She tried to piece together the events of the evening before and all she could remember was goblet after goblet of wine as she thought about Gabe marrying Akiri.

Sophie remembered Bastian asking her to dance and her convincing him to drink with her instead. She was pretty sure they talked about Gabe, and she wondered if she gave Bastian the chance to say anything about himself.

Sophie knew that she had not been good company last night, and would likely not be a good company today either, but that hadn't stopped Bastian from taking her to his bed. Sophie was sure at the time she had been willing to ease her pain with Bastian, the handsome distraction that he was, but now she was dressed, and it was time to go.

She tiptoed to the door and opened it slowly, hoping it wouldn't creak and wake him. It didn't, and she slipped into the hallway undetected. Prince Dominic was already gone, he and Kamara had left last night during the ball. Sophie figured that they returned to the temple where they could be alone. Sophie went back to her room and gathered her things into Leon's pack, including the clothes she had just put on. When her spell was complete and she appeared to be dressed, Sophie headed for the eastern beach. She made a plan to stop at home, say goodbye to her mother and father and then go back to her studies at Lapis Highland. *Maybe there's a spell for a broken heart.* Sophie thought.

The flight back to Blackwater went by so quickly that Sophie made it home before Leon even left for work.

"Hey kiddo," he said as he wrapped her in a hug.

"Dad, can I talk to you?" Sophie asked. She hadn't had a chance to talk to him since she found out what Gabe's assignment was, she just needed to know why. Leon and Sophie walked out back to the garden and sat on the bench in the clearing of lilac bushes and peonies. It smelled so nice in the garden, she could see why her mother loved it so much.

"I think I know what this is about, and I can tell you, it's not what you think."

"So Gabe isn't going to marry Akiri?" Sophie asked. She already knew the answer, but needed to let Leon know that it was exactly what she thought.

"He is going to marry her, but it gives us a spy on the inside. We will know her plans and be warned if she ever decides to attack." Leon said.

"You're paranoid, why would she ever attack us?"

"There are things you are still too young to understand. I have seen what power does to people, it makes them hungry. They always want more no matter how much they have, and how long do you think she will be happy being Queen of that hunk of rock where the only thing that grows is sugar cane from hundreds of years of making rum?"

"You think she is planning an invasion." It was a statement, not a question, but Leon answered anyway.

"Yes, I think she will invade if given a chance, if not here, then Braidwood, or even Hillside, or Aerulean Lake. She did not join the Dragon Alliance, so she is not bound to any rules or guidelines we have put in place to protect you three, and the villagers across the continent."

"Why Gabe? I thought you liked him." Sophie was almost in tears now.

"Akiri sent out a request for suitors. She made a list of qualifications, he had to be around her age, taller than her, never married, and so on. Gabe was the only one in the guild who met all of the requirements so we had his portrait painted and sent to her with an offer letter. We didn't know that she would accept so quickly, but apparently, she is in a hurry to get married." Sophie leaned against Leon's shoulder and sniffled. "I'm sorry, again. I know how much he meant to you, but in time you will meet someone just as great as you are, I know it." Sophie wiped a tear from her cheek as she stood up.

"I should be getting back to the tower, I have to clean up and get some practice in," Sophie said.

"Okay, kiddo. I love you."

"Love you too, Dad." Sophie walked back into the kitchen where her mom was sitting at the table drinking coffee. Sophie put her arms around her and hugged her tightly.

"I will see you soon, I have a lot of work to do at the tower," Sophie said.

"I can come over and help you later this week if you want, sweetie."

"That's okay mom, I think I just need to be alone for a while to process everything."

"Okay, if you're sure," Samantha said. Sophie nodded and kissed her mother's cheek.

16

KAMARA

K amara had her sleeves rolled up and her hair was tied back with a ribbon. She had already done so much to transform the temple from a place of worship into a home. She and Dominic removed the altars from the front room and swept and mopped the marble floor. The room was large and open now and Kamara thought it would make a beautiful sitting room for company.

Dominic ordered furniture from the Silver Talons and it would be delivered soon. He kept watching out the front doors for the wagon to arrive. Kamara had a list of staff positions that she needed to fill. She wrote them on two scrolls, one for the crier in Torzana, and one for the crier in Blackwater.

"I'm going to go deliver these, I will be back in about an hour," Kamara said as she kissed Dominic's cheek.

"Okay, my love. I will be here, waiting for the furniture and hopefully when you get back this place will look like home." He smiled as he said that word, *home.* The temple had always been home to Kamara, but now it was more than that.

Kamara went to Torzana first and handed the scroll to the crier. She didn't stop to talk to anyone else, she had to hurry. Laughlin and Juniper were supposed to join them for tea in the afternoon. She rode on to Blackwater. Usually, the town crier had a bell or at least a bullhorn, but this one didn't and he was difficult to track down. Kamara found him at the entrance to the guild just watching the doors.

"Waiting for someone?" She asked.

"No, what makes you ask that?" the boy answered.

"The way you keep watching the door, like any minute someone you know is going to open it."

"I tried t' get a job there, but they said I's too young."

"Well, I have some jobs open. You do this for me, and I will give you a job."

"What d' I gotta do?" the kid asked.

"All you have to do is tell everyone you know about my temple, it just south through those woods. Tell them I am hiring staff and I can pay them well. I am to marry the prince of Ledora after all."

"Really? You're a real-life princess?" The boy asked.

"Not yet, but I will be, and you could come and work for me."

"That sounds nice."

"Where are your parents? We can go ask them together if it's alright."

"I don't have no parents. They died when I was little."

"I'm sorry, I didn't know." Kamara's heart ached for him.

"It's okay, I have been on my own ever since, It's not so bad once you're used to it; as long as you can find work that is.

Okay, you get that word out and when you and your new friends are ready you can come work for me and I will see you are all treated and paid fairly.

"Gee that's real nice of ya. I wish I met more people like you."

"Well I always heard that good deeds have a way of coming back around, and so do bad ones, so I always try my hardest to be good."

The boy smiled and took off with the scroll reading Kamara's words out loud. Kamara rode as quickly as she could back to the temple. It felt like it took longer to get back than it had to get to town. Kamara wanted to soak her aching muscles in a bath so she filled a cauldron and hung it on the fire. She heard the wagon arrive as soon as she eased herself down into the hot water.

Dominic helped the delivery drivers unload their furniture. Two couches, a rug, a small table, a bookshelf, a couple of lantern stands, and new oil lanterns. Dominic made sure everything he ordered was there and then as promised, by the time Kamara was out of the bath, he had everything put together and arranged.

"Wow, it looks beautiful," Kamara said. She looked around at the reading corner with two chairs beside the window, and the bookshelf along the wall. The handcrafted furniture reminded Kamara of the gold trim on the buildings in Ledora, simple, but elegant.

"Just in time for guests!" Kamara exclaimed as they heard a knock on the door. Kamara rushed to open it and invite Laughlin and Juniper inside. Juniper was glowing with her golden hair and rosy cheeks.

"Juniper, you look radiant." Kamara complimented as she hugged Juniper. "Laughlin, it's so good to see you again." She hugged Laughlin as well. "Please, come in and sit."

"Your home looks lovely," Juniper said as she sat down on one of the sofas.

"Thank you, we just got the furniture today, I will do more decorating as we go. Would you like some herbal tea or water?" Kamara asked.

"Oh, no thank you," Juniper said. Laughlin declined as well as they got comfortable in the sitting room.

"I noticed the horses out there, are you looking to have a stable built? I would be happy to help." Laughlin offered.

"Yes, I was planning to build that here in the next few days so whenever you're available to help I would be happy to have a hand with it," Dominic said.

"Have you guys seen Sophie?" Juniper asked. "Leon mentioned that we might want to check in on her, is everything okay?"

"I guess you heard about Gabe?" Kamara asked.

"No, what happened to Gabe, is he okay?"

"He's fine, but he showed up to the Ledoran Ball with Akiri and they were announced as one of the newly engaged royal couples," Dominic told them.

"Oh no, how did Sophie take it?" Juniper asked.

"She was shocked and angry. We all were, to be honest." Kamara said.

"I asked my friend, Bastian, to check in on her before Kamara and I left and If Leon has already heard about what happened I am guessing Sophie is home now?" Dominic asked.

"Home and gone again, Leon said she stopped in to say quick goodbyes to him and her mom, and then she was off to Lapis Highland again," Juniper said.

"Maybe I should go tomorrow morning and see if she needs a friend. I can take a boat over from Torzana." Kamara thought out loud.

"That sounds like a nice idea. I am sure Sophie would be happy to have another girl there to talk to. Maybe you and Juniper could go, and Laughlin and I could work on the stables?" Dominic suggested.

"Are you okay to travel?" Kamara asked, looking at Juniper's baby bump.

"I still have plenty of time before the baby is due, it would be nice to see Sophie," Juniper said.

"Okay, I will make up the guest room for you and Laughlin and we can leave in the morning."

17

GABE

The six councilmen were already standing when Akiri and Gabe entered the council chamber. Akiri introduced Gabe to them and then hastily got on with the meeting. The arena was earning a lot with the new food vendors and contests. The entry fee to watch the daily joust was only two silver pieces and the stands were filled every day. Knights from other countries that came to compete would rent a horse from the stable master, stay at one of the four local inns, and buy their food and ale from one of the many taverns.

"It sounds like things are going very well, and the people are happy?" Akiri asked.

"Yes, My Queen, they are very happy we are no longer taxing them, and they love the entertainment we are providing with the arena," Nohan said.

"Nohan, you and your soldiers come in contact with the people more than anyone else in the castle, what would you say the rate of joblessness is among the subjects?" Akiri asked.

"I would say there's a good five percent of the population that can work, that don't have jobs currently," Nohan answered.

"Gabriel will be needing his own guards. I would like to take some that you have already trained and employ them here, which will open up new positions with the city guard. Timothy, see to it that Nohan is fairly compensated for his trained men."

"Yes, My Queen," Timothy said.

"Your Grace, how many of my men will Gabriel require?" Nohan asked.

"At least three, four if you can spare them," Akiri answered.

"I will assign them at once, Your Grace."

"If there is nothing else, I will see you at the wedding. Meeting adjourned."

Akiri and Gabe stood first, then everyone else followed suit. They waited for Akiri to take Gabe's arm and exit before they started shuffling about. Gabe heard Nohan grumbling under his breath as they left, he looked at Akiri and knew she heard it too, but chose to ignore it. When they were back in the privacy of their corridor, Gabe stopped and looked at Akiri.

"If it means the city guard will be left untrained, I am fine with not having a personal guard detail. It seems your captain wasn't too happy about giving up three or four of his trained men." Gabe said.

"There are thirty-six men currently working for the city guard, they can spare four and still have plenty. He's only angry because I asked him to train new men to replace them. He doesn't understand that jobless people are the biggest threat to the crown. If I had my way about it, everyone would have a job and be able to take care of their families, but that isn't the way it is." Gabe looked into Akiri's face, he could see that she cared a lot more for other people than anyone knew. He felt ashamed that he had believed the rumors about her before anyone took the time to get to know her. Gabe leaned forward and kissed her and held her in his embrace.

"I'll see you in a little while." He whispered in her ear. His hot breath sent a chill down Akiri's neck and she smiled.

The wedding took place in the garden courtyard in front of a beautiful fountain and the wedding arch was covered in trailing clematis blooms. The ceremony was private, only the castle staff was invited, but the subjects of Ash all gathered at the front of the castle for the first glance at their Queen and her new King. Akiri's dress was white trimmed in teal and made of silk. It clung to her curves and accentuated her waist and hips. Gabe's suit jacket was black with teal trim. His undershirt had ruffles at the center of his chest which made him think of the nobles at the Solstice Ball.

They said their vows and kissed before the witnesses as the castle staff applauded. Akiri and Gabe made their way back down the aisle and up to the second-floor balcony. They waved to the people of Ash for the first time as King and Queen.

Akiri looked up at Gabe and he leaned down to kiss her and the crowd erupted in cheers again. As the noise from the people continued, a strange kind of static filled Gabe's head.

"Is it done? Can you hear me?" Gabe heard Leon's voice cutting in through the white noise that filled his head, the cheers of the crowd and the static blended and made Gabe's head hurt. He winced from the sharp, high-pitched tone that began ringing in his ear.

"Are you okay? What's wrong, Gabe?"

"My head, sorry. Yes, I'm okay. I think maybe it was just too much wine last night, my head hurts." Akiri helped Gabe back inside. As soon as they were away from the cheering crowd, the static faded, and Gabe's mind was clear again.

"I need to get some water, and rest for a bit, could you come to wake me up for dinner? In the meantime, maybe you could pack up your things from your old room to move into our room?"

"Really?" Akiri's eyes lit up and she grinned. "Are you sure?"

"Positive, we are married after all." Gabe winked at her and kissed her softly on the lips. Akiri let out a squeal of delight as she took off down the hall toward her old chamber.

Once Gabe was alone in his chamber he contacted Leon. It made his head hurt, like something inside his mind was tearing.

"It's done, we are married." Gabe pictured Leon in his mind. He could see his face as they talked through their thoughts.

"Have you befriended anyone on the council yet?" Leon asked.

"I haven't had time, we got back here after the ball and the wedding was today, it all moved very quickly."

"What was her hurry to get married?" Leon asked.

"Other than being lonely, I'm not sure. She is just a normal.. well, not *normal,* you know what I mean. She is just alone here, ruling a kingdom. I am sure she fears that her council may want to unseat her. She has six men on it, they probably pushed her to marry so they wouldn't have to take orders from a woman," Gabe said.

"Perhaps, but don't underestimate her, she is very dangerous when she's angry. You all saw her that day on Choddrath," Leon warned. Gabe was sure that what happened on the shores of Choddrath a year ago was a misunderstanding.

"Yes, Sir. I will endear myself to the council and find out their plans. I will report back when I have some intel. Until then, I'm going to mend my broken heart by getting to know my new wife."

"Understood. I will wait for your report, just know we don't have much more time, this connection will only last a few months at best." Just like that, Leon was out of his head, and the sharp pains turned to a dull ache, and finally, as he laid on his bed with his eyes closed, the headache eased too. Gabe wished it were that easy to cure his heartache.

When Akiri woke Gabe for dinner, her maids were with her, their arms filled with things from Akiri's room. They filed into the royal chamber, going about their tasks. Gabe noticed the smile on Akiri's face and he smiled too. They left the staff to work, hanging clothes, and placing Akiri's items and furniture around the room the way she liked them. The kitchen staff had prepared a hearty stew with lots of potatoes, carrots, and beef. Gabe wondered where they got the cow but then thought that maybe he didn't want to know the answer to that question after all, at least not until he ate his fill.

After dinner, Akiri and Gabe walked around the gardens, and then to the beach. It wasn't a nice, sandy beach like the one on Ledora's shore, this one was rocky and covered in shells. Gabe started sorting through the shells. He picked out quite a few that he liked and put them in the pocket of his trousers for later.

"Do you like to read?" Akiri asked.

"I do. I used to be a scribe at the citadel in Blackwater. I will admit I like reading, but I don't want to copy any more books," Gabe said with a chuckle.

"I don't have many books. My mother never liked to read. She was only ever concerned with power."

"Is it true that..." Gabe stopped as he looked at Akiri. He wanted to ask if she had killed her mother. That was the rumor that made its way to Blackwater, but Gabe knew how rumors could get out of control.

"Is what true? That I killed my mother?" Akiri lost the cool tone she had before and her voice sounded a little more hostile now.

"I'm sorry, it's just what I heard." Gabe pleaded with his eyes. He didn't want her to be mad at him already.

"Yes, it's true. People ask me if I regret it sometimes, and I know that I should, but she was an evil woman, who was planning to kill me so that she could take the dragon powers for herself. She was going to have her hired guard kill her daughter. I just beat her to the punch is all."

"I'm sorry. Akiri, growing up with a mother like that must have been difficult."

"The kingdom is better off for it as well. My mother taxed the local businesses so much that they couldn't afford to stay open. They all hated her, and honestly, she didn't even think enough of them to hate them. To her, the subjects were specs of dust too small to even notice."

"It seems like they like you though." Gabe nudged her with his elbow.

"I gave them entertainment, and let them spend their money willingly. I don't tax the people at all, and most of them are healthy and happy. There are still quite a few people who can't provide for themselves or their families and I am working on figuring out what I can do for them."

"You are a good Queen. Ash is lucky to have you." Gabe paused. "*I'm* lucky to have you."

Akiri looked up at him, and he ran his fingertips through her hair to sweep it away from her face. He brought his lips to hers. She melted into his arms as they kissed under the starry sky.

When their lips parted, Akiri shivered. "Let's go get you warmed up," Gabe said as he gently took her hand in his, interlacing her fingers between his own. They walked back to the castle and to their room hand in hand.

The fire in the hearth was about an hour old as there were already red-hot coals on the bottom. They warmed themselves in front of the fireplace until the chill was gone from their fingers and then Gabe began to undress. He took off his tunic and laid it over the back of the chair. He turned the back of the chair to face the fire.

"This way it will be warm in the morning."

"Good idea," Akiri said as she took off her tunic and did the same, never taking her eyes off Gabe's chest. His brown skin under the light of the fire was the most beautiful color Akiri had ever seen. Gabe looked at Akiri in surprise. He did not expect her to undress too. She was bold and daring. He liked that about her. She moved closer to him and walked her fingertips up Gabe's chest, to his neck where she lured him into a slow and passionate kiss. He picked her up and carried her to the bed, unable to pull his lips away from hers.

Gabe's hands roamed down Akiri's body until his fingertips grazed the waistband of her trousers. He tugged at them gently as she playfully bit his lower lip. Gabe groaned as he hooked his fingers into her waistband and pulled down slowly. She lifted her bottom off the bed so he could easily take her pants off. Akiri stared at him with a smile as he took off his as well.

"Let me know if this is too fast," Gabe whispered as he looked down at her. Their faces were centimeters apart and their bodies pressed together. "We don't have to do this tonight if you're not-" Akiri pressed her lips to Gabe's and reached her hand down between them and gripped his sex in her hand. She moved her hand up and down, caressing the smooth skin of his shaft. He groaned into her mouth as Akiri guided his erection into her wet entrance. A moan escaped Gabe's lips as she lifted and pumped her hips to match his speed. Gabe closed his eyes as he moved his hips back and forth slowly, he didn't know why, but he imagined Sophie and her red curls flowing softly over the pillow, and her freckles that lightly speckled off her skin, he imagined that it was Sophie's soft lips on his, and the thought of being inside of Sophie was enough to bring him to a quick climax. He pushed himself deep inside his wife and gave her every bit of his seed. He didn't pull out until the throbbing stopped.

When he opened his eyes and saw Akiri looking up at him, he felt ashamed. He had always imagined his first time would be with Sophie, but he didn't want to have to imagine her when he made love to his wife. Gabe got up and walked to the vanity to get a cloth. There was still water in the wash basin so he dampened a cloth and cleaned himself up. Then he dampened another and took it to Akiri, he was startled when he saw the blood.

"Are you okay? I didn't hurt you did I?" Gabe asked, concerned.

"It hurt a little at first, but it's okay. I have been told this happens your first time," she said. Gabe relaxed a little.

"It was my first time too," he admitted.

"I'm glad it was with you," Akiri said as she cleaned herself and wiped up the spot on the bed.

"Me too," Gabe said, feeling even worse now for thinking about someone else.

Their first time left a stain on the sheets and Akiri stood to strip the bed. She pulled another fitted sheet from the linen wardrobe and Gabe helped her put it on the mattress. They crawled into bed and Akiri laid her head on Gabe's chest. He combed his fingers through her hair until she was sleeping soundly and Gabe stared silently at the ceiling and thought about Sophie until sleep came for him as well.

18

SOPHIE

R yul's room was overwhelming. He had so many
spell books and none of the information was sorted or organized. Sophie tried to make some sense of it
all, to put things in an order that made it easy for her
brain to comprehend the material, but it was like a very
large puzzle, and she had to sort the pieces first to see
where they fit.

The moment she got back to the tower, Sophie wrote
a letter to Ryul. He had not written since he left, and she
hoped that he was just enjoying his time with his family.
Sophie was more hurt than she wanted to admit that
Ryul didn't stay with her. After all, they had spent the
last year together, and Sophie had cared for him like he
was her own grandfather. She never had a grandfather,
so it meant a great deal to her to be able to do this for
Ryul. Maybe he didn't know how much he meant to
her, or then again, maybe he did. Sophie walked down

the newly constructed road from the tower to Alasia. Thanks to Juniper's landslide, people no longer had to traverse Cliffside Pass where Sophie had almost died. She delivered the letter to a merchant caravan that just so happened to be heading to Ravenhall.

While she was in town, she visited the temple where the displaced members of The Order of the Red Dragon were staying, although they were no longer called 'The Order' They were Highlanders now. Members of what would eventually be Sophie's Kingdom; Lapis Highland. She was still their queen even though they didn't have a castle right now and she wanted to take care of them. She asked them to help her build a castle where the tower stood, it didn't have to be a big castle, just enough for them to join her in Lapis Highland. Sophie thought about how she would pay the builders. She had been learning magic for the last year, she had not been earning any coin.

"I could ask my father for a loan from the Silver Talons." Sophie thought out loud.

"Nonsense, My Queen, we have been working our fingers to the bone here in Alasia for the funds to build you a castle worthy of your kindness and beauty. Giles left just now to offer all we have saved to the local builders. You shall have your castle, and it would be our honor to continue to serve you." Ezra, who was the organizer of the members bowed to Sophie deeply.

"Ezra, you have stood by my side, waited faithfully at the base of this mountain, and kept our good people together. I would be honored if you would be my Adviser."

"The honor would be mine, Your Majesty." Ezra bowed to her.

Sophie got a ride back up the long road to Lapis Highland. As soon as she reached the tower, Sophie went to her new room at the very top. She started using her magic to move the stacks of books and papers to the library on the level below, and the furniture to the summoning circle. Sophie wanted to start fresh and fill her room with the things she needed and the spell books that contained spells that she had learned. She worked for the rest of the day, and in her hyper-focus on the task at hand she forgot to eat. When she paused for a moment to admire the empty room, it was dark and her stomach loudly reminded her that she had not stopped to fulfill her needs.

A loud knock on the door startled her as the summoning circle brought Sophie and the furniture to the first floor. She climbed over the bed and squeezed between the chairs to get to the door. It was Ezra and the builders. Sophie looked past Ezra to see a cart, fully loaded with building supplies.

"My Queen, We are going to begin bringing loads of stone for the castle, where would you like for us to unload?"

"Honestly, I do not like this tower. I think we should move everything out, demolish it and start fresh. I would like for the castle to be two floors, but no more than that." Sophie said.

"We can do that for you. I have an idea, why don't you go visit your family and we will send for you when it's finished." Ezra suggested.

"You know what, that is a great idea! I'm going to go to see my friend Kamara though, at the Temple of Ophay."

"Yes, my queen, we will send for you when the castle is finished."

Sophie let Ezra and the builders get to work as she returned to her old room on the first floor. She rummaged through some of her old things and dug out one of the old Blackwater Army rations. Sophie ate what she liked out of it and left the rest in their sealed packages for emergencies. Sophie grabbed Leon's old leather backpack and began filling it with clothing. She packed a lot more than she took to Ledora because she didn't know how long she would be staying there. Sophie crawled into bed and fell asleep quickly. She only slept for a few hours and was ready to fly before the morning light. She would, after all, be flying east and the morning sun could be blinding.

19

GABE

The next morning when he woke up, Gabe stretched and reached out across the bed. Akiri's side of the bed was cold. Gabe sat up and looked around the room. He got up, stretched again, and got dressed. The early morning light had just started to peek in through the balcony archway, and Gabe knew that there was a council meeting every morning. He didn't know why Akiri didn't wake him up, but he was going to find out.

When Gabe got to the chamber, the doors were closed and two guards stood beside the entrance- Akiri's guards. As soon as they noticed Gabe, they shuffled apart and opened the doors for him. Everyone at the table looked up at Gabe as he entered the room and the six men stood up until Gabe took his seat.

"Continue," Akiri said. Ser William Robert looked from Gabe back to Akiri. She nodded at him and finally, he continued.

"As I was saying, No one here has ever seen a dragon egg so we do not know how long they will take to hatch, we don't know if they have to stay at a certain temperature, we will have to use trial and error until we get it right."

"Wait, do you have dragon eggs now?" Gabe asked, confused.

"Assuming that your marriage was consummated, Queen Akiri should be able to take her dragon form now, and by the new moon she should be able to produce a clutch."

"So you're saying that she has to stay in dragon shape until she lays eggs?" Gabe looked at Akiri to see if she was considering this.

"The other option is having a human child who may or may not inherit the gift of dragon shape. As far as we know, The Queen and the other dragons from that day on Choddrath are the only ones left. All we know is learned from studying Queen Akiri." Ser William said.

"What do you want? Do you want to stay in dragon form for weeks to produce eggs that may or may not be viable?" Gabe asked. He didn't know why, but the thought of having a human child appealed to him. He thought about teaching his son or daughter to hunt and fish. He thought about chasing them around the castle and hearing them giggling as they ran from him. He pushed the thoughts away as Akiri started to speak.

"I- I want to try to produce a clutch first, just to see if it can be done. If we have dragons protecting our kingdom no one would dare try to take it from us or try to harm any children we have in the future."

"Is someone making threats?" Gabe asked.

"No, but the history of Ash indicates that when the people become unhappy, they revolt and take the throne by force. I'm ashamed to say that even I took the throne that way. I don't want anyone to take it from our family. I want to protect us, and our future children by giving them dragons." Akiri pleaded. Gabe relented.

"If this is what you want, I will support you."

When the meeting was over, Gabe and Akiri walked out together as they usually did. Akiri kept looking up at Gabe as they walked in silence back to their chamber. A million thoughts ran through Gabe's mind and his heart felt so conflicted. This was an assignment. He was here to monitor the kingdom and ensure that they were not planning hostile actions against the other dragons, Ledora, or anywhere else for that matter. He made a promise to Akiri though, it was a promise that in the eyes of the Gods could only be made to one other person, and then you were bound in this life and the next. It had not been his choice and he could have refused, but then his childhood home would be gone and his mother would have to resort to selling herself to the pirates at the Loose Anchor Tavern.

Family really was everything to Gabe, and maybe that was why he wanted a child, he wanted a real family, not a flock of dragons. *Compromise is important in a marriage, right?* Gabe thought.

"Are you angry with me?" Akiri asked. Gabe let out a heavy sigh.

"No, I'm not angry with you, I'm a little hurt. I just wish we had talked about these plans first, just between us, before involving the council. When you are in that room, I am not your equal. You are the ruler of this kingdom and I am here to support *your* decisions. Here in this room, I am your husband and your friend, someone you can lean on and talk to, someone to share your burdens with, but I can't be those things for you if you make all your decisions alone," Gabe said.

"You're right. I'm sorry. I should have included you in the plan from the beginning."

"Is this why you were so eager to get married? Was this the plan all along?"

"Yes. The plan was to lay a successful clutch of eggs, and hatch baby dragons to secure the throne and the kingdom, and then produce heirs to the throne. Don't think for one second though that I chose you at random. We have been planning this for almost a year, and I have been searching for a mate ever since. I had so many offers- men looking for dragon power, or a throne, but you were the only one who seemed uninterested in all of that. You were wholesome and kind, devoted and determined. I know how you traveled to Choddrath for Sophie. I didn't know what happened between you two that you offered marriage, but I couldn't let the opportunity pass by."

"You knew about Sophie and me the whole time?" Gabe asked.

"I saw you, and the way you looked at her when the black dragon was holding her captive at the top of Dragon Peak. I knew then. I was only interested in claiming my power to end my mother's tyranny here in Ash though, so I left as soon as I saw that the threat was handled."

"Why didn't you join the dragon council?" Gabe asked.

"I'm not interested in the affairs of other kingdoms or living by other people's set of rules. I just want to worry about my kingdom and the people in it."

"I heard that you were unkind. I was afraid at first, but I wanted to get away from all the memories I had in Blackwater."

"I was unkind. My mother was cruel and she was the only example I had to learn from. When I was chasing the orb, I did terrible things, I hurt people, and I let my anger get the better of me. All I wanted was to end my mother's rule. I was going to just force her to give up the throne and exile her, but when her guard told me that she had asked him to kill me and steal the orb the second I got my hands on it, well, I blacked out in a rage and confronted her. I shifted in front of her to show her my power and then I tried to roar at her, for intimidation, only it wasn't just sound that came out and I killed her." Akiri started to cry.

"The worst part was that I didn't feel bad about it. I watched her guard cower in the corner as I shifted back and walked right up to the throne and sat down. I was mad with power and I dreamed about making our enemies pay, but then I had a dream or a premonition of what my life *could* be instead. A life without war, a life with baby dragons, a family, and love. I think this dream was sent to me by the oracle so that I would not end up like my mother, bitter and evil."

"Akiri, I had no idea that you had been through so much. I am glad you have opened your heart and didn't continue down the same path as your mother." Gabe said as he took Akiri in his arms.

"So am I," she said.

"When do you have to... you know, change?"

"The sooner, the better, if it takes as long as they say."

"Let's have one more night before you do. I want to hold you." Gabe leaned forward and pressed his forehead to hers and looked into her eyes. He caressed her cheek and then kissed her lips softly. Every real conversation they had made him feel closer to her, but every step he took toward a life with Akiri felt like a betrayal when he thought of his feelings for Sophie. He wondered how his heart could belong to more than one.

"Let's get out of the castle today, and get some fresh air. We could go to the joust," Akiri suggested.

"That sounds fun, let's do that."

Akiri opened the door and asked one of the guards to have their carriage brought around. He quickly agreed and left to do as his Queen asked. Akiri changed into a white silk dress with twisted green rope trim. She braided her long black hair to one side and then put on her most comfortable sandals. The sight of her took Gabe's breath.

"Gods, you're beautiful," he whispered. Akiri's cheeks turned rosy pink, but she smiled.

"You are too kind, Sir," Akiri said in a playful tone. Gabe picked a tunic to match the green in Akiri's dress. Roland Koffery tasked the maids with measuring Gabe and then purchasing a wardrobe for him. All of his clothing was now fit for a king, even his undergarments and sleeping robes were the finest he had ever seen.

When the Queen and King were ready, their guards, two of Akiri's and two of Gabe's, walked them to their carriage. The guards followed them to the arena in another carriage. When they arrived, the carriage doors remained closed until all of their guards were in position. They walked the Queen and King to their seats in the tower. The villagers stood up as the royal procession walked by and they cheered as Akiri and Gabe waved to them before sitting down.

"Have you ever been to a joust before?" Akiri asked.

"No, how does it work?"

"Two knights on horseback try to unseat each other with a lance. You win if you knock the other person off their horse, otherwise, you earn points by either striking your opponent or breaking your lance."

"Why do you get points for breaking your lance?" Gabe asked.

"You know, I'm not sure. I guess because if you hit them hard enough to break your lance, but don't unseat your opponent, you get points for a good hit at least." They watched as the first two knights were announced.

"Ser Finn Marquee of Hagen against Ser Jarett Weiss of Portage." The announcer's voice boomed throughout the arena and Gabe wondered how he had done it. *It has to be a magic spell*, Gabe thought. The two knights ran at each other at full speed and Ser Jarrett got the first hit on his opponent's shoulder. They took up their positions at the end of the run, their squires checked their armor quickly and they were off again. This time, Ser Jarett shattered the tip of his lance on Finn's shield, but Finn stayed on his horse. In the third attempt, Ser Finn lowered his lance just before striking and it shattered on Ser Jarett's armored abdomen. The blow knocked Jarett backward and he fell to the ground. The announcer walked out into the middle of the arena again as the squires cleared the field.

"Next, we have Ser Boris Madder of Braidwood, and Ser Colby Ricard of Ash."

"One from my continent against one of yours. This should be interesting," Gabe said.

"Care to make a wager?" Akiri asked.

"I don't gamble, but I am sure one of my guards will take your bet." Gabe looked at the guard closest to him.

"Absolutely, My Queen," the guard said.

"Okay, Jack I got two gold on Colby," Akiri said. She handed her two gold to Gabe.

"I'll match that, Your Grace." Jack pulled out two gold and handed them to Gabe as well.

"Good Luck, Jack," Akiri said.

"You too, My Queen."

The knights took position and ran at each other, Boris got the first hit and almost unseated Colby, who dropped his lance, but squeezed the horse with his legs and managed to stay in the saddle. He rode to the end of the list and his squires quickly put another lance in his hand. The second strike went to Colby as he raised his lance and struck Boris in the shoulder.

"Third time's a charm?" Gabe asked.

"Maybe," Akiri said. This time, Colby raised his lance even higher, and not wanting to get hit in the face, Boris got startled and pulled back on the reins the horse made a sharp turn toward the stands and then bucked. Boris fell off his horse with a loud clank as his armor hit the ground.

"Does that count?" Gabe asked.

"No, I don't think so. Wait- what is he doing?" Akiri leaned forward to see what was going on, Boris stomped over to the referee and threw his hands up. He was shouting something at the referee but Akiri couldn't hear because of the shouts from the crowd.

"Ser Boris Madder has yielded!" The announcer said. The crowd went wild.

"So, technically you won?" Gabe handed the gold to Akiri.

"No, no one won, Boris got mad and quit it's not the same." Akiri tried to hand Jack his coins back.

"No, My Queen, you keep it. You clearly picked the better knight." Jack said with a smile. Akiri put the coins in her purse.

They refrained from betting throughout the rest of the joust and when it was over, the guards walked Gabe and Akiri to their carriage.

"That was fun. Thank you for bringing me," Gabe said.

"My pleasure."

When they were back at the castle and had retreated to the privacy of their chamber, Gabe began undressing. He took off his tunic first and tossed it in the laundry bin. He started to take off his trousers, but he felt Akiri's eyes on him. He turned to look at her. She was standing by the chair in front of the fireplace still wearing the silk dress. Gabe moved over to Akiri and took her in his arms. He loved the way her body felt against his. They made love again that night, and this time, Gabe took it slow and made it last. He only saw Akiri. Sophie never even crossed his mind.

20

KAMARA

L aughlin and Dominic began working on the barn at first light. Laughlin, who was used to getting up before the sun to work in the coolest part of the day, roused Dominic and Kamara from their slumber. Juniper was already in the kitchen looking refreshed as she poured black tea into two cups.

"Here ya go," she said as she slid one of the mugs across the table. Kamara got a spoon and some sugar from the cabinet. She didn't like how bitter tea was without it. She hoped that one day, they would have a goat or two so that they would have fresh milk and so she could make cheese and butter.

"Did you sleep well?" Juniper asked.

"I slept fine, it's just waking up that's difficult, what about you?" Kamara asked.

"I meditated in the garden out back for a few hours in the moonlight. It's so beautiful out there," she replied.

"The garden? I thought it was overgrown and dead, I haven't touched it since before..." Kamara didn't have to finish the sentence, Juniper knew she meant; before Baelfire's men came looking for the orb and Kamara was the only survivor.

"I did some weeding last night and uncovered some plants that were still good, and a few that needed some help. You have tomatoes, potatoes, onions, and a bed or two of flowers. I couldn't save the rest of the garden, but we can plant more next spring, or we could plant some hearty winter vegetables," juniper suggested.

"Thank you, you didn't have to do all that."

"I know, but working in the soil under the light of the moon recharges me, so thank you."

A commotion outside caught their attention, and Kamara and Juniper ran to the door just in time to see Sophie land in the only spot not covered by the canopy of treetops. They waited as she took her human form, emerging from her dragon shape with clothes on. Kamara looked at her in confusion but still ran out to greet her.

"Sophie! We were just getting ready to come to the tower for a visit. This is a nice surprise!" Kamara said. Sophie hugged Kamara and then looked at Juniper. Her eyes were drawn to her rounded belly.

"Juniper, you're going to have a baby? I'm so happy for you!" Sophie wrapped her arms around Juniper, careful not to squeeze her too tightly. Dominic and Laughlin waved from the frame of the barn they were working on, but they couldn't stop until the frame was complete.

"Juniper just made some tea if you would like to have some. We can let these guys finish up and we can chat inside. Will you be staying the night?" Kamara asked as she noticed the bag Sophie had brought with her.

"Well, I was hoping I could stay with you for a little while. I have builders constructing a ground-level castle instead of the tower and it might take a while to complete the construction, if not, I can stay with my parents, I just really needed a friend right now," Sophie said.

"You can stay as long as you would like, you are always welcome here." Kamara looped her arm through Sophie's and followed Juniper back to the kitchen.

"You changed a lot in here, it's nice. It feels more like a home than a temple now." Sophie said.

"Dominic and I thought we might live here until he is needed in Ledora. Sorry, we left after the ball, we came here and had a little engagement celebration, just the two of us." Kamara said.

"It's okay." Sophie smiled as her thoughts trailed back to that night.

"Why are you smiling, what happened?" Kamara asked.

"I woke up next to Bastian and had to sneak out without waking him. I had so much wine I don't even remember how it happened."

"You didn't!" Kamara exclaimed. Sophie nodded and sipped her tea.

"I wonder what he thought when he woke up." Juniper raised her eyebrows at Sophie.

"I bet he thought it had all been a dream," Kamara said. "Whenever you're finished with your tea, I will show you around." Kamara walked over to the counter and poured water from a pitcher into her cup to rinse it.

"I'm going to go see if the guys need any help, be sure to take a look a the garden," Juniper said as she filled two cups with water for Laughlin and Dominic.

"I will."

Kamara led Sophie down the hall where the guest rooms were and showed her the room that would be hers. Sophie put her bag on the bed before they continued the tour so that she didn't have to carry it with her. Kamara showed her the sitting room, and the patio that led to the garden, and then she led Sophie to the lair.

"Do you think we can produce more dragons?" Sophie asked when she saw the nest.

"I don't see why we couldn't. I don't know how to do it though, if we need to be in dragon shape, or if our human shape will just create dragonshifters like us. We will use trial and error until we get it right, but we are preparing for every possible outcome." Kamara said.

Suddenly, Sophie felt very lonely. Kamara had Dominic, Juniper had Laughlin and a baby on the way, and even Akiri had Gabe. Kamara noticed Sophie's sullen appearance and she wrapped her arms around her.

"I'm sorry," she said. "I would ask if you're okay, but I can see that you're not. How can I help?" Kamara asked.

"I don't know. I just miss Gabe. I took him for granted and now he's gone, married to Akiri. I will likely never even get to see him again. Everything changed when I went to the tower to train with Ryul," Sophie told her.

"We could always invite Bastian over for tea." Kamara joked. "Awe, I saw you smile!" Sophie rolled her eyes, but Kamara was right, she was smiling. Sophie was thankful Kamara had tried to make her laugh about Bastian instead of urging her to talk about Gabe. Sophie's eyes migrated to the hot spring. She could feel the heat from it and longed to ease her muscles.

"Want to get in?" Kamara asked. "I do all the time. It's like a bath that never gets cold, and the water bubbles up from the underground spring so it's not stagnant and it's always clean."

"That sounds lovely," Sophie said.

"Okay, let's have a soak." Kamara took off her dress and laid it on a dry rock. She stepped into the pool in her undergarments. Sophie let her illusion spell drop momentarily, and then re-cast the illusion of a black bodysuit.

"I wondered how you did that," Kamara said as Sophie eased her body down into the pool of water.

"Did what?"

"Shifted back to human form without appearing naked," Kamara said.

"Oh, yes, the illusion was one of the first spells I worked on with Ryul, basically, I just think about what I want others to see and concentrate my energy on it," Sophie told her. "I could try to teach you."

"I'm afraid I don't have any magical ability, other than being able to shift. Dominic tried to teach me some

magic too and I just do not have the aptitude for it."
Kamara said.

When their muscles were relaxed and their fingers were nice and pruney, Kamara and Sophie got out of the hot spring and walked back to the temple to dry off. Sophie went to her room and put on some actual clothes so she could rest her mind. Keeping up the illusion spell for long periods required a lot of mental focus and she found that it tired her out quickly.

Sophie stretched out on her bed and fell asleep. Kamara and Juniper rode into town to get meat from the butcher, and pick up some things from the market. When they returned to the temple, the barn was half finished.

"You guys have done such great work today. It looks wonderful." Kamara complimented. "I will let you guys know when dinner is ready." Kamara and Juniper carried the groceries into the kitchen. Sophie was already awake and when she saw Kamara and Juniper come in with their arms full she rushed to pitch in and help.

The three of them peeled and cut potatoes, celery, carrots, garlic, onions, and beef. Kamara cooked the beef with the bones to make a hearty broth. After removing the bones, Sophie added the vegetables. They covered it and let the stew cook for a few hours. Juniper added some seasoning, tasting it between pinches of salt and pepper. She used a mortar and pestle to grind up dried rosemary, oregano, and some dried peppers and threw in a few bay leaves and some fresh basil. When the seasoning was just right, Juniper added a cup of flour to thicken the stew.

The smell filled the kitchen and made it feel warm and inviting, It smelled like home to Sophie. When everyone was washed up and gathered at the table, Kamara served the stew in large bowls with fresh dinner rolls and butter from the market.

"This is amazing, thank you for cooking," Dominic said as he tasted his stew.

"It was a joint effort, Sophie and Juniper helped." She said.

"It's delicious," Laughlin said.

After dinner, Sophie washed the dishes and Kamara dried them and put them away. The rest of the evening, they sat by the fire talking, playing games, and forgetting all of the tough times they had been through in the last year. Despite all their struggles, they had each other, and that made Sophie especially happy.

The next morning, Sophie helped Laughlin, Dominic, and Kamara finish the barn while Juniper worked in the garden. By midday, Sophie slipped away into the house and conjured a feast for lunch. She didn't take credit for it when everyone came inside to see it, but they all suspected that it had been her. By evening, the barn was finished, and the horses were happy and safe from the elements inside their stalls.

"Thanks for all your help, I couldn't have gotten it finished without you," Dominic said to Laughlin.

"No problem, It was nice to have help. If you want to earn some coin, I would gladly split the profits of my next job with you if you wanted to help me in town."

"I would like that a lot," Dominic said. He was so much happier now than he had been growing up in Ledora. It had been lonely not having friends and never knowing if people were being nice because they had to be or because they liked you. Here, he was just Dominic. He wasn't a prince or even a future king. It made him wonder how long he would get to live life this way before his father or his council called him home to assume the throne.

21

GABE

The castle was lonely without Akiri. She had left Gabe in charge of handling the council meetings and requested that he only visit once a week, right after her feeding. She didn't know how staying in dragon shape would affect her or her mind, and the last thing she wanted was to see Gabe as a tasty snack. Alone in his chamber, Gabe brought the image of Leon into the front of his mind.

"Commander Rend, it's me, Gabe," he thought. His head began to ache, it was dull this time, but he could feel the neural link stretching and connecting across the distance. It wasn't as strong as before, and Gabe thought the connection might be nearing its end.

"Yes, Gabe, what's the report?" Leon asked. His voice sounded far off and static-filled.

"Akiri is currently in dragon shape, she will be for at least the next four weeks while she tries to produce a clutch of eggs."

"What does she plan to do with the eggs?"

"She told me she wants to raise the dragons to protect her family and kingdom."

"Hopefully she doesn't decide to conquer other kingdoms, we are in a treaty with Ledora, and we have to honor the call for aid should Akiri plan an attack, Dragons for Ash could mean war for the rest of us, be careful. Keep me posted. How are you holding up?"

"Better now," he thought. "I will message back when Akiri has made progress with a clutch." Gabe didn't want to allow Leon to bring up Sophie, so he dropped the connection on the link for the time being so that his thoughts could be his own.

As the weeks passed, Gabe settled into a routine. Following the same schedule made things easier. Gabe didn't give himself a lot of free time. He scheduled sword fighting lessons, Archery lessons, even though he was already pretty proficient with a bow, he took ballroom dancing lessons and then requested copies of certain tomes from the elven citadel in Ravenhall.

Gabe spent his evenings reading by the fireplace in his room. He was reading books about dragons, what they ate, how they grew, and how to train them. He did as Akiri requested and only visited after she had eaten. On his third visit, Akiri moved away from the nest to show him a clutch of five green eggs. The shells were covered in scales, but they looked as if they were breathing because Gabe could see them moving.

"Do you have to stay in dragon shape for them to hatch?" Gabe asked.

Akiri didn't answer, he didn't know if she was even capable of speaking in dragon form. She couldn't lay on top of them because her size would crush them, instead, she curled up beside them and wrapped her tail around them. Gabe sat down beside Akiri's tail and placed his hand on one of the eggs. He could feel movement beneath the scales.

"What if we sent two of our guards down here to keep an eye on the eggs, they could switch out every twelve hours. Then you could come inside." Gabe looked into Akiri's eyes. Her eyes were different in this form. The pupil was thinner and came to a point at the top and bottom, the iris was bright gold in the middle and turned a darker golden red on the outer rim. Akiri's human eyes were a stormy gray that turned to a light bluish gray when she was happy.

Akiri uncurled from the eggs and shifted back into her human form. She bent down to pick up one of the eggs from the nest. She lovingly stroked the scales with her fingertips and the creature inside responded to her touch.

"We created these. Every one of these eggs has a baby dragon inside. Do you know how much people would pay for these? Dominic, Kamara, me, and Sophie are the last known dragons in this world, and we have the ability to create more. I fear that money and power would cloud the judgment of men. I am not sure I can trust anyone enough to not be tempted to take one of our children for themselves."

"I understand that, but do you even know how long they will take to hatch? How long are you willing to live in this underground tomb? What if it takes years for these guys to hatch?"

Akiri looked back at the nest and then she looked back to Gabe. She relented. Akiri knew he was right. "We need a heavy steel door," she said, finally. "It will need to be locked and protected with magic. Then I might feel safe enough to leave them with guards at the door," she said as she gently placed the egg back into the nest.

"No problem, I will see it done today, My Queen." Gabe took her hand in his and kissed it as he bowed to her. Goose flesh rose on her arm and spread across her body. The way he said "My Queen" made her melt. When others said it, their words blended together and it sounded more like m'lady, but when Gabe said those words it felt like he was telling her that she meant more to him than anything else and that she was his *Queen*. Not just in title, but the queen of his heart too.

Gabe found a blacksmith and requested that he come to the castle to measure the opening to Akiri's lair. The nest was far enough back into the lair that it could not be seen from the entrance, so as long as he didn't try to wander down into the cave, no one would know what was down there until Akiri was ready for them to know.

"The openin' is a little bigger'n what I thought it was gonna be, to be honest, carrying that much steel up here whole will be impossible. I'd need a forge here to do a job this big."

"Whatever you need, we will set you up. Go ahead and gather your supplies and tell this guy what you need and he will get it for you." Gabe told the blacksmith as he gestured to the guard nearest him.

One of the guards stood at the entrance and Akiri stayed in the back of the cave with her eggs. Gabe still had to find a wizard to protect the door when it was finished. He went out into the city, he asked all of the locals he could find, but the wizard that used to teach Akiri when she was young, disappeared. The only spells Akiri had ever learned were offensive attack spells which did not come in handy in this situation.

Having no luck, Gabe went back to the castle and straight to his room. He reached out to Leon.

"I need a wizard who can do protection spells for the lair," Gabe told him.

"Hello to you too, Gabe. I take it that Akiri was successful in producing a clutch, but now doesn't want to leave the nest?" Leon asked.

"Yes, there are five eggs in total and they are all moving. We could have five dragons soon, although none of the texts I got from Ravenhall say anything about how long it takes a dragon egg to hatch."

"I will reach out to a contact in Northport, I am assuming that Sophie is out of the question," Leon said. It was not a question, but a statement.

"Yes, sir. We didn't part on the best of terms last time." Gabe said as he thought back to his last interaction with Sophie.

"I'm sorry about that, I am, but the information you have given us already is proving very valuable. The fact that humans and dragonshifters can produce eggs- is truly fascinating. Keep up the good work, Gabe." Leon said.

"Thank you, let me know when you find a wizard." Gabe disconnected their mental link before Leon could continue. Gabe disliked being reminded of Sophie every time they talked. He just wanted to move on. He forced the conversation, and Sophie from his mind and instead, went to the storage closet and gathered two bedrolls and pillows. Then he grabbed two robes and arranged for Mister Koffery to bring him and Akiri dinner in the lair.

The blacksmith was working diligently on the door as Gabe approached. The large steel door was almost completed. It was not solid, but rather, the top of the door looked more like the cell doors in the dungeon. If they put a solid door on the lair, there would be no airflow and Gabe worried that the eggs might not survive if cut off from the fresh air.

Gabe walked down the stairs, and around the corner to where Akiri sat beside the nest, humming to the eggs. He laid out the two bedrolls and pillows side by side. Akiri looked at him curiously.

"What's this?" She asked.

"Until the door is finished, I thought I would stay down here with you, to help you watch over our babies," Gabe said as he placed a hand gently on one of the eggs. "I have already arranged for Mister Koffery to bring us dinner, and I brought our robes, so we can be comfy." Gabe watched Akiri's face turn from surprise to awe. She stood up and walked over to him as a tear ran down her cheek.

Gabe took her in his arms and held her close as he reached up and wiped the tear from her cheek with his thumb. "Please, don't cry."

"I'm sorry." She said.

"What do you have to be sorry for?"

"I just don't understand my feelings. You are so sweet and you make me so happy, but then the thought of possibly losing you makes me feel like a piece of me is gone. When I think that this must have been the way Sophie felt about you, and the way you felt about her, I am ashamed that I took that from you both."

"No, the situation with me and Sophie was beyond anyone's control it was her choices and mine that led me to you and I don't regret a single thing that happened. This feeling that you're talking about, that's love, this is what love feels like. I don't want to lose you either, not for anything in the world. I'm not going anywhere. I'm yours, Akiri. I love you." His voice was deep and soft in her ear and it sent a shiver down her spine. Her skin prickled as Gabe ran his fingertips up her bare back and in what seemed like an instant, but forever at the same time, he kissed her. It was slow and soft.

Gabe ran his fingers through her long black hair as he deepened the kiss. The room felt like it was spinning to

Akiri, she felt woozy like she had the very first time she had wine. Gabe's fingertips explored the curves of her body as he trailed kisses down her neck. They forgot anyone else in the world existed until they heard someone behind them loudly clear their throat.

They jumped, startled by the sudden noise and Gabe rushed to grab the robe he brought for Akiri. Gabe's guard, Jack turned his back while he waited for Akiri to slip the robe on and tie it at the front.

"Yes?" Akiri asked as she adjusted her robe and brushed the hair out of her face.

"Sorry to interrupt, My Queen, I just wanted to let you know that the door is finished. This is the key and it is the only copy. Keep it with you, we can't open the door without it." Jack said as he handed the key to Akiri. Jack turned and left the lair.

Akiri looked at Gabe. She saw the obvious sign of frustration about the interruption. She smiled as she stood on her tiptoes to wrap her arms around his shoulders.

"What do you say we lock up here, and go finish what we started in our bedchamber?" she whispered.

Gabe agreed enthusiastically.

22

SOPHIE

Time seemed to move so quickly. The first day, turned into three, then before Sophie knew how it happened, she had been with Kamara and Dominic for more than two weeks. They settled into a routine. During the week, Sophie and Kamara would spend their morning gardening while Dominic worked on various building projects. The horses now had a fence that spanned the entire left side of the property, which included a fresh spring to drink from and plenty of pasture to roam. They also obtained goats for milk, and pigs for bacon, ham, and sausage, of course, it would be at least a year before any of the pigs were ready for the slaughterhouse- which Dominic still had to build.

On the weekends they flew to Ledora and spent time with the king during the day and they enjoyed court life at night. Kamara, as the Princess, knew almost everyone and often introduced Sophie to people she thought she might like. Sophie became quite popular with the noblemen at court, but the whispers she overheard were contrary. It was usually the women. She knew they were talking about her because when she would approach, they all stopped talking and would look guilty when she spoke to them.

On more than one occasion, she had women approach her and they tried to engage politely in conversation, only for Sophie to realize that they were really only fishing for information about why Sophie had turned down proposals from several of the nobles of Ledora. It had been a week since the last occasion and already a new rumor was circulating the court. Sophie overheard the whisper this time in the powder room.

"I know why she turns down every man who tries to court her, she's Prince Dominic's mistress. She even lives with them in their new castle, If you can even call it that."

"They have a new castle?"

"Well, not *new*. They just fixed up that old temple where all those religious people were murdered outside Blackwater."

"I swear that town is a curse."

"I know! Positively a curse, you know that's where Sophie is *from.*" Sophie had heard enough, she opened the door to the privy and walked right over to the girl starting the rumors. When she saw Sophie all the girls went silent, they knew she had heard every word.

"What's your name?" Sophie asked as she reached up to touch the brooch of the girl's family crest that she had pinned on her chest. The girl remained quiet. "This is such a pretty pin." Sophie gave it a quick tug and the back of the pin popped open and it came off in Sophie's hand.

"Actually, I haven't accepted a proposal because I like to sample everything at the buffet. I get bored of the same old thing all the time and unlike you, I run my own Kingdom and am not forced to choose a husband just for the sake of being married. Secondly, I am sure Prince Dominic would love to hear how you're implying-no-flat out *telling* people that he has taken a mistress and broken his vow to Kamara before they have even wed. How would the king feel about these rumors you're spreading about his only son and heir? If I were you, I would take more care with your tongue, before you lose it. Oh, and I'm keeping this." She held up the brooch. "Let me hear you say another word about me or my friends and they will be the last words you speak."

Sophie didn't wait for any of them to respond, she walked out of the powder room with her head held high. She could feel all their eyes on her as she left. Sophie rounded the corner quickly, in a hurry to find Kamara and tell her what happened and she bumped right into someone. She almost fell but he caught her.

"Woah, careful. Sophie, it's so good to see you," he said as he helped her stand upright again. She knew his voice before she even looked up to see his face.

"Bastian, I- uh... hello." Sophie stumbled on her words. She hadn't expected to see him again after their drunken night together at Dominic and Kamara's engagement. His blue eyes sparkled like sapphires and his blond hair, which was now long enough to put in a ponytail was tied back with a black ribbon. To the right of them, Sophie saw a maiden with her fan drawn up to her chin. She looked at Sophie with envy and then batted her eyelashes as she looked back at Bastian.

"Would you please dance with me?" Bastian extended his hand to Sophie. She nodded and gently placed her hand in his as he suavely swept her onto the dance floor. He twirled her around so that her back was to him and ran his fingers up the sensitive part of her arms as she raised them above her head. Sophie brought one arm down slowly, caressing the side of Bastian's face. Just before their lips touched, he twirled her out again, this time, just beyond the edge of his reach. She twirled away from him as his steps lightly followed her. She paused, looking away from him, and he put his arm around her from behind, resting his hand on her abdomen. He slowly turned her chin to look at him with his other hand and she gazed up at him as their lips grew closer. He dipped her smoothly, staying so close that she could feel his breath trail all the way from her lips to her breasts as she leaned back in his arms. When he guided her body back up, his hands roamed her body and his face was almost touching hers. She wanted to kiss him, but he controlled their every move as he led the seductive dance. Everyone watched them as their bodies told a story of desire and longing. The crowd that gathered around the ballroom burst into applause when the song was over. Bastian's lips still never even brushed hers.

His seductive dance had worked. She wanted him. This time, she was completely sober and the magnetic draw she felt to him was undeniable. He bowed to her and then kissed her hand.

"Thank you, Sophie. I hope I see you again."

"What do you mean? Are you leaving?"

"I am, I was already on my way out when I ran into you, but-" His words cut off, but Sophie could tell there was more he wanted to say. "Never mind. It was really good to see you again." He kissed her cheek and then quickly turned to make his way back through the crowd toward the exit.

Sophie stood there in shock as he disappeared into the sea of people. *Wait, that's it? Really?* Sophie thought. Their dance had left her almost breathless and needful. She tried to follow him through the ballroom, but by the time she made it across the room and through the doors leading outside, he was gone. *How did he disappear so quickly?* Sophie thought.

She stood outside for a while, looking off into the distance, trying to calm her racing thoughts, and let the strange feeling of arousal pass. She had spent the night with Bastian when first they met, and this time it seemed that the second things started heating up between them, he was in a hurry to leave. Sophie was about to head back inside when the doors behind her opened and Kamara came out to join her.

"Did you just need some fresh air? I would, after that dance. Sss ow!" Kamara touched Sophie's shoulder with her fingertip and pretended that her skin sizzled and burned, her sound effects did make Sophie smile.

"Bastian left. He was already gone by the time I made it to the door like he just disappeared. I don't understand how he vanished so quickly." Sophie told her.

"That's strange. I don't know him other than from the ball so I am afraid I won't be much help, but, we could go back in and dance." Kamara smiled and took Sophie's hand. "I mean- I doubt that I'm as seductive a dancer as Bastian, but I will try my best." Kamara winked at Sophie and just like that, Sophie moved the thoughts of Bastian to the back of her mind and was actually grinning. She followed Kamara back inside and onto the dance floor.

That night as Sophie slept, her mind was filled with strange dreams. The sky was filled with heavy, dark, rain clouds and the air was cool. Sophie didn't know where she was, the town was strange-looking with twisted alleyways filled with dark wooden houses that were all shuttered up. Not even a lantern illuminated her way. The full moon shined down through a part in the clouds. Sophie watched the moon to see if she could tell which way the storm was going, but the clouds didn't move. It was like they were magical in nature and used to engulf the city in shadows.

Sophie walked down the narrow cobblestone path toward the sound of a cawing raven. She saw the bird perched on an old stone wall beside an iron gate. When the bird noticed her drawing closer, it cawed again and flew away. She ran after the sound of flapping wings, into a graveyard. She tripped over a small headstone and fell to the ground. She stood up and ran through the cemetery until she reached the other end of it. The raven perched on the wall again and it seemed to look at her as she approached. Sophie reached out her hand to touch the bird and it squawked angrily. It flew at her face quickly and she reacted too late, the bird's talon scratched her on the side of her neck as it swooped past, it swooped like a bat-not a bird. *How odd.* Sophie thought.

Just then, Bastian stepped out of the shadows and he seemed to float over to where she stood holding her neck. She looked at her hand and saw blood. Bastian didn't say a word, instead, he looked at her with his piercing eyes. Sophie felt irresistibly drawn to him and in an instant, she closed the gap between them and kissed him. He pulled back only a little as he brushed his lips against hers in the most teasing way, then he kissed the corner of her mouth, her cheek, her jaw, and then her neck. She moaned softly as she felt his tongue on her neck, and just as abruptly as he had disappeared from court, the dream was over and Sophie woke up. She groaned loudly in the frustration of her empty bed and tried to remember what had happened between them the night of Kamara and Dominic's engagement. Why couldn't she remember anything besides waking up next to him and why did she need him so badly now?

Damn it, Sophie, pull yourself together. She scolded herself. She tried as hard as she could to fall back asleep, but it evaded her. When she tried to think back on her dream she found that it was gone from her memory. She knew it had been about Bastian, and that it had made her crave him more than ever, but the details beyond that were gone.

She was usually not even attracted to Bastian's type, really, she had only ever been attracted to one other person, and that was Gabe. Bastian and Gabe could not be more opposite. Gabe was shorter, he was also outdoorsy with a dark brown complexion and dark hair. He liked to wade in the creek, skip rocks, fish, and gather herbs in the forest. Sophie only reached Bastian's shoulder, he was poised and proper, well-dressed, and well-mannered most of the time. His hair was long and blonde, and he had piercing blue eyes. He was the very embodiment of the social elite, a great dancer, diplomatic, and yet there was something so mysterious about him.

Hours passed and Sophie still couldn't sleep, so she stopped trying. Instead, she took a walk. She wandered aimlessly through the gardens, stopping now and again to smell the flowers. She couldn't see the moon, it was cloudy now, so the only light came from the flickering oil lanterns that hung on shepherd hooks at the end of every flower bed.

Sophie sat down on a bench beside a bed of stargazer lilies. Even in the dark, the bright pink flower stood out against the stems and leaves of green that filled the rest of the flower bed. The wind whispered softly through her hair and chilled her arms. She shivered once but quickly recovered as she rubbed the back of her arms with her palms.

"Couldn't sleep?" Sophie looked up to see Dominic. She smiled and shook her head.

"No, what about you?"

"I always take a night flight before I go to sleep, it helps me relax."

"Where's Kamara?" Sophie looked around, but she didn't see her.

"She fell asleep already and I didn't want to wake her. So, what's on your mind? Why can't you sleep? Is it Gabe?" Dominic took a seat on the bench beside Sophie.

"Surprisingly, it's not Gabe. It's Bastian. The night you and Kamara got engaged, I somehow ended up in his room-in his *bed*. I don't remember what happened, but when we danced tonight it felt like a spark, like a magnet pulling us together and a heat between our bodies that could melt steel. Then he disappeared and I don't know why," Sophie told him. Dominic's eyes widened. He looked like he had seen a ghost.

"What?" Sophie asked. He knew something about him, she could tell.

"Nothing, I mean, I thought you were out here pining over Gabe, I'm just surprised you moved on and I didn't hear about it sooner." He managed a smile. "Bastian seems nice, I know him from court, and we are friendly enough, but now that I think about it, I don't know anything about him other than his first name. It's strange."

"Well, I should be getting back inside, I need to try to get a little sleep before tomorrow evening when we fly back," Sophie said.

"I'll walk you to your room." Dominic rose to his feet first and offered his hand to Sophie. She took his hand until she was on her feet and then she pulled away quickly. She hadn't meant to and she hoped he wouldn't notice, but he did.

"What's wrong?" He asked, worried.

"There were some girls in the powder room today, they were spreading rumors. They thought that I was your mistress. I was just afraid if they saw us holding hands, or walking too close that the rumors would get worse.

"Since when do you care what anyone thinks? You are Queen Sophie Rend of Lapis Highland, Wizard of the North, and one of my very best friends. They can think what they want, let them speak badly of you in front of me and I will hand you their tongue." Dominic nudged her with his shoulder.

When they got to Sophie's room, Dominic embraced her warmly. "Sleep well, Soph. I will see you in the morning for breakfast." Sophie closed the door as Dominic walked down the hall toward his room. She fell asleep as soon as her head touched the pillow and didn't wake up until the morning light was shining brightly into her eyes.

23

AKIRI

G abe and Akiri jolted awake to the sound of a dragon screeching as it passed by their bedroom window. Akiri jumped out of bed with her heart pounding
and threw on a dressing gown. She was already out of
the room and down the hall before Gabe could even
get out of bed. Akiri ran out the back doors and across
the southern courtyard. Her heart dropped and she
screamed as she surveyed the scene. Loud clanging from
the bell tower told Akiri that someone noticed the fire
and was at least alerting the castle.

Smoke billowed from the door of the lair and Akiri
bolted from the back of the castle to the steel door. It
was hot to the touch, but she grabbed the handle anyway. She screamed for Gabe as she cried and frantically
tried to open the steel door but it was stuck and her hand
sizzled as she gripped the hot metal handle. She roared
in pain as she pulled her hand off. She looked at her

right hand which was now missing the top layer of skin in the shape of the handle. Gabe made it outside just in time to see Akiri burn her hand and he quickly grabbed a bucket of water and rushed it to her. She plunged her hand down into the bucket and muffled a scream as the water took the heat from her wound.

Another ear-piercing roar rang out as a large, dark shadow passed over them. Gabe and Akiri looked up to see a large black dragon flying south with a bag hanging from its mouth.

"It can't be. I thought he was dead?" Gabe wondered aloud.

"The eggs! The eggs!" Akiri screamed.

Gabe ran to the training yard on the western side of the courtyard and grabbed two swords from the rack. When he got them back to the door, he ran both of them through the handle of the door in opposite directions. He took off his tunic and ripped it in half, he wrapped both of his hands in the fabric to protect them from the blades. He grabbed the handle and blade of each sword and pulled back as hard as he could.

"Can you cast any water spells?" Gabe asked as the door flew open. A wall of heat and smoke poured from the opening, causing Gabe to recoil as he felt the heat singe the hairs on his skin.

Akiri was still frantic, crying as she looked at the entrance to the lair. She carried the bucket to the doorway and emptied the bucket as she flung the water through it. It made little difference to the flames that burned at the bottom of the stairs. She put her hand in the empty bucket and tried to cast a water spell but the bucket would not fill. Her casting hand was injured and the spell wouldn't work. She screamed again and threw the bucket down the stairs, she listened to the thin metal pail clank down the stairs until it too reached the bottom and disappeared in the flames.

"This is your fault," Akiri screamed at Gabe. "I wanted to stay with the nest, I wanted to stay with our babies, but you... you," she couldn't finish her sentence, she fell to the ground and cried. It was the most mournful sound Gabe had ever heard. She knew it wasn't his fault-not entirely, but she still felt like he had clouded her judgment.

"How could this even happen? Weren't the guards supposed to be here?" Gabe asked.

With no way to fight the flames, Gabe sat down on the ground next to Akiri and tried to comfort her. He had no words that would cheer her up so he placed his hand on her shoulder. She was curled in the fetal position, sobbing. She shrugged away from his touch.

"Akiri, I'm sorry. I didn't know something like this could even happen. I promise I will get to the bottom of it." Gabe said.

Akiri got up from the ground and shifted into her dragon form. She braved the flames and went down into the lair. Her breath weapon was an acidic sludge, which would do no good. Akiri pushed her way through the flame; her scales protected her from the heat. Akiri heard a *crunch* as she stepped on something. She backed up to look down and saw that she had crushed a human skull. The skin was melted off of the corpse, but she would recognize the armor anywhere, this was one of her guards. *He must have died trying to protect the nest,* she thought.

Akiri made it to where the eggs should have been and found only broken shells in the remains of the nest and scattered around the floor of the cave. There seemed to be fewer shells than she expected for five eggs. *Some of them must have turned to ash in the flames.* She thought, *either that or the black dragon took what he wanted and burned the rest.*

Akiri ran up the steps and took flight into the sky, leaving Gabe on the ground below. The castle staff had gathered and formed a chain from the well to the lair as they filled bucket after bucket of water and tried to put out the fire.

Akiri flew until she reached Ledora. She landed on the western beach and walked to the castle gates without care that she had arrived naked; better that, than showing up in dragon form, which after the way she treated King Haki last year, could be perceived as a threat. A coughing fit took over her as she approached the gates and she caught the attention of the two castle guards standing on either side.

They both rushed to help her. One of them took off his cape and wrapped it around her. He checked her face for bruises, cuts, or any other sign of violence.

"Who are you running from, Miss?" he asked with concern.

"I need help, I need to see Prince Dominic and Princess Kamara please," Akiri said. The other guard took off toward the castle while the other tried to keep Akiri engaged in conversation.

"Have you been hurt?" He noticed her hand and the soot on her face. *That's a stupid question. Of course, she's been hurt, look at her.* The man thought. "I mean, who hurt you?"

"I'm not sure. I- uh..." She wasn't sure if she should tell the guard about the eggs or not. Prince Dominic and Kamara would probably try to have children soon, so she needed to warn them.

"Can you tell me what happened? We want to help you. Did it happen here in the city?" Akiri shook her head.

"No, it happened at my castle in Ash, but I would rather wait for Prince Dominic and Princess Kamara, it's a personal matter."

Just then, the other guard returned with Dominic and Kamara. When they saw Akiri in the state she was in, Dominic rushed to her and offered his hand to help her up.

"It's okay, we have her from here. Thank you for coming to get me."

They led Akiri through the front doors of the castle and into one of the guest rooms located on the second floor and down the right-side corridor. Kamara asked one of the maids to find Akiri some clothes and Dominic heated some water for a bath. Akiri was seated in the chair beside the hearth, still wrapped in the guard's cloak. Kamara grabbed her a dressing robe and sent the guard's cloak with one of the castle maids.

"What happened, Akiri?" Kamara asked as she pulled the other chair closer to Akiri's.

"He's back. The black dragon I mean- he destroyed my nest and my clutch of eggs." Akiri sobbed.

"Are you talking about Baelfire? We killed him, that can't be right, can it?" Kamara asked.

"I guess so, but he was very much alive when he destroyed my babies and then flew off toward the south with a bag of something hanging from his mouth, My guess would be he stole an egg." Kamara looked at Dominic, "We should tell Sophie."

"Would you mind if we asked Sophie to join us?" Dominic asked Akiri.

"I- I'm not sure she will want to see me, given the history she has with Gabriel."

It was strange hearing her call Gabe by his full name, he never used his full name, not in Blackwater, or during their journey to Choddrath last year.

"I can ask her if you want, but we don't have to."

"I don't mind, I just want to find the bastard who hurt my babies, and I can't do it alone," Akiri said.

Kamara nodded and got up. "Dominic and I can go talk to Sophie and in the meantime, you can clean up and get dressed. Meet us in the kitchen when you're ready, we will leave a guard outside your door to show you the way when you're finished." Kamara placed a friendly hand on Akiri's shoulder.

"I know we have never been friends, nor have we ever really worked together, but I would like to change that," Kamara said softly. She smiled at Akiri before she turned to follow Dominic out into the hall.

Akiri went to the bath and slipped the robe off. She stepped into the large tub cautiously. The water was still quite warm and it stung her skin as she eased herself down into it. She did not put her burned hand into the water, instead, she used a cloth to gently clean around the wound as best she could. When she was finished washing her body, she stood up, the water was black with soot from the fire and smoke. She pulled down on the handle that pulled the stopper up from the drain and watched the black water get lower and lower until it swirled around in a circle at the mouth of the drain.

She found herself wondering where the water goes as the tub emptied. Her maids still had to empty her bath by hand. She felt a lot better after her bath, except for her had which had begun to blister now. Akiri opened the door to find the guard standing beside it as Kamara told her he would be.

"I'm ready, Sir," Akiri said. The guard nodded.

"Right this way." He turned and walked down the hallway. Akiri loved the way the golden trim brightened up the castle walls, it made it not as dark and scary looking as the dark halls of her castle. The guard led her to a set of double doors that opened into a large kitchen with several workstations. The pots and pans dangled from the rack above the kitchen island. Sophie, Kamara, and Dominic were sitting at a small table in the corner of the kitchen and there was a chair left for her. They had heated a kettle of water for tea and waited for her before they began.

"Please, join us," Dominic said, as he gestured to the empty chair. As she sat down, he poured water from the kettle into their cups.

"We want to help you, but we need to come to an agreement first," Sophie said.

"What kind of agreement?" Akiri asked. She feared that it might have something to do with Gabe, but she was never so relieved to be wrong.

"A year ago, we formed the dragon alliance between us and The Silver Talons Guild. It is our job to protect the interest of dragons, by assuring peace with humankind. If humans fear us, they will hunt us, and no one wants that. Humans who commit acts of violence or threaten dragonkind will be brought to justice by the guild. My father is the leader of the guild, so believe me, the punishment will fit the crime. We will only help you if you join the alliance with the Silver Talons Guild and agree to follow these rules." Sophie slid a handwritten book bound in leather across the table to Akiri.

"Okay, I agree," Akiri said without hesitation or even opening the book. She wanted to find who was responsible and bring them to justice, she would do anything to see that happen, even join a guild.

"Great, looks like we are heading to Ash. We can wait until sundown and then we will go, if you need to rest up or eat, do it while we have time to spare. We will meet on the western beach at sunset." Dominic said. Sophie started to stand up, but Akiri put her uninjured hand on top of Sophie's.

"I hope that we can be friends," Akiri said. She had wanted to say that she was sorry about Gabe, but Akiri knew that hearing his name from her lips would cause Sophie pain so she didn't. Sophie pulled her hand away.

"Just take care of Gabe and we will have no problems," Sophie said. She walked away, not offering any expression or other hint as to her thoughts. Akiri looked at Kamara and Dominic.

"She needs more time, Gabe was her best friend since they were children, and she is helping you as part of the dragon alliance code, if you want anything more than that, you will have to earn her trust."

"Gods know I don't deserve yours after Choddrath, and what I did to your father last year," Akiri said.

"Lucky for you, I believe in second chances. I don't want enemies when I take the throne, I would much rather have friends and allies," Dominic said.

Akiri winced in pain as she tried to rise from the table, she had accidentally placed her hand, palm down on the table to push up from the chair and instant regret filled her as she collapsed back into her seat.

"Let me take a look at that" Dominic held out his hand to Akiri. She showed him her palm. It was blistered and red and still looked dirty. Dominic waved his free hand over the wound and whispered an incantation. As his hand encircled hers, a blue crackling of lightning surrounded her hand like a bubble. The particles of dirt and smudges of soot lifted from her hand and floated away into the magical sphere.

"All I can do is clean it out, you need to see Clarice in the infirmary. Come on, I'll take you."

Dominic stood and reached for Akiri's good hand to help her up.

"While you show her to the infirmary, I'm going to go talk to Sophie," Kamara said. Dominic kissed her softly. And whispered something in her ear. She leaned in, placed her hand on his chest as she listened, and smiled.

"I love you too," she said back to him as he led Akiri out the door.

The infirmary smelled like every herb all at once. The wall to their right was lined with shelves of tinctures, potions, salves, and the wall to the left was lined with beds. An older woman with gray hair and an apron stood to greet them as they came in.

"How Can I help you, My Prince?" she asked with a curtsy.

"She has a pretty bad burn on her hand, she needs healing." Clarice looked at her palm. She closed her eyes and began to chant in a language Akiri had never heard. As she spoke, new skin began to form and covered the burn in soft pale flesh.

Akiri looked down at her hand in amazement, she opened and closed her fist, turned her hand up-side-down, and inspected the back of it as well.

"That's amazing! I've never seen magic like this, it's like it never happened. Thank you."

"Yes, of course, this is my purpose. The Goddess gifted me with this power so that I could help others." Clarice explained.

"You should get some rest before we go, It has been a traumatic day for you," Dominic said.

Akiri nodded, although, traumatic did not even begin to describe it.

24

SOPHIE

Anxiety took over and Sophie paced back and forth across her room biting her nails. The coppery tang of blood hit her tongue before the pain signal made it to her brain and she looked down at her fingertips to see that two of them had started to bleed.

"Sophie, can I come in?" Kamara's voice came from the other side of the door. Sophie rushed over to open it and invite Kamara in.

"I don't understand, we *killed* Baelfire. I saw him turn to dust, he can't be back." Sophie began pacing again as Kamara closed the door and walked over to join her.

"Maybe there was another black dragon. We thought we were the only four until Baelfire emerged, so maybe he wasn't the only one." Kamara suggested.

"How can we find him? It's not like we're going to find an enormous sign that points us to his lair."

"Sophie, stop, come sit down before you pace trenches into the floorboards." Kamara patted the end of the bed next to her. Sophie sat on the bed next to Kamara but she continued to bite her nails, and her leg bounced rapidly.

"I'm worried for Gabe, Akiri left him there alone, what if the black dragon comes back before we get there?" Sophie asked.

"If that happens, I hope Gabe can fortify himself somewhere safe. We can leave as soon as the sun sets. We will be flying west, so we won't be able to see until twilight at least." Sophie nodded, but she was still filled with worry. Kamara was worried too, Sophie could see it.

"I'm going to get some rest, you should too; try at least," Kamara said as she walked toward the door.

"I will," Sophie promised.

Sophie pulled out her spell book and practiced some incantations, without the hand movements, the spells were ineffective, but her pronunciation needed work on some of the spells. She could cast fire in a bolt or an area, she could cast simple illusions such as the appearance of clothing, and she could create food and drink, and she could even turn invisible for a short time, but only in human form. She was unable to cast at all in her dragon form.

When Sophie was finished practicing, she kept to her promise and tried to rest. She closed her eyes and tried to force sleep, but it would not come. Instead, thoughts of Gabe and Bastian mingled in her mind and kept her awake. *Why can't I get him out of my head?* Sophie thought. She tried to think of that day under the willow when she had kissed Gabe. She thought of his soft lips on hers, but when she closed her eyes again she was no longer kissing Gabe, now it was Bastian. In her fantasy, Bastian was strong and passionate and took what he wanted instead of waiting for her to make the first move. Maybe that was why she couldn't stop thinking about him.

No matter how hard she tried, she could not remember what happened between them the night of the engagement ball. She remembered kissing him, Gabe interrupting, and then she woke up next to Bastian. She didn't remember walking to his room, undressing, or getting into his bed.

Ugh, this is useless. Sophie thought as she threw back the covers and sat up. The wood floor beneath her feet was cold, she looked toward the hearth and noticed that the fire was out. She put a few pieces of wood in there and got the fire going again. As soon as she stood, there was a knock on her door.

"You couldn't rest either?" Sophie called through the door. She expected to see Kamara again, but it was Bastian. Sophie looked at him in surprise but moved back so that he could enter. He looked at her so intensely that it made her heart flutter and her face flush. Sophie closed the door and locked it.

Bastian moved closer to her, his blue eyes staring deep into her soul. He didn't hesitate any longer, in an instant, his lips were on hers and they started tearing each other's clothes off and letting them fall to the floor. He picked Sophie up and pressed her back against the wall as his lips explored her. Sophie could feel that he was aroused and just teasing her as he pressed against her. Bastian carried her to the bed, their lips only parting long enough to take in a breath. He laid her down gently, carefully placing her long hair to the side of the pillow so that he wouldn't pull it by accident. He trailed kisses down her body. He cupped her breast in his hand and rubbed his fingertip across her nipple. He slowed down and looked her in the eyes as he ran his fingertips down her sides, and then her hips.

"Is this real, or am I dreaming again?" Sophie managed to ask.

Bastian smiled, "You've been dreaming of me?" He asked. Bastian kissed her stomach, her belly button, and then lower, and lower until his mouth found its prize. His hot breath warmed her as he flicked his tongue on the secret spot that made Sophie moan his name. She gripped the bed sheet in each hand with a white-knuckle grasp and arched her back. He kissed his way back up her body until he reached her breast and then he took her nipple in his mouth and sucked gently elongating and hardening it. He played with her nipples and teased them with his tongue until Sophie's desire was too strong and she could bear it no longer. She reached between them and took his length in her hand, gripping as much of him as she could in one palm, and positioned him at her entrance.

Bastian watched her face as he slowly slid inside of her. She gasped and no words came, but she moaned softly as he moved his hips back and forth slowly, pushing himself deep inside her and pulling out to the very tip before inserting his length again. Bastian lifted her hips and pulled her toward him as he thrust faster and harder until he felt her contracting. He let himself reach climax deep inside her, and he stayed inside her until they both stopped throbbing. He looked down at her soft red lips and her eyes which reminded him of a doe. Bastian rolled over onto his side, still admiring Sophie. Her rosy pink skin glistened with perspiration and he traced constellations in the freckles that speckled her shoulders and chest. Bastian curled a lock of her hair around his finger and then pulled his finger out of the curl and watched it bounce back into place, *a perfect ringlet on a perfect girl.* Bastian thought.

Sophie rolled over and kissed his lips. Bastian held her body to his as she accepted his tongue into her mouth. His body responded to her passion and she felt him harden as his erection pressed against her inner thigh, and she felt a pooling of wetness in her center. Bastian turned her onto her back and positioned his face between her legs. He licked up and down her sex as his arms wrapped around her thighs and held her in place. He could feel her trying to squirm as he swirled his tongue around her clit and sucked it into his mouth as he flicked his tongue back and forth. She moaned his name and begged for him to enter her.

Bastian sat up and pulled Sophie onto his lap. She straddled him as he kissed her passionately and tangled his fingers in her hair, pulling gently to tilt her head back. He kissed her chest and her neck as she moved back and forth, sliding his cock between her lower lips, feeling him on her core as his sex slid against hers. He bucked his hips as Sophie started to move forward and he thrust himself inside of her.

"Oh goddess, you feel so good," Sophie told him. Bastian gripped her ass, lifted her up, and slid her back down giving her every inch of his passion. She screamed as her pleasure mounted and called out his name as she reached orgasm. He felt her sex pulsing around his and he let himself climax with her again.

After that, sleep did not evade either of them.

When Sophie woke up, the sky was deep orange. She sat up quickly and this time, her movement woke Bastian. He tried to pull her back into the bed as she tried to get up.

"I'm sorry, I have to go, but I will see you here next weekend, I hope," Sophie told him.

"Maybe I could come to visit you before that?" She couldn't resist him, although she tried.

"My castle isn't complete yet, I am staying with Prince Dominic and Princess Kamara."

"Your castle? Are you a Princess" Bastian asked.

"No," she replied. Bastian looked at her confused. "I'm a Queen, actually," Sophie said with a smirk.

He pulled her in close and growled softly in her ear, "A *Queen.* That's so hot. I guess that makes me the Queen's Consort."

"Or the Queen's Plaything." Sophie teased.

"I can't say I'm disappointed by either title." He kissed her neck and rolled her on top of him, gripping her thighs. Sophie's red curls cascaded down over her breasts and Bastian stared at her as she felt him harden beneath her. She made a deep, inarticulate sound filled with desire and regret as she swiftly moved from the bed and cast the clothing illusion.

"I'm sorry, I have to go. I'll be here next week, and I want to see you again." Sophie said with a commanding tone.

"Yes, *My Queen.*" The way he said those words; a half-whisper and half-lust-filled groan, drove Sophie crazy, if she weren't so worried about Gabe, she might be tempted to stay longer and have her way with him again, but she gathered all her strength, and her bag, then headed for the beach.

The flight to Ash was shorter than Sophie expected, but the landscape was exactly what she heard it was; flat farmland for miles and a small town near a dark, looming castle carved from the stone of the only mountain on the island. Sophie instantly felt sorry for Gabe, that this place was now his home. She thought that he must miss the forest and the streams. She wondered if he might even miss his job at the citadel.

They landed on a rocky beach, it was dark and everyone else had to get dressed. Sophie picked up a rock and whispered an incantation to it. The rock lit up like a full moon and they had to shield their eyes from it as Sophie tossed it a few feet down the beach. The area where they stood was now dimly lit and everyone could see to get dressed.

"Thanks, Sophie. Magic sure comes in handy doesn't it?" Dominic asked. Sophie chuckled and nodded.

"Sometimes."

When everyone was dressed and ready to continue, they took a dirt path leading away from the beach and between the neglected fields. It was a longer walk than it appeared, and when they finally got to town, everything was already closed. They walked up the cobblestone street toward the castle in silence. Akiri led them through the front door, around the left corridor, and through the back doors that overlooked the southern courtyard. She picked up an oil lantern on the way so they could see once they passed the courtyard.

Sophie could smell the ash and smoldering remains as soon as they stepped out the back door. The scent intensified the closer they got to the entrance to the lair. The three of them followed Akiri down the steps into the underground cave which had been carved out by hand tools, much like the rest of her castle, and the mountain keep on Choddrath. Remnants of metal armor and weapons remained, but not much else.

"This is where my nest was, I laid five eggs. They all had movement inside. I would have had children, but they were murdered, or perhaps even stolen. There were broken eggshells down here, but it didn't look like enough to be all five eggs." Akiri turned to face them with tears streaming down her cheeks. Sophie didn't know how to feel. A year ago she would have thought Akiri was incapable of feeling. The way she had claimed her power and left the rest of them to take care of Baelfire alone.

Now here she was, crying and broken because someone had taken everything she loved away from her. Sophie knew that she had a habit of harshly judging others in the past. She once thought Kamara was too naive to survive the real world, and that she had not been hurt by it enough to be cautious in her actions. She had been wrong to think that though because Kamara had been hurt by the world more than any of them when Baelfire's men stormed her temple and killed everyone she knew. She had been lucky to escape, and smart to stay with the guild even after delivering the orb.

"Sophie." Kamara's voice brought her back from her thoughts of the past and she looked up to see them all standing at the base of the stairs. "Ready to go?" Kamara asked.

"Oh, yeah. Sorry." Sophie followed them back through the courtyard and into the castle. Gabe was waiting for them just inside the door. When Sophie saw him she wanted to run to him and throw her arms around his neck, but that seemed inappropriate now, with him being married and all.

"How are you, Sophie?" Gabe asked.

"I'm good. I would ask how you are, but that seems like a silly question given the circumstance." Sophie said gesturing to the lair. Gabe nodded and turned toward the guard standing to the left of the entrance.

"Jack, would you please ask Mr. Koffery to make some tea and bring it to the dining hall?"

"Yes, Your Grace," he replied with a quick bow and hurried off to do as Gabe asked.

"You have adjusted to royal life well," Sophie said.

Akiri put her arm through Gabe's and the two of them led the way to the dining room. The table was modest with only eight chairs. Akiri sat at one end, and Gabe at the other.

"Please, sit wherever you would like," Akiri said. Sophie chose a seat in the middle and Kamara sat next to her, closest to Gabe so Dominic walked to the other side of the table and sat in the middle across from Sophie.

Kitchen maids served them tea and brought in a tray of sugar and milk. The teacups were made of some kind of smooth black stone. It held in the heat, even after the fresh milk was added. They waited for everyone else to leave the room, and when they were gone Akiri cast a magical dome around them.

"Don't worry, this is just magical soundproofing. Only those of us sitting at this table will be able to hear our conversation." She finished the incantation and paused before speaking again. "I saw the black dragon fly south from here with something hanging from his teeth like it was carrying a bag. I suspect they might have taken an egg or two before they destroyed my lair." Akiri said as she sipped her tea.

"It can't be Baelfire, we turned him to dust," Dominic said.

"There's more. A seer told me that someone on my council would betray me. She didn't say how, or who, but she knew that it was going to happen. I haven't seen her since she made the prophecy."

"You think it might be her?" Kamara asked.

"No, but she knew someone would betray me and she is now missing. I have looked for her in the city and turned up nothing, I have had the city guard looking for her, as well as the sailors down at the port and so far, everyone has come up empty-handed."

"What's her name?" Sophie asked.

"Agatha Stone, although, She was often called Madame Stone," Akiri told them. She left out the part about how she only used to call her 'witch' or worse.

"So where do we go from here? We could fly south and look for clues, or we could re-create the situation, and tell everyone you have a new lair, and this time you are not telling anyone where your lair is. Then, you can confide in each council member privately and give them each a different location. Then we watch those locations, and if the dragon shows up at one of them, whoever you gave that location to is the betrayer. Does that make sense? I know I kinda rambled for a minute." Sophie said.

"I think that will work, Sophie, you're a genius!" Akiri said.

"Yeah, good idea, Sophie." Gabe smiled as he looked at Sophie, but then quickly looked away. She knew that he was trying to keep things friendly between them.

"This plan will take months to execute, It will also require me to be away from Ash, and away from the council during my ovulation period. I hate to ask, but would you know of somewhere I can stay, where I can remain hidden during this time?" Akiri asked. Kamara looked at Sophie, and she nodded back to her.

"You can stay in one of the guest rooms at the castle Ophay with me. Dominic will return to Ledora, Sophie will return to Lapis Highland, and Gabe will remain here in Ash. We will still need two more locations and people to watch over them." Kamara said.

"I can ask Juniper and Laughlin to go to Northport, and my dad can send men to Stonehold Keep," Sophie suggested.

"It sounds like a plan. You can all sleep here tonight and we can fly northeast tomorrow afternoon. I will let Gabe show you to your rooms, I'm going to let the kitchen staff know to prepare extra breakfast." Akiri said. The shimmering veil that surrounded them dissipated and became no more than specs of dust as Akiri dropped the spell.

Gabe stood up and waited for the others to join him. "Right this way," he said as he turned to lead them from the dining hall. The castle seemed eerie. Sophie wondered if it were this lonely during the day too, or if it were just because they arrived at night time. Gabe stopped and opened the door to a guest room.

"Kamara and Dominic, this room is yours," Gabe said. "If you need anything, my room is just across the hall," Gabe said. Gabe returned to the hall and looked at Sophie. "Your room is a little farther down." They walked to the end of the hallway and around the corner to the left. Gabe stopped at the first door in that hallway. The rooms were all on the right because the left looked out over the central courtyard.

Gabe walked into the room and Sophie followed. He looked at Sophie with his eyes full of sadness. She had to look away. She hated seeing him like this.

"I'm sorry about the eggs," Sophie said.

"Thanks." Gabe didn't know what else to say. He wanted to say so much to her, he wanted to hold her. He wanted to rush over and kiss her. He had tried so hard to stuff these feelings deep inside and forget about Sophie. Being so far away from her had helped in that regard, but now that she was here in front of him, his heart felt like it might explode. It was as heavy as a boulder and it felt like it was crushing him.

"My room is around the corner at the end of the hall if you need anything," he said. Sophie nodded, and Gabe had to force his feet to move back to the door before his heart could convince him to stay longer. He closed her door on the way out and let out a heavy sigh before he walked back to his room.

Sophie listened to the sound of his footsteps receding away from her room. She hated this. Gabe was miserable. She knew him better than anyone and she could tell. Sophie longed to have back those days beneath the willow now more than ever.

She cried herself to sleep that night, and in the morning, her head ached. Sophie rolled over to get out of bed and noticed a tray that was not there when she went to sleep. It had toasted bread, berries, a small bowl of oatmeal, a pitcher of water, and a cup. Sophie poured a cup of water and when she lifted the cup she saw a note. She unfolded it and saw that it was Gabe's handwriting.

The rose is beautiful and sweet. It was almost a line from Sophie's favorite poem. The line said; the rose *was* beautiful and sweet. It was a poem about a metaphorical flower given as a symbol of love, losing all of its petals because it was neglected by the person it was given to. Sophie wasn't sure what he meant by this. *Is he trying to tell me that he is happy?* Sophie wondered. She was touched by the fact that he remembered that it was her favorite poem. She had first read it in a book of poetry that Gabe copied from the citadel. Most of the poems were anonymously written, but they were all beautiful and filled with so much emotion. It was one of the greatest books Sophie ever read. She thought she might ask him about it today if she could find a moment alone with him before they left.

25

GABE

A t the meeting of the council that morning, Gabe studied the mannerisms and words of each man intently as Akiri questioned them about what happened to her lair. Had he known from the start that Akiri suspected one of them might betray her, he would have been watching them closely the whole time. Most of the men at the table, not counting Gabe were well into their fifties, except for two. Nohan Arach was perhaps in his twenties, and Timothy Ackerman had just celebrated his thirtieth day of birth.

"My guard, Michael Roman is dead, burned alive in my lair. My eggs were destroyed. I want to know where all of you were while that was happening." Akiri demanded. They all began speaking at once, denying their involvement or knowledge of the event.

"Stop. You first, Ser William. Where were you when the black dragon came and destroyed my lair?"

"Your Grace, I was in town, doing the weekly shopping, by the time I got back to the castle, you were gone and King Gabriel was fighting the fire, one bucket of water at a time so I gathered the household staff and all the buckets we could find and we created a chain from the well to the lair to put the fire out," William said.

"Mister Ackerman, what about you?" Akiri asked.

"I was not feeling well the night before, ate something that didn't agree with me and I was finally asleep after spending all night in the privy." Timothy looked embarrassed as he admitted his whereabouts.

"Nohan." Akiri continued questioning around the table.

"Your Grace, I had the night off, so I visited the brothel and spent the night there, several girls can account for my whereabouts." He looked particularly proud of himself, but Akiri wore an expression of disgust.

"Mister Koffery."

"When the fire broke out, I was holding the staff meeting that I hold every morning just after the council meeting. We use that time to plan out the day and delegate tasks. As soon as I heard the commotion, I ran out to help," He said.

"Very well, Bertram?"

"I was repairing a broken stall door at the arena, and then I went to check how far along construction was on the new town square. I didn't arrive home until that evening."

"Was anyone a witness to your presence there?" Akiri asked.

"I suppose the locals were all aware I was there, but if they will remember seeing me I cannot say, Your Grace." He looked nervous and let out an inaudible sigh of relief when Akiri moved on.

"Mister Stewart?" Akiri nodded to her guard.

"Your Grace, I was outside your room when I smelled the smoke. I investigated the source of the smell and when I saw where the smoke was coming from, I ran to the bell tower to ring it."

"I do remember hearing the bell as soon as I saw the smoke coming from the lair. Thank you, your quick action helped extinguish the flames, but unfortunately, we did not act fast enough to save my eggs. I want you all to be extra vigilant. Bertram, can you stay behind? I would like to speak with you privately. Everyone else, you're dismissed." Akiri watched as everyone else got up from the table. When Bertram and Gabe were the only ones left in the room, Akiri closed the doors and returned to her seat.

"Bertram, I asked for privacy because I want this to stay between us. You are the leader of the builder's guild and I know you have some engineers within your company. I was hoping you could design and have them build a weapon capable of shooting a dragon from the sky. I'm thinking something *like* a bow and arrow, but bigger and made of something that can pierce a dragon's skin." Akiri said.

"I will see what I can do, Your Grace," Bertram said.

"Thank you. I'm also going to be gone for a while and will be leaving Gabe in charge, I'm not telling anyone else, so please keep this to yourself, but I am making a new lair far away from here, but in case you need to reach me, and I do mean *only* you, I will be going to Stonehold Keep. It's been abandoned for years, it's the perfect place for a lair." Akiri said.

"I'll not tell a soul, My Queen," Bertram said.

"Thank you. That is all, when you have a prototype of the weapon let either me or King Gabriel know immediately. I would like for it to be built on top of the castle."

"Absolutely, Your Grace." Bertram waited to be dismissed and when he was he hurried off to begin his task.

"First seed is planted. I think I need to take a rest already, I'm still a little tired from the stress of the last couple of days." Akiri said.

"Me too. Would you like for me to lay with you for a while?" Gabe offered.

"I would like that very much."

On the way back to their room, they saw Sophie walking down the hall toward their room.

"Is everything okay, Sophie?" Gabe asked.

"Yeah, fine. I'm just going to go out for some fresh air, maybe walk around town for a bit before we go later this afternoon."

"Okay, will I see you before you leave?" Gabe asked.

"I- uh, if I make it back in time. I'll try." Sophie said. She hurried down the hall and toward the grand foyer.

"Come on," Akiri gently pulled on Gabe's arm as she led him into their bedroom. She directed him to the bed and told him firmly to sit down. "It's not fair. I want you to look at me the same way you look at her. I want to know what it feels like. Akiri's fingers started to glow with a green light. Gabe was nervous. She whispered an incantation and as she waved her hands over her body, she morphed into Sophie. Every detail was the same, down to the last freckle. She walked over to Gabe and straddled him as she pressed her lips against his. He pulled away.

"What's wrong? Isn't this what you want?" She asked.

"Not like this, I don't need you to become *her.*" He said the words, but they held no weight against his desire as he looked back at this woman who was Sophie in almost every way. Akiri knew, too because she felt his arousal beneath her as she stared down at him. Gabe swept her fiery red curls behind her shoulders as he kissed her lips. She stood up and slid the straps of her dress off of he shoulders and let it pool to the floor around her feet.

"I want you, Gabe. Take off your clothes," she commanded. He couldn't resist. He undressed faster than he ever had before and when he was finished, Akiri walked over to him and pushed him down on the bed. She walked her fingers up his stomach, to his chest as she mounted him. She hadn't even needed her hand to guide him inside her. He was more aroused than he had ever been before and Akiri knew why. She rolled her hips forward and back as she watched Gabe admire every inch of her. She moaned with pleasure as he held her hips with his hands and pushed deeper inside her. In a swift movement, he rolled Akiri over and positioned himself back between her legs. He lifted her hips as he thrust himself inside of her again. Gabe stared down at her as he slowed his pace. He leaned down and kissed her gently as his free hand cupped her breast.

"I love you, Sophie," he whispered. He hadn't meant to say it, but after the words left his mouth he couldn't take them back. Akiri dropped the illusion and looked at Gabe angrily. He tried to apologize but she cut him off.

"I knew you were still in love with her."

"This is on you. If you knew how I felt why did you turn yourself into her visage? I told you that I didn't need you to become her. Do you not think it possible that I could care for you both? Godsdamn it, Akiri, I'm trying here. I was in love with Sophie since childhood, and that doesn't just go away, but it also doesn't mean I can't grow to love you too. The real you, not you trying to be her." Gabe got up and started dressing.

"Where are you going?" Akiri asked. Her face was stone. Gabe had expected some emotion other than anger, but if she felt any, they didn't show.

"I don't know, right now, just away from you." He slammed the chamber door as he left. Gabe walked out the front door of the castle with his guard following behind. Gabe turned to face him and put his hand up.

"I'm fine, I don't need an escort, I need to be alone," he said. The guard paused and looked as if he were considering following anyway. "That's an order, stay here," Gabe told him.

"As you wish, Your Grace."

Gabe watched him start walking back to the castle and Gabe went toward town. He had not been to town since his first tour around the kingdom, he doubted if the subjects would even recognize him without his royal armor.

He walked down the cobblestone streets past the shops and when he came to a tavern in the center of town, he was drawn in by the music. They never had music at the castle and Gabe had not realized how much he missed it. He walked in and sat down at the bar. When the barkeep asked him what he would like, Gabe ordered the best ale they had. He had never tried ale before, but the way everyone talked about it, he thought it might be good.

The barkeep handed him a mug of dark brown liquid with a thin layer of white foam on top. Gabe took a big gulp and started coughing as soon as the ale slid down his throat. It tasted bitter and robust, like coffee, but with a taste of copper and herb. As he choked on the ale, the other patrons at the tavern laughed at him.

"First time eh? Yea that'll put th' hair on ye chest won' it?" Gabe turned toward the voice that spoke to him.

"It will do something, that's for sure," Gabe replied.

"Ya get used to it after a bit. It ain't the taste ya drink it for, it's to forget, and it looks like you got some'n you wanna forget."

"I do."

"Don't we all?" The man gestured around the tavern to the other patrons, no doubt all there drinking to forget something.

"M' name's Kendrick, but mostly people call me Ken. I got the cow farm o'er there by those old sugar cane fields," Ken explained.

"I see, I'm Gabe."

"Gabe, the King?" Ken's eyes widened as he looked at Gabe.

"Shh, keep it down, I don't want anyone making a fuss." Gabe said.

"So what's a king like you drinkin' to forget?" Ken asked.

"It's kinda personal, I had an argument with someone today and I feel bad about it, but I also feel like I'm not wrong."

"Well I don't know much about diplomacy, but it sounds like you could patch things up with a little communication, but you'll never fix anything if you look for all your solutions at the bottom of a pint glass."

"Thanks, Ken, that's not bad advice." Gabe chuckled as he pushed the ale back toward the barkeep to signal that he was finished with it.

"Hey, if yer not gonna drink that, I will, no point in wastin' it," Ken said.

"What about all that 'don't look for solutions in a pint glass' talk?" Gabe joked.

"I'm not looking for solutions, just numbness. It's too late to get back what I lost, but it sounds like you still have time." Ken chugged the last half of Gabe's ale and put the mug back across the bar when he was done.

"Hey, thanks for the talk, I'm going to go see if I can't patch things up." Gabe smiled as he pushed in his bar stool and started back toward the castle. Before he made it out of town, Sophie spotted him from across the street.

"Gabe!" She called. He turned to see her already on her way across the street to him.

"Hey Sophie, how are you?"

"I'm fine. I got your note this morning. What did you mean by it?" Sophie asked, getting right to the point.

"I knew you liked that poem is all."

"You know that I can always tell when you're lying." Sophie playfully nudged his shoulder.

"I was just saying that you look happy. I hope that you are," he said.

"Do you want me to be honest, or do you want to feel good?"

"Please, be honest. Always."

"When I came back to Blackwater, I came back to tell you how I felt. I was finally ready for us to be together. When you said you were leaving and didn't know if you would be coming back, I was devastated. Then when I saw you and Akiri among the newly engaged royal couples I was heartbroken. Now, I know I should stay away, and I know that being your friend is infinitely harder with my feelings being what they are, but I can't lose you again."

"I should have told you from the start how I felt about you, but I was afraid you didn't feel the same, and I would lose even your friendship. Then all this happened with my mom and the guild. I messed everything up and I'm sorry," Gabe said.

"It's okay, I could never stay mad at you. Even if you are a complete bonehead."

"I have to get going now, there are a few things I have to take care of before you guys leave. I will be there this afternoon when you go," Gabe said.

Sophie nodded and hugged him tightly, not knowing if she would be able to later when his wife was on the beach with them.

26

SOPHIE

Later that afternoon, Sophie met the other dragons on the beach. Kamara and Akiri were going back to the temple Ophay, Dominic was going back to Ledora, and Sophie would be returning to Lapis Highland. She hoped that the castle was finished, or at least her bed chamber. Gabe was there to see them off, just as he said he would be.

"I made these for us." Sophie handed each of them a quill. And a notebook. "They are all connected by the same magical spell. When you write in the notebook, the ink appears, then disappears like this," she demonstrated by writing her name into her notebook. All the other notebooks began to glow. "Go ahead, open them," Sophie said. When they opened the notebook they saw Sophie's name written in their notebooks. "When you close the book again, the messages disappear, so make sure you only open the book when you have time to read it, but this way we can quickly get messages to each other from anywhere. If you want to message only certain people, just write their name first and underline it, like this," she wrote Kamara's name, underlined it, and then wrote a little note. Only Kamara's notebook lit up. When Kamara read the note she giggled. They all packed their notebooks and quills into their bag which they brought for traveling. For Sophie, it was her father's backpack, which was beginning to show signs of wear on the straps from being carried in her teeth.

"This is a great gift, Sophie. Very thoughtful." Kamara said as she packed it.

"I agree, thank you, Sophie." Gabe and Sophie's eyes met and his gaze lingered a moment too long and he heard Akiri huff. He quickly looked away. "Safe travels, everyone. Hope to see you soon."

When he moved forward to kiss Akiri goodbye, she turned her face and his kiss landed on her cheek. Sophie looked away quickly, not wanting to insert herself in the obvious spat they had going on. They shifted into their dragon forms, Dominic the majestic gold dragon with the power to exhale lightning, Sophie, the fierce red dragon with fiery breath, Kamara, the silver with the ability to bring ice and frost upon the land, and Akiri, the dark green dragon who could spit acidic sludge and melt metal with it. Sophie knew that if the four of them were on the same team, there would be no force strong enough to take them on, not even the black dragon would stand a chance.

Gabe watched as they took off into the sky. He thought it must be so freeing to be able to fly wherever you wanted to go in no time at all. Traveling by ship sometimes took weeks compared to the trip from Ledora to Ash which only took a couple of hours.

Sophie felt weightless in the sky, which was quite a feat for a dragon. She loved soaring through the clouds and beside the birds. She felt so free of everything when she was flying that she wished she never had to come back down to the ground.

Even though she loved staying at the Temple Ophay, with Akiri there now, she was glad to be going back to Lapis Highland. It was dark when she landed, but she could see that Highland Castle was now complete. When the guards saw her, they bowed immediately.

"Welcome back, My Queen." Sophie heard as she approached the castle doors.

"Thank you," she said as she continued inside.

"I would like to call an emergency meeting. If the throne room is completed gather the Highlanders and have them wait in there. I'm going to make myself presentable." Sophie turned to the other guard, "would you mind showing me to my chamber?"

"Right this way, My Queen." He led her up the grand staircase, which opened into a small library and sitting room. Comfortable-looking chairs stood in front of large windows with bookshelves in between them. They turned right down a hallway and the guard stopped.

"This entire wing is yours. You have your chamber here," he pointed to the first door on the left, "and then you have your study. All of your magical items and components have been stocked and are in your study for you. There is a secret passage that leads from your bedchamber to the lair and from the lair to your study. I will leave you to explore, but please, My Queen, if there is anything you need, I will be right here." He pointed to the corner of the hall and the library. "I have been assigned to be your guard unless you choose another, Your Grace."

"I feel like if we are to be working so closely together, I should know your name," Sophie said.

"My name is Thomas, Your Grace," he said. The boy was no older than Sophie, but he was muscular and looked like he could win a fight.

"Thomas, do you know how to use that sword?" Sophie gestured to the short sword sheathed at his hip.

"Yes, My Queen, I have trained every day since I could hold a blade."

"Then you will make a wonderful queen's guard, Thomas." Sophie smiled and retreated to her chamber, taking notice of the boy's prideful expression as she left.

Her bed chamber was beautifully decorated with a carved mahogany canopy bed with red and black curtains, a matching chest of drawers, and matching bedside tables. A silver chandelier illuminated the room with flickering candlelight. The nightstands each held a beautiful oil lamp, as well as the vanity and the writing desk. The bath chamber was the most surprising, She didn't know how they did it, but the marble tub had a metal spout and handle that pumped hot water into the tub. The water drained from a hole in the base, no one would have to carry buckets of water to fill or empty her tub.

Even with all of her magic, this was one of the greatest things she had ever seen, at least that was what she thought until she saw the privy. There was a tank of water on the back and a chain connecting the tank to a handle. When Sophie pulled it, the water drained from the tank into the bowl and the bowl filled momentarily and then washed down the large drain. *Wow*, Sophie thought.

She quickly cleansed herself in the bath and dressed in a lavish gown. She put on her obsidian crown which was made for her on the island of Choddrath, inside the mountain keep. She exited her room and approached the guard.

"Would you please, escort me to the throne room?"

"Of course, My Queen." Without another word, he did as he was asked and led her to a set of carved double doors. When he opened them he walked in before her.

"Please stand for Queen Sophia Rend, The Red Dragon," Thomas announced. Everyone stood up and turned toward the center aisle to see Sophie enter. She walked confidently to the throne and when she sat down, everyone else did as well.

"I know you might not be aware of recent events, but A black dragon has attacked the kingdom of Ash. This dragon destroyed something very important and irreplaceable to the Queen. If you see the black dragon, you are to report it immediately. Anyone caught knowingly concealing the dragon's identity or human form will be sentenced to death. I do not know if this black dragon is Baelfire, I thought for sure he was dead, but know that I am your rightful Queen and anyone who does not swear fealty to me, here and now can leave the Highland and never return." Sophie stood and walked to the edge of the platform.

"If you are true to your Queen, take a knee at this time and promise to defend Lapis Highland and the Red Dragon from all enemies." Sophie had never seen an entire room of people kneel so quickly. There was not a single person left standing.

"My Queen!" They all declared.

Over the next few weeks, Sophie settled into a routine. She chose a small council and found a way to make money selling potions and magical items that she created in her study. She was becoming more practiced in wizardry and her new shop in Alasia Outpost, the shopping district of Alasia, did very well on its grand opening. The shopkeeper, a Highlander by the name of Gladys was an experienced caravan operator and she sent her people out in all directions selling Sophie's enchanted items to people in every town they traveled to.

It was around her third week back at Highland Castle, that Sophie began feeling ill. She was throwing up like she had a stomach bug and was tired all the time. The healer brought her things like plain toast and ginger, but nothing seemed to help. Everything she ate or drank came back up. When another week passed and she did not get her blood with the new moon, she thought of Bastian. *Oh no, what have I done?* Sophie thought of the last day they spent together. A tear rolled down her cheek as her hands protectively felt her stomach for signs of movement. There weren't any yet, but the bottom of her stomach felt hard and just a little bloated. It was not much bigger than normal, maybe the same as it was after a large meal. *I need to keep this to myself for now,* she thought.

27

AKIRI

Kamara was a gracious host. Temple Ophay was beautiful and homey. It wasn't large like a castle, but it did have plenty of guest rooms and Akiri's favorite part, a gorgeous lair with bubbling hot springs. Akiri liked the forest, it was a lot better than the dry island of Ash. She thought of Gabe and hoped that he was doing well.

Before she left, Akiri had already given three of her council members false locations, and Gabe was feeding the other three information. He was also in charge of watching the councilmen making sure they weren't discussing the locations with each other and uncovering their lies. The plan counted on them not finding out that they each had a different location. Weeks passed and Kamara and Akiri spent much of that time talking and getting to know each other. Akiri had been good at concealing her sadness in the first few days, but her thoughts weighed on her until they became too much. Kamara saw her expression and couldn't stand it any longer.

"Akiri, would you like some tea?" Kamara asked.

"No thank you, I just need someone to talk to." Akiri was in the sitting room on the end of a sofa nearest the fireplace. Kamara walked over and sat down beside her.

"What's wrong?" Kamara noticed a redness in Akiri's eyes.

"Gabriel is still in love with Sophie. I tried to overlook it because I wanted a clutch of eggs, I wanted children, but now I realize that I only want love-*his* love. The way he looks at her... he'll never look at me that way." Akiri wiped a tear from her cheek.

"That sounds difficult, I can't imagine how hard that is for you. Is he at least trying?" Kamara asked. Akiri nodded. "Perhaps in time, he will come to love you just as much," Kamara added.

"Maybe, I don't deserve his love. Honestly, the only reason I accepted his proposal was that he was a Silver Talons Guild member. I thought having him in Ash would gain me leverage. I thought he might be able to call the Guild Army to his back should Ash need to defend itself. Then when I got to know him... I just wanted him to like me as much as I liked him, but I blew it."

"Maybe not. Gabe is honorable and determined. He made a promise to you and I don't see him breaking it, he will try to work things out when you get back, I know it." Kamara was trying to comfort her, but it was hard to shake the feeling that she had messed everything up.

"I have another cloak with a hood here somewhere, we could go into town and find something to do. I don't think anyone here would recognize you."

"I can do better than a cloak." Akiri used her magic and turned her hair blonde, and changed the shape of her face. She looked like a completely different person.

"That's impressive!" Kamara said as she looked at the girl in front of her who looked nothing like Akiri. "What should we call you?"

"My nanny when I was young, her name was Margaret, She was my favorite, I think I will go by 'Maggie' in her honor," she replied.

"Maggie, it's nice to meet you, are you ready to go to town? I know just the place to wash those blues away!" Kamara said.

They took the horses and a short ride later, they rode out the western Blackwater gate toward the docks. When they reached the Loose Anchor Tavern, Kamara hitched the horses out front and pulled their oat bags over their snouts.

Jovial music and the pounding of heels against the wooden floorboards greeted them before they even opened the door. Akiri had never been to a Tavern like this. The one in Ash was quieter, more like a place of lament than celebration.

"Come on, Maggie!" Kamara called as she danced her way through the crowd to the bar.

"Two honey ales please!" Akiri heard Kamara say when the barkeep approached her. "I normally don't like ale, but their honey ale is delicious!" Kamara was talking very loudly so that Akiri could hear her over the sound of the music and dancing.

When the barkeep slid their drinks across the counter, Kamara handed him a silver piece and then waited for Akiri to try the ale. "It's good huh? I told you!" Kamara smiled and took a big gulp. When they finished their drink, Kamara pulled Akiri out onto the dance floor. They blended in with the crowd and were as invisible as they had hoped to be. They had a few more drinks until they felt tired and like it was hard to hold their eyes open. A few times, Akiri felt like the room was spinning, or maybe she was spinning.

"I need to sit down, in the fresh air," Akiri said, as she stumbled to the exit.

Her heart was pounding, and so was her head, and Akiri had only made it a few steps out the door when all the ale came back up. She did at least manage to turn away from the footpath and vomited into the bushes instead. Kamara walked out of the tavern right behind Akiri in time to see the aftermath of her honey ale.

"Oh, I'm sorry, I guess we had a little too much. What do you say we get back home? You might want to put your hood up, I think your spell has dropped, you look like yourself again." Kamara said. Akiri's hair was once again raven black, and her skin was ghostly pale. Akiri drew her hood and mounted the horse as best she could. Kamara helped her and strapped her feet into the stirrups. She hooked the horses together as if they would be pulling a cart and then mounted her horse.

"You know, When we first got these horses, I did name one of them, but I forget now what I named it. What are some good horse names you think?" Kamara asked. If Akiri weren't completely drunk, she might have recognized that Kamara was just trying to keep her awake.

"Umm, Ale and Rum," she said, pointing from Kamara's horse to the one she was riding.

"Is that because you like rum?"

"Nah, it's 'cause Ash was... its history... the uh, rum runners and um... What was I talking about?" Akiri wasn't used to her mind working so slowly, and not being able to think of the words to say what she meant.

"The names for the horses, Ale, and Rum," Kamara chuckled.

"That's right! I forgot. Ale for yours, and Rum for this one." Akiri said. There was a long period of silence between them after that as they listened to the birds in the trees and the shuffling of the horses' hooves through the debris on the forest floor.

"I think a nice long soak in the hot spring sounds lovely when we get back," Akiri said longingly.

"You're right, that does sound nice, If you can put the horses in the pasture, I will make us some tea and meet you in the lair. The silvery temple had just come into view and they both sighed in relief at the thought of spending the rest of the evening relaxing.

When they dismounted, Kamara handed the reigns of her horse to Akiri and they went about their separate tasks. Kamara started a fire in the hearth and heated the kettle on the hook over the fire. When the water was hot she made a cup of tea, both for herself and Akiri.

Kamara strolled through the back garden with a cup in each hand. She wasn't close enough to see inside the lair, but she had a feeling that something was wrong. She called for Akiri as she got to the mouth of the cavern but received no response. Then she saw them, boot prints too wide and long to be from Akiri's small foot. Someone had been in her lair. Kamara set the tea down quickly. She rushed to the hot spring and looked around the empty lair. *Oh no, oh no, what's happened?* Kamara thought as she ran back out to the entrance of the cavern. Then she saw it, it was the tiniest bit of evidence, but it was evidence nonetheless, a blood-stained rock discarded carelessly to the side. The boot prints seemed to go no further than the entrance.

28

DOMINIC

The King was happy to have his son home again, he had of course wondered why his son had not brought his Princess with him. Dominic had said that she was feeling under the weather and that she chose to stay at the Temple Ophay. He told his father that he had come to practice his royal duties, this made the King very happy and of course, he had commanded a banquet in his son's honor. He set the date of the event three weeks in advance to give all of the guests enough travel time.

On the night of the banquet, Dominic wore his royal uniform the coat was a royal blue with gold embroidery along the buttons, and his collar was an elegant white lace ruffle that covered the top half of his vest which matched the coat and trousers. Dominic's father was not the only one to take notice of the fact that his wife-to-be, Princess Kamara had not accompanied him, and as they usually do, the whispers began to spread.

"Prince Dominic!" The Prince whirled around to see Bastian approaching him with outstretched arms and a smile. "It's been too long." He said as Dominic took his hand in a firm shake and clapped his other hand on Bastian's shoulder.

"How are you, Bastian?" Dominic asked politely.

"Honestly, I've been better. I'm lovesick. I was hoping that Sophie would be here but I haven't seen her." It was more of a question than a statement, Dominic could tell that he was hoping that Dominic would offer up some information as to her whereabouts.

"I haven't seen her either, not for a few weeks," Dominic said. Bastian looked forlorn. "But hey, there are plenty of ladies here tonight, perhaps you can find one to help you forget?" Sophie had never confided in Dominic her true feelings for Bastian, but he thought if she wanted to be with him then she would have invited him to travel with her.

"I don't want to forget. Sophie is the one I want. I think I'm in love with her," he said dreamily.

"Has she told you how she feels about you?"

"Not with words, but I know she feels the connection we have."

"I'm sorry, I wish I could help you, but my father is calling for me. I wish you and Sophie the best of luck!" Dominic called as he maneuvered his way through the crowded banquet hall. He stopped at the series of buffet tables along the wall on which, sat beautifully arranged

212

and delicious delicacies for snacking. He picked up a plate and selected some strawberry tarts, pineapple chunks, a couple of samosas, and some kofta made with ground beef and lamb, mixed with herbs and spices, skewered, and grilled over the fire. When his plate was full, he took his place beside his father at the center of the banquet table. The King raised a chalice and toasted to Dominic and the Kingdom of Ledora. The crowd cheered as they all took their seats at the table. The servants brought course after course while musicians played music on stringed instruments.

When the banquet was over and most of the castle had retired for the evening, Dominic found himself thinking of Kamara. He thought about going back to the temple to see how things were going, but he couldn't tell anyone in Ledora about the black dragon.

"My son, why do you look so glum?" Dominic hadn't heard his father approach and he startled slightly at his voice.

"Oh, sorry, I'm just missing Kamara."

"What's going on? Why has she not joined you? You have been away for weeks now and to my knowledge have not even received a messenger from her." King Haki sat down beside Dominic and prepared to listen to his woes. Dominic did not tell him of the notebook and that he had been talking to Kamara regularly.

"Honestly, things between us were great, we were setting up a home at the temple. It's easier for us to work with the guild this way, but truthfully, I am here, and she is there because we are on assignment. We are trying to lure out a rat," he confided.

"I see, that is a demanding assignment, to be away from the one you love." The King showed empathy.

"I think I am going to take a walk and get some fresh air," Dominic said.

"Should you need to talk again, you can always talk to me, no matter the time." The King rose to his feet and hugged his son before they parted ways.

The night-time air in Ledora was cool, a blessed reprieve from the scorching sun of the daytime hours. Dominic walked from the castle through the Golden City, then out the eastern gate toward the beach where he and Kamara always landed. The moon, although not full, still cast the beach in a soft white glow. A low, rumbling sound stopped Dominic in his tracks. He tiptoed up behind the dunes and peeked out across the crest. He saw a cloaked figure shift into the form of a black dragon.

Dominic gasped and then, afraid the dragon might have heard, clasped his hands over his mouth and ducked down behind the dune. He waited, anticipating the sound of the dragon's footsteps in his direction, but instead, he heard the beating of two large, leathery wings as the dragon took flight to the northwest. He had to get back and use the notebook from Sophie, he had to let all of them know that the dragon was in Ledora.

Dominic ran across the beach toward the western gates of the Golden City. His feet sank into the sand as he ran and slowed him down. By the time he reached the steps of the castle, he was gasping for breath. He rushed to his bedchamber and bolted the door behind him.

The notebook was in his bag, he grabbed it and dumped it on the bed. He opened the notebook and scribbled; *The Black Dragon was just spotted at the Lair in Ledora.*

Not long after he wrote the message, his notebook lit up. *I know who it was, it was Akiri's guard, Horace Stewart. I will handle it on my end. Meet here as soon as possible. -Gabe* Right after the message from Gabe, another message appeared. *Akiri is gone, they've taken her. I'm headed to Ash right now.* It was from Kamara.

29

SOPHIE

Sophie was in a deep slumber when the sound of heavy armored boots marching down the corridor stopped at her chamber door. She was already up and on her way over when the metal armor clanged against the wood.

"Your Grace, I am so sorry to disturb you at this hour, but there is a gentleman at the front entrance who is very insistent upon seeing you," the guard explained through the door.

"Did he give you his name?"

"Bastian, Your Grace." Sophie's heart leaped. She was so happy that he had found her. After Sophie left Ledora to go to Ash she wondered how long it would be before she got to see him again. Sophie tied her dressing robe around her waist and ran to the stairs and took them two at a time to get down them faster. When she reached the front entrance, she was out of breath but threw her arms around Bastian's neck at once. The guards averted their eyes as this stranger handled their queen in such a familiar way, grasping her backside as he lifted her off the ground and parted her lips with his tongue. One of the guards cleared his throat. Remembering that they were not alone, Sophie led Bastian up the stairs to her room. He tried to kiss her again as soon as they crossed the threshold, but Sophie stopped him.

"I want to see you undress," She commanded. Bastian began quickly untying his tunic, but again she stopped him. "Slowly." Sophie sat down on the edge of the bed and watched him intently as he pulled at one string very slowly and the knot came untied with an almost inaudible pop. He slid his fingertips under his tunic, letting his hands showcase his abs and chest as he lifted his tunic over his head. He walked up to Sophie, positioning the tie to his trousers close to her mouth. She touched him, running her palms from his chest down to his hips.

She kissed the sensitive skin between his belly button and his trousers and then took the end of the string in her teeth and pulled the bow loose and then quickly pushed him backward. He hooked his thumbs into the waist of his trousers and then slid them down. Sophie watched with anticipation as her prize was slowly revealed.

Sophie stood up, untied her robe, and pulled the silk belt from the loops. As she glided over to where Bastian was standing she could tell that he was imagining her shape beneath her robe which hung open, barely obscuring her breasts. Sophie put the silk belt around the back of Bastian's neck and used it like reins to guide him to the bed.

She pushed him back onto the bed and then slipped out of her robe as she crawled onto the bed after him. "Put your arms up." She commanded.

"As you wish, My Queen." His eyes never left her as she used the silk belt of her robe to tie his arms to the headboard of the wooden canopy bed. She trailed kisses from his lips, to his neck and down his chest, then his inner thighs. He writhed beneath her, as she paid attention to every part of his body except for his sex which was throbbing with desire. He moaned as her breasts grazed his skin as she kissed her way back up his thigh and then took him into her mouth, swirling her tongue around the tip which was salty with the first drippings of his seed. She stopped then, leaving him wanting more as she crossed the room for no other reason than to let him desire her as she stood out of his reach.

"Sophie, please," he begged.

"I didn't say you could speak," Sophie said quietly. She stared at him intently as he continued to squirm, and move his hips in an attempt to relieve the pressure. She smiled as he moaned and begged for her without daring to utter another word. She crawled onto the bed again, this time she straddled him. She leaned over to kiss his lips as she let him slide into her. He groaned as she rolled her hips slightly, arching her back as she rode him. He longed to touch her body, fondle her breasts, and thrust into her deeply, but she was in complete control.

When she was satisfied, she reached up to untie him. In an instant his hands were all over her, his left hand was squeezing her buttocks and his right grasped her breast. He gently flicked her nipple back and forth with his thumb which caused her to cry out. She then turned around on her hands and knees and faced the foot of the bed. Bastian quickly rose to his knees and entered her from behind. He grabbed her hips and pulled her toward him as he thrust into her. He moaned as he felt her muscles contract around him and it made him thrust harder and faster. He pulled her toward him slightly so that he could run his hands up her belly to squeeze her breasts and his right hand went further still as he held her throat. He loved the way her curly hair grazed the small of her back as she rose from all fours to her knees with him still inside her.

He turned her around so that he could look at her as he pushed into her again, slowly this time, teasing her with the tip and then finally giving her a good deep thrust. He watched her face as he did this, noticing the way her mouth fell open when he was deep inside her and the way her eyes rolled back when he only gave her the shallow, quick thrusts, and the way her nipples hardened and lengthened at his touch. He moaned her name as he reached climax and pumped inside her until he slid out soft and satisfied.

"I love you, Sophie," he said as he gazed down at her.

"I-" She started to speak but a faint light from the desk caught her eye. It was the notebook. *Oh no, how long has it been lit up?* she wondered.

"Hold that thought," Sophie said as she scrambled up off the bed. She opened the notebook and read the messages from Dominic and Kamara. "I'm sorry, I have to go." Sophie didn't bother packing a bag, she used the illusion spell to dress in the bath chamber and then ran out to the side of the castle, She prepared her body to shift and tried, but it wouldn't work. She tried again, this time, focusing on her hands, stretching her fingers to make them grow into talons. It was no use. She couldn't shift. A fluttering in her lower stomach told her why. The sudden fear of having to tell people why she couldn't shift took over her mind and she began to cry, but dried her eyes as best she could before returning to her room to face Bastian.

"Is everything okay, should I leave?" he asked as he tied his tunic.

"Everything is okay, don't leave. We need to talk." All the joy left his face at those words.

"Oh, is this the 'it's not you, it's me' talk, or the 'we need to see other people' talk?" he asked.

"This is the 'I'm pregnant, what are we going to do about it?' talk," she replied.

Bastian sat back down on the edge of the bed, his eyes wide, and his hand over his mouth.

"I mean, We didn't exactly do anything to prevent it, so it was inevitable. How do you feel about it?" Bastian looked at her.

"I'm not sure." Sophie thought about shifting, she couldn't get to Ash, if she sailed, it would take her weeks to get there because she would have to sail around The

Barren. She went to the desk and grabbed the notebook and the quill and wrote;

Can't make it, I can't shift. I will explain later, handle the guard and then let's meet here.

Sophie closed the notebook, placed it in the desk drawer, and then sat on the bed beside Bastian.

"I thought you were leaving, I didn't know if I should stay with you not here," he said. Bastian had his boot in his hand but put it down when Sophie came over to sit beside him.

"You don't have to leave. I would prefer you stayed." Sophie leaned her head on his shoulder. Moisture began to gather in the wells of her eyes. She didn't know why she was suddenly overwhelmed with sadness, but Bastian put his arm around her and softly kissed the top of her head. He rested his head on hers.

"Would you like to lie down? Maybe you need to rest?" Bastian suggested.

"That might be a good idea." Sophie dropped the illusion spell and crawled beneath the covers of her bed.

"Would you like for me to stay in a guest room?" Bastian asked.

"No, I want you to hold me and tell me everything is going to be okay," she replied.

Sophie was finally able to sleep when the last of her energy was cried out. Bastian held her most of the night. She didn't feel him slip out of bed, but he was gone when she woke. Sophie pulled on a robe and walked about the castle looking for him. The guards stood in their places and nodded as Sophie walked by.

"Did Bastian say where he was going?" Sophie asked the guard standing at the front doors.

"Yes, My Queen. He said he was going to go into town to go shopping."

"How long ago did he leave?"

"He left before the sun came up, Your Grace."

"Thank you," Sophie didn't remember the guard's name. The castle staff had been hired by Ezra. He ran the underground keep for Baelfire but swore fealty to Sophie when Baelfire was killed. He gave Sophie no reason not to trust him and she knew that it was because of him, and his rallying, that she now had this castle. Ezra was a good man. Giles too. Giles was the first to swear fealty to Sophie when the keep fell. He had whispered to her in secret that if anyone could free them from Baelfire it was her. Giles was a yes man, he was too afraid of punishment to outright disobey, so he always did as Baelfire commanded without question. In the time Sophie spent in the mountain keep of Choddrath, she witnessed Baelfire's mistreatment of those he felt were beneath him. He treated her like a princess, of course, his daughter- the heir to follow in his footsteps and carry out his plans. Too bad for him that Sophie's plans included her family- her real family- Leon, and Samantha.

Sophie wandered to the kitchen and put on a kettle for tea, she loved being able to get water from the pipe over a large basin. Even with all of her magic, this still seemed like sorcery to her. She sipped her tea, she wanted to wait for Bastian, but she needed to head to the courtyard to meet Dominic, Kamara, and Gabe.

30

GABE

The throne room was dark; black stone floors, dark gray stone walls, and the arched stone windows faced the north and were shaded by large trees. Gabe walked around lighting the torches in the sconces around the room. The only light that came in from outside, came from a round skylight above the throne that illuminated it as if the sun were shining directly on that spot.

Gabe walked onto the throne platform and behind the throne to the rope that hung from the bell tower. He pulled the rope at least eight times, the clanging of the bell vibrated through the rope and he could feel it. He took a seat on the throne as everyone in the castle began filing in. They sat on long benches lined up on both the left and right of the center aisle. It reminded him of a wedding, but no one would be getting married today. He waited for the guards and the small council to be present, and when most of the castle staff had taken their seats, he let them know the reason for the meeting.

"It has come to our attention that the incident that happened last month with the Queen's lair and her eggs, was an inside job. One of you knows something, one of you knows the black dragon that killed our children. I intend to reveal this traitor to the crown, and they will be dealt with accordingly, before I call the guards upon this individual, I ask that you would beg for mercy from the Queen, and admit to what you did."

"The Queen isn't here though, where is she? She left us here with this outsider sitting on the throne, ruling *our* kingdom while the Queen hides," said a gruff man with long greasy hair. He stood in the back with his arms crossed.

"I hear your frustration, and believe me, I did not intend to be ruling without Queen Akiri, but the attack on her children can not be forgiven, and it is our goal to protect the queen until the guilty party is brought to justice. Without further wait, Guards, please arrest Horace Stewart." Angry outbursts erupted from the crowd. The guards moved up behind Horace and seized him by each arm. They brought him over in front of Gabe and put him on his knees. Horace's face was filled with shock and confusion. "We have evidence to believe that you gave sensitive intel to the black dragon so that he might find the Queen's lair. Have you anything to say for yourself?" Gabe asked.

"My King, I have only ever served Queen Akiri loyally, I am not the betrayer. The burden of proof may not be on my side, so I would ask your mercy and that I might stay locked in the dungeon until you find this black dragon and dispatch him so that it can be the Queen herself to decide my fate." He bowed to Gabe so deeply that all he could see was the tip of his boot.

"Very well, guards. Lock him in the dungeon, we will let Queen Akiri decide what to do with him when she returns. You all are dismissed." Gabe sat down on the throne as everyone filed out of the throne room- all but two.

When the throne room was empty, Kamara and Dominic approached Gabe. He looked at them, confused for a moment. "Where's Akiri, and Sophie?" Dominic and Kamara looked at each other.

"You haven't read the last couple of messages, have you?" Dominic asked.

"No, I went to sleep last night after I sent my message and I left the notebook in my desk drawer this morning, why, what's happened?"

"Akiri has been taken, we aren't sure how, or who, but there were boot prints in the lair, which means her kidnapper was human. Even if they were a dragon, when they shift in and out of human form they're naked, they wouldn't have boots on."

"How did this happen? You were supposed to be watching her!" Gabe shouted at Kamara.

"This isn't her fault." Dominic put his hand up to prevent Gabe from getting any closer to Kamara.

"I was making us tea and we were going to soak in the hot spring." Gabe took a breath and thought about what this meant.

"If the dragon was in Ledora, and the Temple, there has to be more than one traitor among Akiri's councilmen. I will try my best to get someone to slip here, you guys go to Sophie and make sure she is okay. Please, don't let anything happen to her." Gabe said.

"We will do our best," Dominic promised. He wrapped Gabe in a quick hug to comfort him and then looked at Kamara. "Can you lead the way? I have never been to Lapis Highland before." Kamara nodded.

"I can lead us there, but we wait until the evening sun is gone, otherwise we will be flying blind," Kamara said.

That evening, after Dominic and Kamara left, Gabe called an emergency council meeting, expecting all five councilmen in attendance, minus Horace Stewart, who was in the dungeon. Gabe was seated in Akiri's chair at the head of the table. He waited fifteen minutes past the time he commanded them to be there, and one of the men was still missing.

"Where is Nohan Arach?" Gabe asked. The men looked at each other. "Bertram, send guards to the city watch barracks and see if he is there. He is to be brought here by any means necessary, we will continue without him for now." Gabe waited for Bertram to come back inside the room and take his seat. "Is the weapon finished, Bertram?"

"Yes, we have placed it on top of the northeastern tower. We have plenty of bolts already made and even more in production."

"Good. Inform everyone, if the black dragon is spotted flying over Ash, the triggerman should fire immediately. Do we have a plan of defense should there be an attack? What will we do with the women and children?" Gabe asked.

"We have turned the old dungeon into an underground stronghold. We are stocked with supplies enough for the city to survive for a year at least without the need to go above ground. We have a mushroom farm down there for protein and an entire storeroom of fifty-pound bags of rice. There is a mountain spring that runs fresh water down there, and there is only one entrance so it is easy to defend." Roland Koffery said.

"Perfect, Alert the villagers, have them ready to run at the first sign of trouble."

"Yes, My King," he replied.

"Okay, if anyone sees Nohan Arach, he is to be taken directly to the dungeon and come get me immediately. Dismissed." Gabe thought about Nohan, Gabe was sure that the captain of the city guard was the same age as he was, if he was older, it couldn't be more than by a year or two. Akiri had told Horace Stewart herself that her Lair would be in Ledora and the black dragon was spotted there. But Gabe had told Nohan that the lair was at the Temple Ophay, and Akiri was taken from the temple. *What am I missing? It has to be one of them if not both, doesn't it?* Gabe thought.

31

AKIRI

When she opened her eyes, she saw only darkness. Akiri lifted her hand to the back of her head and felt the lump that had formed there while she was out. It was painful to the touch and the size of a plum. Her hair was sticky and matted with what she could only assume was blood. The floor beneath her feet was made of stone and seemed to be swept clean, there was no debris or dirt beneath her that she could feel. Akiri tried to cast a spell for light, but as she tried to cast, the manacles around her writs glowed a faint green and absorbed the magic from her hands. Her ankles were chained as well, she could get up and walk around, but when she got a few feet away from the wall, the cuffs around her ankles pulled her back and almost tripped her.

She was naked, but she didn't remember undressing. She searched her memory for what had happened. *We got back from the tavern, I stalled the horses, and closed up the barn; Kamara went to make tea. I went to the lair...* All she could remember after that was darkness. It seemed like hours before she finally heard footsteps approaching and could see a lantern in the distance. Akiri moved back toward the wall as the figure grew closer. She could now see the outline of their shape, a hooded figure in dark robes, and a dragon mask that hid their face and made it impossible for Akiri to recognize her captor.

"Please, why am I here? What do you want from me?" she demanded. As they approached, her captor hung the lantern on a hook on the wall.

"This is your new lair, what do you think?" Akiri tried to place the voice, but it sounded distorted as if some magical interference carried it from somewhere else entirely. She couldn't even tell if the voice was male or female.

"Who are you?" she asked.

"It doesn't matter who I am, I am no one. I am here to make sure you are taken care of." With a whisper and a wave, a few small berries appeared in the captor's hand. "Eat one," they said. Akiri backed away, shaking her head.

"Girl, don't be a fool. You cannot escape, no one knows where you are, and even if you did manage to make it out of this cell, I assure you that you will not find a single morsel to eat on this island. Oh, and I forgot to mention, we have cast a spell on you that will keep you from shifting, until we want you to, that is."

"I don't understand, why are you doing this?" Akiri asked. "I just want to go home."

"Our master needs a mate. He cannot produce eggs, but you can. You have been wasting your birthright with that human boy, creating abominations that are half dragon, half human without the ability to shift."

"How do you know- You took one, I knew the dragon took one." Akiri reveled in her realization.

"You will never get what you want if you continue to mate with the human boy, he is not special. I would show you the result of your union with the human, but we already disposed of it."

"You're monsters, those were my children," Akiri spat.

"No- those were monsters who would have been chased from the villages with torches and pitchforks. No one would have trusted them, or loved them. What kind of life would that be? One where you are hated by everyone, everywhere, for your whole life. We are offering you better children, dragons that will be feared by all and make your kingdoms the strongest in the realm."

"You can't just kill my children and then expect me to..."

"It's your choice, you can stay here forever, unable to get back to those you love, or you could do this one simple thing, and produce a clutch of eggs for us and then you can take half and go free," the captor said.

"I will never let him touch me."

"Then you will remain here until you die." The captor left a single berry on the floor in front of Akiri. "You'll want that when you get hungry." They left it just out of Akiri's reach and grabbed the lantern from the wall. Akiri listened to the footsteps retreat. Her magic was useless with the barrier up, there were no rocks, weapons, or anything else near that she could use to break the chains. Kamara and the others were her only hope. They had to be looking for her by now. She curled in the fetal position and cried herself to sleep. She hoped for dreams, but even those seemed to abandon her.

When she woke up it was still completely dark, she had no indication as to what time of day it was. No light came in from outside, and the temperature was always the same. She hated that her captor was right, but now that she had slept, she was hungry. Akiri held out as long as she could and when the pain became too great she stretched and reached for the berry. She wiggled her fingertips and lengthened both her arms and legs as much as the chains would allow until finally, she was able to reach her breakfast.

She rolled it in her fingers, and she remembered from seeing it in the lantern light that it had been a red berry, smooth and round like a blueberry, but deep red. She put it into her mouth and chewed it up. The taste was dry but strong; it was tart and bitter at the same time and not as soft as she had expected it to be, but it was also not crunchy like some dried fruit. Once she swallowed it, she felt full; like she had eaten a whole meal. She also was not thirsty anymore-which she didn't understand since the berry had been dried.

A little while after, the captor returned. Akiri watched the lantern swing back and forth as the captor walked closer. "I see you've eaten, good girl," they said. "Have you given any more thought to our request?"

"It wasn't a request, was it? You say that word like I was given a choice, but the only choice is to do what you want, or die." Akiri said bitterly.

"I never said it was a good choice, but you do have one," the captor said.

"I have another question, this black dragon is your master, yes?" The captor looked confused. "Is he Baelfire?" Akiri asked.

"No, not even close. First of all, Master is dark green, not black, and second, Baelfire? No one follows him anymore."

"So then how does this green dragon still have his powers? I thought that all the power was given up when the ancients contained the magic in the orbs?"

"The island of Immernacht where Master was born holds many secrets. Magic that affects the rest of the realm does not penetrate the barrier protecting Immernacht. When all the other dragons lost their power, Master was saved from that fate. He and his brothers, although his younger brother left Immernacht well before the age of seventeen to squire for some noble family, as you know, the power of the dragon lays dormant in a shifter until they are seventeen. It's because the body is too weak before then to handle the shift. When we realized that Master still had his power, he promised that he would restore dragons to our kingdom so that we could finally see the sun again."

Akiri thought about the darkness in the room where she was, and the fact that she had seen no light at all since she got there. "Are we in Immernacht now?" she asked.

"Our time is up, no more questions. Master will be back in a few days, you should think about the offer. I think he is being pretty generous," the captor said.

32

SOPHIE

The morning sun was just peeking over the horizon when Kamara and Dominic arrived at Highland Castle. Sophie met them in what would eventually be the western courtyard with robes for them to wear.

"I'm going to have changing stalls built here, and in the eastern courtyard as well, that way when you come to visit you don't have to walk very far without clothing, or worry about where you can get dressed. I didn't know if you brought clothes with you, so I brought you these," she said as she handed them the robes. She had brought three robes out with her, but Gabe had not come with them.

"Gabe had to stay in Ash, with Akiri gone, he is the King there and he can't leave, there is no one he trusts enough to rule," Dominic said. "Otherwise, you know he would have come."

"Are you okay, Sophie? Why can't you shift?" Kamara asked.

"I'm pregnant," Sophie said. She felt it was better to just rip the bandage off.

"Oh my goodness, Sophie... Who-"

"Bastian."

"That's wonderful, Sophie! Isn't it?" Kamara saw the apprehension on Sophie's face and then wasn't so sure that she was ready to celebrate the news. Dominic looked even more shocked than Sophie.

"I just saw Bastian in Ledora, he was looking for you."

"He found me. He's here now," Sophie said.

Dominic looked confused. He was trying to process through the shock how Bastian could be in Lapis Highland already, but he thought it best to continue thinking for a while. He didn't want to alarm Sophie. She guided them from the unfinished courtyard to the stone walkway that led to the front doors of Highland Castle.

"I'm sorry, I know it's not much yet, but after some landscaping and gardening, it will be as beautiful a castle as I ever dreamed." Sophie smiled.

They entered the grand foyer and saw the staircase that opened into a small sitting library, but Sophie led them to a meeting chamber with comfortable chairs and a large round table. She sat down and waited for Dominic and Kamara to take their seats too.

"Do either of you have a plan or any leads as to where they might have taken Akiri?" Sophie asked.

"No, but there were very few footprints near the lair or inside it, so either the kidnapper is extremely light-footed, or they can fly," Kamara said.

"Do you think it was the black dragon that took her?" Sophie asked.

"It's possible. I think our focus now should be, finding out who this black dragon is." Dominic looked at Sophie. "I saw Bastian, just the other night in Ledora, by ship the trip from Ledora to Blackwater Bay takes at least four days on a direct route, then from Northport, it's another half a day's walk... How is he here so fast? Did you see him arrive?" Dominic asked softly. Sophie looked horrified as her mind came to the same conclusion as Dominic's.

"You don't think that Bastian is the black dragon do you?" Sophie looked as if she were about to cry. "It can't be true, there has to be some other explanation, tele-portation circles, or maybe even a polymorph spell that could turn him into a bird, something... not that." Sophie clutched her stomach as the tears pooled in the corner of her eyes. She felt the hot tears roll down her cheeks. "How could I have been so stupid, I never should have-"

"Sophie, none of this is your fault. We will find her. We just have to figure out where he might have taken her. Did he tell you where he was from?"

"We never really talked about his past, at least I don't remember if he mentioned it."

"What did you guys talk about?" Dominic asked.

Sophie tried to remember actual conversations, but all she could think about was how he made her feel when they were together in her bed. She didn't recall having any meaningful conversations about him, or even about herself. She looked ashamed as she shrugged at Dominic. Kamara put her arm around Sophie's shoulder.

"Don't worry Sophie, everything will work out," Kamara said. "In the meantime, we can give you a ride back to Ash if you want, so you can see Gabe."

"I have to deal with Bastian first, we can't just leave him here, and we can't expect my castle staff to stop a dragon, I have an idea, we will take him with us, but I need to brew a pretty strong sleeping potion first." Sophie stood up and almost ran to the staircase. Dominic and Kamara followed Sophie to the study upstairs. This was where Sophie spent most of her time, creating magical potions and magical weapons, necklaces, and rings.

"Wow, this is a pretty amazing study," Kamara commented.

"Thank you, it's not finished yet though, I have more things in storage that I don't have shelves for yet," Sophie said as she grabbed some ingredients from a cabinet. She began mixing herbs and powders in a miniature cauldron that she hung over a candle flame. She added some water from a jar with an amethyst tied around the mouth of it. She added in a glowing teal powder and a deep blue smoke rose from the cauldron as the contents started to boil.

Dominic and Kamara watched her with amazement as she created the potion. When she was finished, she strained the liquid into several small vials. The potion inside was a shimmering dark blue. It looked like the night sky filled with millions of shimmering stars.

"Will that work?" Kamara asked.

"If we can get him to drink it, he should sleep for a few hours. We might have to give him another dose mid-flight, depending on how long it takes."

"From Ash to here it was about seven or eight hours, We left in the evening, and arrived at sunrise," Dominic said.

"I will give him a little extra, hopefully, it will last until we can get to Ash." Sophie stuffed the vials into the pocket of the robe she was still wearing just as Thomas, her guard stepped into the room.

"Bastian has returned, Your Grace," he said.

"Thank you, Thomas, these are my friends, Dominic and Kamara, they are free to roam the castle as if they live here, with no restrictions."

"As you wish, Your Grace."

Sophie looked at Kamara and Dominic. "Perfect timing, give me an hour and then meet me in the western courtyard." Sophie walked toward the door and Thomas moved out of the doorway so that Sophie could exit. She went downstairs and greeted Bastian in the foyer. He held out a bouquet of bright pink lilies and kissed her cheek as she took them.

"They're beautiful. I should get these in some water, and I was just about to make some tea, do you want a cup?" Bastian nodded and Sophie looked at him the way she always had, but was nervous that he might sense that something had changed. Sophie and Bastian walked to the kitchen, with Thomas following a few feet behind to guard the door. Thomas stood with his back to the kitchen to give them the semblance of privacy.

Sophie found a vase for the flowers and then put the kettle back on the wood stove, the fire was burning low so she placed another piece of wood onto the hot coals and stoked it to get the flames going again. She took one of the vials out of her pocket and held it tightly in her hand.

"Would you mind asking Ezra for some milk from the cold storage? Thomas can direct you to him, it's just a few doors down." Bastian smiled and got up from the table. He kissed her before going about his task. As soon as he was gone Sophie uncorked the vial and poured the contents into his cup. She cast an illusion spell on it to make it appear empty and then carried both cups, spoons, and sugar to the table. She lifted the strainer from the kettle to check the color of the tea inside, it was dark, just like she wanted it.

When Bastian returned with milk, they both sat down at the table. She offered the milk to Bastian first, which he refused. Sophie was relieved, the color of the tea might be slightly off with milk in it and then he might know something was strange. She poured her cup first, and then as she poured Bastian's cup she dropped the illusion spell as the dark liquid mixed and covered the potion. Bastian put some sugar into his tea and stirred it.

Sophie sipped her tea eagerly, since it had been poured from the same kettle into two seemingly empty cups, Bastian would have no reason to distrust her and refuse the tea. Finally, he raised the cup to his lips and sipped it.

"This tea is really good, where did you get it?" Bastian blew onto the surface of his drink to cool it.

"I bought it in Alasia from the tea shop, it's a special blend of elven tea from Ravenhall," Sophie said as she took another drink. "I think after we finish our tea, we should take a walk in the courtyard, maybe pack a basket and have brunch beside the ocean," Sophie suggested. Bastian's eyes were filled with nothing but stars for her as he enthusiastically agreed. They finished their tea, and Sophie conjured a basket of delicious treats to take to the cliffside. Sophie dressed quickly and made sure to stash the extra vials of sleeping potion into the pocket of her trousers.

"Ready?" She asked Bastian when she came back downstairs.

"I'm feeling kind of sleepy all of a sudden, maybe we should take a nap first." Bastian yawned.

"I'm sure you'll get your energy back once you eat something," Sophie said.

"You're right, I am a little hungry." He carried the basket for her with one hand and held her hand with the other. Sophie couldn't help the overwhelming sadness she felt, not only because of the deceit but because of the way things could be if Bastian were not suspected of treachery.

As they reached the back of the western courtyard, Bastian began to stumble. "What the-" Sophie gasped and tried to help him sit down, but he pushed her hand away. "What was in that tea?" He looked at her as if he were in a daze.

"Nothing, I feel fine, it must be something else, did you eat or drink anything while you were in town?" Sophie dropped to her knees at his side. Bastian was sitting on the grass near the edge of the cliff.

"Everything is spinning, I don't... I think I need to lie down." Bastian fell backward and Sophie caught his head in her hands and lowered it gently to the ground.

"Bastian!" She called his name a few more times and when she was sure that he was sleeping soundly, Sophie called to Kamara and Dominic who were waiting around the corner of the castle out of sight with a large coil of rope.

"Let's hurry," Dominic said as he shifted. The sun illuminated his golden scales and he had never looked so magnificent before. The golden dragon bowed down to accept his rider. Sophie called for help from the castle guards and asked them to hoist Bastian onto Dominic's back.

The guards were apprehensive about the dragon at first, and with good reason, since they had all been at the battle of Choddrath, but they did as Sophie commanded because she was their Queen. Kamara and Sophie tied Bastian to Dominic's back with the rope and then Kamara shifted as well. Sophie climbed onto Kamara's back and found a couple of handholds near the silver dragon's neck.

They took flight into the sky, even though the sun was just above them, they knew the way now, and there was no time to waste. They flew below the clouds because at least the clouds gave them a little coverage from the sun and they could see well enough to know that they were on course. Sophie had never flown on dragonback before and she decided then and there that it was not her favorite mode of transportation. She loved to fly, but she needed to have control. She kept watching Dominic. He flew straight and steady, but despite the smooth flight, it looked like the ropes were loosening, and Bastian was slipping. She hoped that it was only a trick of the light, but when Bastian slipped to the other side of Dominic's back, the golden dragon rolled sharply to try to keep his rider on, but despite his best effort, Bastian began to fall. Dominic tried to turn around and dive down beneath him, but he was not fast enough, his enormous dragon body would not allow him to turn as quickly as he needed and Sophie screamed as Bastian plunged into the ocean below.

"No! He's in a magical sleep, he'll drown!" She screamed. Dominic had never dove into the ocean in his dragon form, he wasn't sure if he could swim, but he went after Bastian who was sinking beneath the waves as his lungs filled with the salty water. Dominic needed to breathe. He breached the surface, took a breath, and then tried to dive down again, but Bastian was now too deep for Dominic to see, the darkness claimed him.

When Dominic flew up out of the water without Bastian again, Sophie let out a wail. It was a sorrowful sound,

Kamara and Dominic knew that despite their revelation that Bastian might be the dragon that kidnapped Akiri and destroyed her lair, Sophie was in love with him. Dominic was about to dive down again when a loud rumbling sound came from beneath him, he flew up out of the way and watched as a dark dragon emerged from the water. He spotted Sophie on Kamara's back and flew straight for them. Dominic got in between them and swung his tail at the dragon that could only be Bastian. Dominic's tail caught Bastian in the neck and Bastian tumbled backward through the air.

"Go!" Dominic shouted to Kamara. Sophie heard Kamara's voice inside her head tell her to hold on tightly as Kamara accelerated quickly. Sophie screamed and held onto Kamara's scales as tightly as she could. Sophie leaned forward, almost laying down completely against the back of Kamara's neck, but she wanted to look back, she had to know if Bastian was okay. Dominic flew toward them, but stayed a safe distance away, as he waited for Bastian to attack again.

Kamara flew as quickly as she could, she was not able to look back without slowing their progress, but Sophie kept trying to turn around and search the sky while still trying desperately to maintain her grip. She hoped that Dominic was okay, but she also secretly hoped that Bastian was too. Her heart was shattered. How could he do these things, destroy Akiri's lair, crush her eggs, kidnap her... no, this didn't sound like Bastian at all. There was no denying that he has been keeping the fact that he is a shifter a secret from everyone, including Sophie.

They heard nothing but the beating of wings, roaring, electricity, and screeching behind them as the wind battered their faces, but Kamara didn't stop until she reached the rocky shore of Ash. Kamara laid as flat as she could so that Sophie could climb down. When Sophie backed away, Kamara looked at her and she knew that Kamara wasn't going to stay with her, she was going back to help Dominic.

"Be careful!" Sophie called, as Kamara ascended into the sky once more.

33

DOMINIC

Bastian roared at Dominic as a cone of fire erupted from his mouth and stopped short just before it reached him. Dominic kept his eyes fixed on the figure in front of him. They hovered in the air, and the beating of their wings began to turn the clouds into a funnel as they faced off against each other. Bastian darted forward and then suddenly rolled right. Dominic was expecting some kind of trickery and rolled left to head him off. Dominic's body crashed into Bastian's. The bright light of day made it hard for Dominic to see much of anything and in dragon form, he couldn't even squint to shield his eyes from the sun. He relied on his other senses, he could hear Bastian's wings beating to his left so Dominic again, darted to the left and rammed into Bastian's body with his own.

Bastian screeched as he tried to blow past Dominic to chase after Sophie and Kamara. Dominic drew in all the air he could hold and used all of his might to strike Bastian with his lightning breath. Dominic saw the smoke rising from Bastian's back as the black dragon spiraled out of control and fell beneath the clouds. Dominic flew toward Ash as quickly as he could, there was no way that he was going to leave Kamara and Sophie unprotected.

Dominic kept listening for the sound of beating wings, or Bastian roaring after him, but the sky stayed quiet which was both unsettling and suspicious, but there was no time to stop, he had to get to Ash. When he finally did hear the beating of wings, Dominic drew in a breath and prepared for a fight, but it was a silver dragon that emerged from the clouds. He let out a sigh of relief which came out sounding like a sorrowful roar. Once she saw that Dominic was okay, Kamara turned around and led him back to where she had left Sophie. They landed on the rocks and shifted back to their human forms.

"Sophie!" Kamara yelled. She scanned the beach, tall rocks towered like jagged spires from the earth and it occurred to Kamara that Sophie could be hiding behind one of them. Kamara took off running across the beach, calling for Sophie as she passed each rock. Dominic ran to the beach in the opposite direction, calling Sophie's name as he searched. When Kamara and Dominic reached the opposite ends of the beach with no luck in finding Sophie, they ran back to each other.

"Maybe she already started making her way to the castle, we have to go, I don't want to be the one to tell Gabe if she didn't make it there though," Kamara said.

Dominic and Kamara exchanged a glance and looked away. Dominic knew that she felt it too. The same nagging guilt that he felt. They promised to keep Sophie safe and now they had no idea where she was. They started walking toward the castle that loomed in the distance like a dark cloud of despair. Kamara was silent as they walked and Dominic knew that she was fighting back tears. He took her hand and gripped it tightly. He couldn't reassure her that the situation would turn out fine, but he could reassure her of his love and support.

By the time they reached the castle steps, their feet were bleeding and sore from the broken shells and sharp rocks on the beach and the walk to the gates with no shoes. When the guards spotted them, they knew immediately to fetch buckets of water for their feet, gowns to cover their bodies and the healer from the infirmary.

"Please, we need to see King Gabriel, It's important." Kamara pleaded.

"We will have him come out to you, Princess." The guard said as he placed a pail under each of Kamara's feet and then slid the next two buckets under Dominic's. The water stung as their feet soaked. Kamara winced.

"I know, Princess, but the herbs in the water will clean your wounds and save you from infection." He gave each of them a white dressing gown to slip on, and just as they covered themselves Gabe entered the guard post.

"What happened? Where's Sophie?" His heart sank. Dominic could see the pain in his face already. He was hoping that Sophie had already made it to the castle and that this conversation would not be as grim.

251

"We found out who the dragon is, we drugged him with a sleeping potion and tied him to my back in his human form. We were going to bring him here, but as we were flying over the ocean he began to slip off. He fell into the ocean, but he emerged as a dragon and tried to go after Sophie. Kamara flew here as quickly as she could with Sophie on her back, while I headed off the black dragon and impeded his progress, I hit him with my lightning breath. Kamara left Sophie on the beach to come back to help me take care of him, but we didn't see him anymore, so we rushed back to the beach and by the time we got back, Sophie was gone, we hoped she had come straight here." Dominic explained.

"I'm sorry, Gabe, I know I shouldn't have left her, but I thought that she would be safe and that Dominic was the one in danger. I was only trying to protect them both."

Gabe's face twisted in anger. His eyes welled with tears. He opened his mouth to speak several times, and Dominic could see him working through what he wanted to say to them. They were friends, but Dominic knew how betrayed Gabe felt. Gabe turned and walked back toward the castle without saying anything at all. Kamara looked at Dominic.

"Maybe we should keep looking. I mean, where would they have gone? They didn't fly past us, and Sophie can't shift so there is no way she would go with him unless she wanted to, they have to still be here on Ash."

"Maybe," Dominic said.

34

AKIRI

A kiri didn't know how long it had been now, three days, four? It was always dark inside the lair. The person in the dragon mask had come to check on her every day and each day they left her a single berry. When Akiri ate the first one, it had given her the sensation of being full as if she had eaten a large meal. It also quenched her thirst. She knew that the berry would be the only source of food, and with no other options, she accepted it daily.

When the captor arrived today, their interaction was different. They didn't offer her a berry, instead, they inspected her body. "You look healthy. That's good. Today, you will shift. This lair was designed to disable your dragon's breath, so don't get any ideas. Also, the tunnel is too small for you to escape in dragon form, and once you shift, you will not be able to shift back until we drop the spell. If you perform your duty for us today, you will be rewarded. If you do not, you will be punished. Do you understand?" Akiri nodded, but a tear rolled down her cheek.

"Turn around and face the back wall and don't look anywhere else but the wall." The captor commanded. Akiri did as she was told. She heard another set of footsteps enter the lair behind her, and then the cracking of bones and the roaring of a dragon.

"You may turn and look on the face of your mate." The captor said.

Akiri turned to face the dragon. He was large, possibly a year or two older than she was judging by his size. His scales were dark, almost black, but the captor had said he was dark green, not black. Akiri was afraid.

"Turn back around." The captor commanded. When Akiri faced the wall again, the captor removed her manacles. The chains clanked to the floor in a pile. "Now shift." Akiri did as she was commanded to do. She wanted to go home. If this was her only way to go free, she would do it. She shifted, her fingers stretched first, bending into long and sharp talons, then her arms bent and cracked as her bones grew and changed shape. She felt her face elongate and her back stretch into the shape of her dragon body. She felt her tailbone grow into the length of her tail and then the scales became hard and more defined, like armor.

The dragon wasted no time in mounting her, rubbing her tail with his back leg until she lifted her own to accept him. His front legs wrapped around hers and she was pinned to the floor, unable to move her upper body.

She lifted her tail by rolling her bottom half slightly to the right. He entered her sideways, holding her to him as he drilled into her again and again. His roar was a low rumble that shook the earth beneath them which would have resembled the groan of a climax if they were in human form. She remained silent and unsatisfied by the captor's pet. Before he got off of her, the captor placed one of the manacles around her back talon, above the knuckle so that it could not come off without damaging her talon.

"Within a few weeks, hopefully, you will be able to lay eggs, if not, we will have to repeat this until you can produce. Now, keep facing the wall." the captor commanded. Akiri heard the dragon shifting back into human form so that he could leave through the tunnel. Akiri knew she was risking everything, but she had to know who it was. She turned her head and she saw him wiping himself off. The captor was facing him, but they saw Akiri move out of the corner of their eyes. Akiri roared in anger and tried to shift, but she couldn't. She didn't know if it was the manacle, or a spell placed on the lair, either way, she was stuck.

"I told you to face the wall and not to look back," the captor hissed. "Now I have to punish you."

"No need, so she has seen my face, what does it matter if we get what we want?" Akiri looked at him, Nohan Arach, Captain of the City Guard of Ash, and member of her council. It was him all along. Akiri felt so stupid for not seeing his ambition before. She wanted to cover them both in her acid breath, but of course, she couldn't do that either.

"If she produces a clutch for us, we can just kill her and no one will ever know," Nohan said coldly as he walked around to look her in the eye. "Then we will kill her human husband in Ash, and I will finally take the throne as I was always meant to do with a thunder of dragons at my back." Nohan looked at her and laughed. Smoke flared from her nostrils, and she swiped at him. He backed away, but not quickly enough to escape her talon and a red gash opened on his chest. It wasn't deep enough to cause him real harm, which Akiri felt was unfortunate. He looked down at his chest and the scratch which was now beading with droplets of blood from his left collarbone to his right pectoral. Nohan turned and left without another word and the captor followed him, leaving her alone. Now that they were gone, she realized that she was hungry, and her outburst and disobedience were surely the reason the captor had not left a berry.

Akiri inspected the manacle on her back talon. Her body was too long, and she couldn't get the talon to her mouth, no matter how she tried, it would be the equivalent of trying to lick your elbow in human form, such things were impossible due to physical limitations, yet it did not stop children from daring each other to do it and laughing at them when they tried.

Akiri rolled over onto her back and tried to get one of the talons from her free leg under the manacle. She would rip off her talon at the knuckle if she had to if it meant she could escape and get back to Ash to warn

Gabe, but it was tight to her skin, and her thick talon could not even get under the iron. She cried until she fell asleep.

The next morning, the captor brought her a berry. They looked at her. Akiri could see their eyes, but the mask still obscured their face. Akiri wanted to ask them what their name was, but no words came out when she tried to speak, only low rumbling roars. She didn't understand how dragons had their own language if they couldn't speak, or maybe it was something they had to be taught to do and Akiri just never had anyone to teach her.

She waited for the captor to leave, and then Akiri flicked the berry across the room. She would not eat another bite. Maybe after a week of starving herself, she would be able to slip her talon out of the manacle. Akiri paced as much as the manacle would allow and flapped her wings as much as the size of the lair would accommodate. She worked out all day until she was too tired and sore to move, then it was time to go to sleep so she could do this all over again when she woke up.

Akiri dreamed of returning to Ash, preparing for war, and hatching a clutch of dragons to protect the kingdom for generations. She dreamed of Gabe and his soft brown skin, and brown eyes. She missed the feeling of his arms around her, and his lips on hers. She wondered if Nohan was still sitting in the council chambers, pretending to serve the kingdom, pretending to serve Gabe, biding his time until he could have an army of dragons to steal her throne and destroy everything she loved.

It was hard for her to sleep, even when she cried for hours at a time. Her head pounded and her eyes felt puffy even under the tight reptilian skin of her dragon form. She tried for hours to sleep, but it would not come to her. She paced the lair some more until finally, the captor returned with a berry, which told Akiri that another day had passed. She realized that she could keep track of how many days she was there by counting the berries. The one she flung across the room and the one the captor gave her today made two, and she had been there at least three days before that, although she wasn't sure about that. *Five days total so far.* Akiri thought.

Akiri placed the berry along the wall and scraped dirt over it. When she first got here, the floor had been clean, but her exercise and the beating of her wings stirred up the dust and dirt from the walls and the corners. The berry looked like a small pebble now that it was covered in dirt, but she would know what it was. *It's been two days since my last meal.* Akiri thought. She tried to slide her talon out of the manacle, it was looser now, and it was almost loose enough to get a talon from her free claw under the metal. *A few more days should do it,* Akiri thought. She continued exercising, ignoring the pain in her abdomen and the loud growl of her stomach.

35

SOPHIE

Sophie tried to scream as she watched her friends separate from each other on the beach, she couldn't hear them, but it was obvious they were searching for her. She tried to scream to get their attention, but they couldn't hear her either. Bastian had grabbed her and then it was like they blinked out of existence, but the world around them went on. *Why can't they see me?* Sophie wondered.

"Sophie, I'm sorry. I wanted to tell you- I..." Bastian started to explain, but Sophie cut him off.

"No. You don't get to say; *Sophie, I'm the bad guy, sorry I didn't fucking tell you.*" Sophie was sure her face was red, and she couldn't remember a time when she wanted to punch someone's face more than she wanted to punch his right now, but as angry as she was, she could never be the one to bring harm to him.

"I'm *NOT* though, that's what I'm trying to tell you. I'm just a dragonshifter, like you. We were raised to never tell anyone our secret because the humans would hunt us to extinction, but the problem is, we are going to go extinct anyway, because the only dragonshifters that survived on the island of Immernacht, were male. A couple of them tried to mate with humans, hoping their mates would birth more shifters, but instead, the babies were born with a human shape, but the scales of a dragon, destined to live their lives as outcasts from both human and dragonshifter societies because how could we keep our secret with half dragon children?" The subject seemed like a painful one for Bastian to talk about, but Sophie needed to hear the rest of it.

"What happened to the children?" Sophie asked.

"Baelfire took them years ago, they tried to scrape off their scales to look more human but resorted to wearing masks in the end. Baelfire said he found a way to restore dragons to the earth. He told us that we had to stay on Immernacht until we heard of the dragon's return, and then we must leave and find a dragon mate."

"When you say we- how many of you were there, and how did you get there? You're not Baelfire's *son*... are you?" Sophie tried to hold back the urge to vomit, but her stomach turned and she put her hands on it. She felt the fluttering of life inside her.

"No, but our mothers were all taken to Immernacht before the ancient dragons took power away from the remaining dragons. We were spared the curse on Immernacht because of the wardings over the island. I lived there, in the dark for eighteen years, never seeing the sun, green grass, or blue skies. Then last year, we finally heard that it was safe to leave the island and I went to Ledora. I read about the Golden City, and the lavish balls that King Haki liked to throw. I knew I had to see it for myself. Six months after my first trip to Ledora, I came back, and I met you. That was the best night of my life, and when I woke up in the morning and you were gone, I felt broken. I thought maybe I could stay away, but I couldn't. When I came back and we danced, I felt myself being drawn to you like a magnet, and I knew that if we continued on that night I would wake up alone again, so I left. I flew out of there to clear my head. Sophie, I love you. I can't explain it, but it feels like there's a huge hole in my chest when I'm away from you. I *need* you." Bastian embraced her and kissed her forehead. Sophie cried into his chest. It made his skin warm and wet with her tears.

"Who was it then?" Sophie asked.

"What?"

"Who destroyed Akiri's lair, and kidnapped Akiri?"

"I don't know, I had no idea about any of that," Bastian said.

"How many black dragons are there?"

"I'm the only black dragon, but Nohan is dark green and often is mistaken for black, the other dragons are brown and gray," Bastian told her.

"We have to get to the castle. We have to tell them. It has to be this Nohan guy, I have heard his name before,

I think he might be on the staff at the castle." Sophie's voice was urgent.

"They will kill me. I can't go."

"Not if we talk to them, and tell them what you told me, if you help them stop Nohan and find Akiri, I promise we can show them that you are not what they thought." Sophie pleaded. She didn't want to go alone, and she cared about Bastian, she didn't want to leave him again. He finally nodded and dropped the spell that shrouded them from the outside world.

Sophie cast the illusion spell on Bastian so that he would appear dressed. He looked down at himself and even he could see the cream-colored tunic which tied in a pattern of x's at his chest and ruffled at the bottom of the sleeve. His trousers were black and well-fitted and the boots were nicer than the formal shoes that he wore to the ball. He followed Sophie to the castle gates and when the guards approached them, they looked shocked.

"Queen Sophia, the King, Prince Dominic, and Princess Kamara have been looking for you. I will announce you at once. He led them to the front doors of the castle and the door guards directed them to the council chamber. When the doors opened, Gabe got up from his seat and stared with his mouth open like he was seeing her ghost. He ran to Sophie and took her in his arms. Gabe held onto her until Bastian cleared his throat.

"What is he doing here?" Gabe demanded. "Sophie, did he harm you?"

"What? No. We came to tell you that he is not the one responsible for the attack, we know who it was, it was-"

"Nohan Arach." Gabe said.

"That's right, you already knew?" Sophie looked at Gabe and anger flashed in her eyes, but she stuffed it down, she didn't want to be angry at Gabe, she missed him too much. He was her best friend after all.

"We suspected, but this just confirmed it. If Bastian were responsible, there is no way you could have convinced him to come here. Bastian, where would Nohan have taken Akiri?"

"Nohan was one of Baelfire's loyalists. I would guess that he would have made a lair in the last place he knew Baelfire to be..."

"Choddrath," they all said in unison.

"Okay, we know where we need to go, all we need is a plan. Why don't we get some sleep and meet here in the morning, we can discuss a plan then. Jack, can you show Bastian to a guest room? Dominic and Kamara already know where their rooms are, I need to talk to Queen Sophie, I will show her to her room myself." Gabe said to his guard. Bastian looked like he wanted to protest, but he didn't.

"Yes, Your Grace." Gabe's guard gestured to the door and waited for Bastian to exit, then led him down the eastern wing and left around the corner to the third room in the hall next to the central courtyard.

"Sophie, I missed you so much. If he hurt you, you would tell me right?" Gabe asked.

"Of course, and no, he hasn't."

"So what's going on, why can't you shift?"

"I- uh…" The words were harder to form than she had anticipated. Why did she have a feeling that this news would hurt him? Was it because his chance at having children died in that lair, or was it because she knew, deep down that Gabe was still in love with her? Mostly, she thought it might be because even though she tried not to be, she was still very much in love with him.

"Sophie, you can tell me anything," he said.

"I'm pregnant," she couldn't hold it in, the words fell out of her mouth like crumbs.

"I see. I assume, Bastian is the father?" Gabe's voice was cool and even. "I mean, I see the way you look at him. The way you looked at me the day we kissed under the willow, do you remember?" Gabe pulled out the chair for Sophie so she could sit back down, he took the chair beside her and held her hand.

"Of course, I remember, it seems like a lifetime ago, you got married and I did what I could to ease the pain. At first, Bastian was just a distraction, but the more time I spent with him, only made me crave more time with him." Sophie said.

"It was the same with Akiri and me. It was a duty at first, a way to fulfill my debt to the guild, but then I saw her, I *really* saw her for who she was, not who she wanted to appear to be. Everyone thought that she was evil, and yes, she did do some of the horrible things she was accused of, but she told me the reasons and showed remorse for the ones that weren't justified. I soon found out that my heart was capable of loving two women at the same time."

Sophie smiled, he was right, because she also loved two people at the same time. Bastian, and Gabe. She looked into his deep brown eyes, they were kind and soft, and his hands were gentle and loving. Why could she not have them both? She felt that sometimes, life was cruel to give her a soul mate who was always just out of reach.

"I should get some rest," Sophie said.

"Would you like a room of your own, or would you like me to take you to Bastian?" Gabe asked. Sophie noted that his voice sounded different, almost sad to have to ask her that, so she asked for a room of her own. He led her down the Eastern wing and into the same hallway as Bastian.

"Bastian's room is the third one, you can take the first one. If you need anything... Above all else, I just want you to be happy, Sophie." Gabe kissed her cheek and left her there at the door to the guest room. When the sound of his footsteps was gone, Sophie closed the door to her room. She would have gone to Bastian, but it would not be fair to him when all she could think about was Gabe.

She stared at the ceiling for a long time before she finally fell asleep. She dreamed of the willow tree in Blackwater, and the way she and Gabe used to play in the forest. She dreamed of the kiss they shared and the life they could have built together, if only she had chosen him over her ambition to train with Ryul at Lapis Highland. In her dream, they were married and had two children, a boy, and a girl. Neither of them had the power to shift that they knew of, but that was okay. Sophie worked with Delilah at the infirmary and made healing potions, tonics, and salves. Gabe still worked for the guild, but he got a job training recruits to fight with a sword, which meant that he got to come home every night. There was something just so mundane about it though, there was no action, no adventure, just working, and raising children.

She woke up to the sound of someone knocking on her door. She opened it to see Bastian's face filled with worry. "Are you okay? It sounded like you were having a nightmare."

"You could hear me through the room between us?" She asked.

"Yes, that's why I'm here, to make sure you're okay," he said. Sophie pulled him inside the room and threw her arms around his neck. He held her firmly like he never wanted to let go. She pressed her lips to his and parted his lips with her tongue; she need him, now. She felt an insatiable hunger for him any time he was near, she couldn't help herself. He took off his dressing robe, pulled Sophie's tunic up over her head, and tossed it. She was already removing her trousers by the time her tunic hit the floor. Bastian took her in his arms, holding her bare skin against his. Her nipples hardened at the touch of his skin and she could feel his sex pressed against her own, beckoning to enter her. Sophie wanted him so badly, she *needed* to feel him inside her again. Bastian lifted her and sat her on the edge of the chest of drawers so that he could guide himself into her wet, hot sex. She moaned with pleasure as he began thrusting in and out of her. The dresser wobbled back and forth and banged against the wall in a steady beat. Sophie tried to lean back to even the weight on it and when she did, Bastian bent down so that his face was between her legs, he used his tongue to flick the nodule of flesh just above her opening. He sucked the nodule and swirled his tongue around it and Sophie gripped the dresser with both hands as he kissed and licked every inch of flesh between her lower lips. When he suckled her pink button once more and flicked it with his tongue, she felt herself explode in his mouth. He stood up and carried her to the bed, covering her neck and face with soft kisses as he held her in his arms. Her red curls cascaded across the pillow as Bastian laid her down gently and positioned himself between her legs. He lifted her hips and then rubbed the tip of his sex against that same pink piece of flesh that turned her into a puddle moments ago. She moaned his name with carnal need and he finally gave her what she was begging for and slid his hard erection deep into her. He filled her with his length and girth. Sophie's back arched as every nerve within her felt alive. He looked into her eyes as he moved slowly deeper inside her, and then pulled out and slid the length of his sex over her pleasure center, that amazing, tiny bean! She looked up at him as they made love, and he gently touched every inch of her with his fingertips, bringing out the goose flesh on her skin. When he kissed her, his lips were tender and tantalizing.

He kissed down her neck and shoulders, then he turned around, sat on the edge of the bed, and pulled her on top of him. Sophie slid onto his cock as if they were made for each other; like a lock and a key, they were a perfect fit. He kissed her breast and gently swirled his tongue around her nipple; he felt it elongate and harden in his mouth. He did the same to her other breast as Sophie began to roll her hips, feeling him from every angle, her sex contracted and he could tell that she reached an orgasm. Her pulsing sex stimulated his, and he couldn't contain his desire. His mouth fell open, and he hugged her tightly as he reached his climax. She felt his hard cock throbbing inside her as his orgasm filled her and then spilled out between them.

"I love you, Sophie, and I don't want to live another day without you. My Queen, My Mate, My Love." He closed his eyes and kissed her deeply. "I am yours until my last breath," he vowed.

36

AKIRI

S he didn't remember falling asleep, but Akiri woke to the sound of the captor's voice. They brought her another berry. *Three, plus the one across the room, that's four. I've not eaten in four days.* Akiri thought. When the captor was gone, Akiri hid the berry along the wall with the other three and tried again to slip her talon under the iron. It worked! She was overjoyed, but now she had to perform the hard part. Breaking the talon of her back leg would be like breaking her toes all at once. It was going to be painful, not only right now, but painful to walk out of the lair, and that was assuming that she could shift after the manacle was removed.

Akiri decided to do it quickly, she hooked her talon under the manacle, counted to three, and then pulled it as hard and fast as she could. Her strength surprised her as she looked at the aftermath, her whole back claw was covered in blood and the back talon was laying across the room with the manacle still attached to it. She wanted to scream in pain, but adrenaline coursed through her and she could think of nothing else but escape. She rushed over to the wall and looked at the berries, they were covered in dirt, but she thought she might find a place to rinse them on her way out. *Okay, the moment of truth...* Akiri closed her eyes and thought of her human body, two legs, two arms, smooth skin, no tail, and she shifted. *Thank the Goddess.* Akiri sighed, pleased to be back in her own body and that the anti-magic spell was only on the manacles and not the lair itself. She cast a disguise, giving herself the appearance of blond hair, blue eyes, clothes, and shoes.

Her foot was in excruciating pain as she knew it would be, but she still ran through the winding tunnel until finally, she saw a light, the bright light of the sun, beckoning her to soak up the rays. She walked cautiously to the mouth of the cave, shielding her eyes from the light she had been deprived of for days. Akiri recognized the ruins of the volcano, and the black obsidian fields brought back the fear and anger Akiri felt the last time she was there. Her mother sent a guard to kill her and steal the orb for herself, and at that time, Akiri had no one loyal to her.

Across the black stone earth, Akiri saw a new keep. It wasn't large, or fancy, but she knew that it was where her captor, and possibly, the black dragon were staying. She hesitated for a moment, the urge to fight and attack them while they weren't expecting it sounded almost like a good plan, but getting as far away as she could, sounded better. She dropped the berries, the only water around was the salty ocean and she knew it would only take her a few hours to get back if she just flew South, she made this trip once before while carrying a prisoner, and she was sure that this trip would be even quicker.

Without looking back again, Akiri soared through the sky and flew as fast as her wings would carry her. She needed to make it to Ash before sunset, it was hard to see, but luckily, Akiri knew the way. She was hungry, and thirsty, but determined to make it back to Ash and gather all the power of the dragon alliance, and the city guard. Akiri hoped that they wouldn't realize she was gone at least until morning.

The sun was directly above her when Akiri reached the Northern shore of Ash, but she didn't land until she reached the castle. She heard screams and people scattering as her enormous shadow darkened the landscape. As soon as she was close enough to the ground, she shifted and limped as quickly as she could to the castle doors.

"Gabe!" Akiri screamed through the hall, the room started to spin, and then a bright white light took over. She heard the guards and Gabe as they approached her body, but they sounded far away like they were in a tunnel, or perhaps she was in a tunnel.

Akiri was in the infirmary when she came to. Her foot was cleaned up and she sat up to inspect the damage. Her big toe and her middle toe were missing. The last three were still there and she wiggled them slowly. It was more difficult without her other toes. She sat up and slid to the edge of the infirmary bed. She planted her unscathed foot on the floor first and then pushed herself up off the bed. She was surprised that when she stood, it didn't hurt, but she had no grip on the floor with her injured foot, and her first steps were shaky as she wobbled to the infirmary door.

"Woah, hold on there, Your Grace." A woman wearing a blue dress with a white apron brought Akiri a walking stick. It wasn't a staff, but more like a Noble Lord's cane. "Lean on this," she said as she placed a gentle hand on Akiri's back to steady her.

"Who are you?" Akiri asked softly. When she was here last, Ash did not have a cleric, or a healer and the infirmary was an empty room with a few bandages on a shelf. Now the room was stocked with shelves of potions, salves, medical tools, and this kind woman.

"I'm Nadine Garrison, I came from Blackwater. King Gabriel said that Ash needed a healer. I was trained by Delilah, the cleric in Blackwater, I am not a cleric, but I can perform first aid and know many herbal treatments for pain and warding off infection." Nadine walked with Akiri down the hall from the infirmary to the council chamber.

"Will I always need the cane?" Akiri asked.

"When you are in your human form, you might always need it for added stability, but I don't think it should affect your flight at all," Nadine said.

"Thank you so much. It's a pleasure to have you here, but I fear we don't have much time, I need to call a meeting, I would like for you to be here too," Akiri said.

"Yes, Your Grace, I will have Mister Koffery ring the bell." Nadine quickly walked down the hall and Akiri hobbled to her seat at the head of the table. The bell rang moments later and it took no time at all for what was left of the council, Gabe, Dominic, Sophie, Kamara, and some new person to join Akiri in the council room.

"Who is this?" Akiri asked.

"I an Bastian Delacroix, of Immernacht, Your Grace." He bowed to her.

"What is your purpose at this council meeting?"

"I am a dragonshifter and I am here to offer my service to the Kingdom of Ash and its Queen." Bastian did not rise until Akiri told him he could. He was respectful, she liked that.

"Where is Horace Stewart?" Akiri asked as she looked at Gabe.

"I am having him brought up from the dungeon, We have only just learned that the dragon we saw on the beach of Ledora was Bastian, and not the dragon responsible for the attack on your lair, or your abduction. Since he was the keeper of Ledora, we assumed that he had sent the dragon there looking for you." Akiri knew that by 'keeper' Gabe meant that he had told Horace that Akiri's new lair was on the beach in Ledora.

"I understand your confusion in that situation and you did the right thing. Here's the deal, I know you do not know what happened to me because I have not had time to fill you in, nor do I have time to go over all the details right now, but Nohan Arach is our enemy. He is currently staying on Choddrath and when he notices that I am gone, I am sure he will attack Ash. Gabe, I would like for you to alert the city guard and the royal fleet. Have them prepare the ships to evacuate the city. I want women, children, elderly, and disabled people shipped out, possibly to Ledora if that is okay with you, Prince Dominic?" Akiri paused for him to nod his confirmation and then continued. "Every able-bodied man will be given a sword or a bow and whatever armor we can find. We also need to man the large bow on the Eastern tower and have it ready to fire. That's all I have for you right now, let's prepare for war, dismissed." Akiri had to lean on her cane as she stood. She motioned for Nadine to wait for her as everyone else started filing out of the chamber to fulfill their tasks.

"Nadine, I want you to be safe, but I also know that we will require your services if things don't go as planned. We have a storage room beneath the castle where I would like for you to set up your supplies. I will have some of the staff help you move everything down there, the trapdoor is under the rug in the kitchen. After the supplies are down there, I will give you a choice, you can board the ship, or you can stay."

"It will be my honor to stay with you and help the people of Ash, Your Grace." Nadine bent to one knee and swore service to Akiri.

"I appreciate your service. Thank you, Nadine."

As the afternoon turned to evening, Akiri walked outside, the city had been evacuated in record time, the last ship was about to set sail within the hour and the Kingdom was eerily quiet. It was almost peaceful, she would have enjoyed the quiet if not for the sense of impending doom weighing on her chest.

"Hey. How are you?" Gabe asked as he came up behind his wife.

"I've been better, but I've also been worse," she let out a halfhearted chuckle as Gabe wrapped his arms around her.

"What happened? Did he hurt you?" Gabe asked. Akiri didn't want to answer. She thought about being in that dark cave, and what she had to do to get home. She didn't want Gabe to be angry or put himself in danger on her behalf. Gabe wasn't a dragon, he didn't practice magic, he *was*, however, an excellent swordsman, but what good was a sword against the breath or weight of a dragon?

"No," she finally answered. "I'm okay." Her eyes gave her away, Gabe could tell that she was holding back, but he didn't press the matter and that came as a great relief to her.

"Let's go inside, I want to lay in our bed and hold you. I missed you." Gabe let her lean on him, rather than the cane. She had missed him too. He was a good man and every day she became more thankful to have chosen him over the other suitors.

37

SOPHIE

"Please, get on the ship, Sophie," Bastian begged. "I couldn't bear it if anything happened to you and you can't shift right now."

"I can still hold a sword. I wielded Destiny, my father's magical greatsword, and I can also use magic. I can still fight," Sophie argued.

"Think about our baby, it's not just you that I am trying to protect, it's both of you." He embraced her and placed one hand on her stomach. And pressed his forehead to hers. "You are my whole world and the thought of losing you shatters my heart, please, get on the ship," he whispered. Hot tears fell from his eyes and onto Sophie's cheeks. She felt the tugging of his heart on hers. She hated it, but he was right.

"What about you? What if something happens to you? Come with me." Sophie urged.

"You know I can't, I vowed my assistance to the crown and I am nothing if not a man of my word."

"I know, I *know*. I just wish we had more time together, we have not spent more than one night at a time together since we met and now I need you more than ever. Please, be careful. I will go, but only if you promise that you will meet me in Ledora when it's over."

"I promise that I will see you again." Bastian pressed his lips to Sophie's and stroked her cheek with his thumb. He didn't know if he was wiping Sophie's tears from her face or his own.

"I love you, Bastian."

"I love you more," he said.

The ship was packed and it was hot and smelly below deck already. It would take two days to get to Ledora by ship, and that was if they happened to have favorable wind. The bouncing of the ship over the crests of the waves made Sophie nauseous but she held back the urge to vomit. Dinner was just rice and beans, it didn't offer much in the way of flavor, but Sophie was sure it was because rice and beans were cheap, shelf-stable, and could feed a lot of people. She was given a bedroll and slept on the deck of the ship that night under the starry sky. A crescent moon hung just over the starboard side of the ship and Sophie gazed at it until she drifted into the land of dreams, lulled by the gentle rocking and hushed lapping sound of the waves.

She didn't wake up until sunrise, and what a glorious sunrise it was, the sky was still dark blue at the top, then it was purple, pink, and finally, red just above the horizon. She wished that she could paint so she might capture the beauty of the sky reflected on the surface of the still ocean, but that was a skill she never learned. Below deck, Sophie heard infants crying, and young children yelling for chamber pots. Soon, the ship was bustling with life, and just like that- the peaceful sunrise was over.

Breakfast was rice and beans, the cook mixed the leftovers from the night before into the new batch. Sophie gave her portion to a young boy who was complaining to his mother about still being hungry, his mother had eaten almost all of her breakfast and was ready to give him the rest when Sophie approached. "Here, take mine," she said. "I'm still full from last night." Sophie handed the boy her bowl. The mother looked thankful that she would get to finish her breakfast and silently nodded her thanks.

"What's your name?" Sophie asked the boy as she sat down beside them on the steps between the upper and lower deck of the ship.

"Patrick," the boy said with a mouthful of beans and rice.

"Patrick, don't talk with your mouth full," his mother scolded.

"Sorry," he swallowed and then asked; "What's yours?"

"I'm Sophie." The boy's eyes widened.

"You mean Queen Sophie? Is it true you're a dragon?" He was so excited that he forgot about his breakfast.

"I'm a dragonshifter, I can turn into a dragon," she explained.

"That's.. wow! So why didn't you fly to Ledora?" he asked.

"Well, I can't shift right now."

"You sick 'er somethin'?" he asked as he took another bite.

"What did I say about talking with your mouth full? Show Queen Sophie some respect, son. I am so sorry, Your Grace." Patrick's mother seemed mortified.

"He's just a boy, it's quite alright," Sophie told her.

"I'm not sick, I'm going to be a mother," she smiled at the boy and his mom.

"If you have a boy, you should name him Sam." The boy said.

"That's interesting, why did you choose that name?"

"I had a puppy named Sam, but Mama said we couldn't bring him with us."

"My mother's name is Samantha, I think Sam is a wonderful name, sometimes people call my mom that when they're in a hurry because it's faster than saying, Samantha." Sophie could tell that the boy was trying not to worry about his pet. "I hope that Sam will be happy to see you when you get back," Sophie told him.

"Me too." The boy smiled at her.

"Take care, Patrick, and listen to your Mama."

Sophie walked to the bow of the ship and looked across the water. Ash was already a day behind her and all she could see was the ocean and sky. She was worried about her friends and Bastian, she had never really been the religious type; so many deities and none of them had ever sent her a calling, but at that moment she could think of no better Goddess to ask for her favor than Freyja, Goddess of love, fertility, and battle.

Please Freyja, protect those in the Kingdom of Ash and guide their swords, arrows, and bodies in battle. Protect my child and my body, the vessel in which my baby grows. Protect the love between us all and leave none of my friends brokenhearted. Sophie wiped a tear from her cheek as she ended her request to the Goddess. Sophie decided that when she got to Ledora, she would make an altar and light a candle. She hoped that the goddess would accept her offering and give them all divine favor.

38

AKIRI

A kiri felt the rise and fall of Gabe's chest and listened to the rhythmic thumping of his heart, his
skin was warm and soft against hers. He was still awake,
neither of them could sleep on what might very well be
the eve of battle. He turned over on his side, looking
deep into Akiri's eyes. He gently stroked her long black
hair away from her face.

"You are so beautiful, I want to remember this moment for the rest of my life." His eyes surveyed every
inch of her face like he was engraving it into his memory.
Akiri pulled his lips to hers and his sensual kisses sent
a shiver down her spine. He brushed his fingers up and
down her arm, awakening every part of her. He loved
the juxtaposition of his brown skin against her creamy
complexion, he wanted to kiss every inch of her, but he
wanted to make it last. He kissed her cheek, and her
jawbone, then very slowly he moved to her neck and

then her collarbone. She exhaled heavily as he kissed her chest, and then her nipple, it felt like torture, but she didn't want him to stop. She was filled with need and desire for her husband as he kissed her stomach, then her inner thigh, and then when he kissed her hot, wet, sex she moaned, and when he inserted a finger into her opening, she moved her hips slowly as he moved his finger at the same pace in an out a few times until he was able to work in his middle finger too. She called out his name which only intensified his erection and he could no longer delay his pleasure. Gabe slid his erection inside of his wife and groaned with pleasure as her muscles squeezed him. Her nipples were hard and pointed and grew slightly painful as her desire mounted. She pushed him back. "Lay down," she commanded.

Gabe was stunned but did as his wife, The Queen, commanded. She mounted him and his eyes rolled back as she slid down onto his erection. He looked at her body grinding on top of him, her rhythm matching that of a seductive belly dancer like the ones he saw perform at the Loose Anchor Tavern when he was younger. Gabe moaned her name as he exploded inside of her and she came to climax at the same time.

"Akiri, that was amazing," Gabe sighed. Akiri smiled and nodded in agreement. She was too out of breath to speak. She curled up beside him, resting her head on his chest again.

"I don't think I will be able to sleep tonight, I'm scared. I know Nohan is going to be angry when they realize I am gone, and I have no idea what kind of followers he has amassed, the one other person he had with him, called him Master, like he was a God or something."

"Maybe they are the only follower he has, and this will be easy if he even shows up at all." Gabe hoped that he was right about that, but he had a feeling there was going to be nothing easy about this fight. Akiri's mind wandered to her lair and the eggs that had been destroyed. She knew it wouldn't be tonight, but she wondered if she might lay a clutch soon. She decided that she would shift in the morning, in preparation for an attack, they all would, and she would stay in dragon form until the new moon came again, if she had not laid a clutch by that time, then she would give up her dream of having baby dragons, and she would give Gabe the human children his heart desired. He deserved to have a family, he was kind and strong, loving and patient. She knew that he would make a great father.

Akiri looked out the arched windows on the northern wall and watched the clouds roll across the starlit sky, she watched as the stars began to disappear. It was time to get up. She tapped Gabe, who had managed to fall asleep, but only just, and whispered that it was time to prepare. He got up quickly and began to dress. Akiri didn't need to dress, she was going to shift.

"I'm going to head to the front courtyard, and have Dominic, Kamara, and Bastian meet me there," Akiri said. Gabe nodded and kissed her as he rushed off to begin waking the castle. Akiri shifted in the courtyard and waited for the others as she kept her eyes fixed on the sky to the North. The others joined her, shifting into their dragon forms as they reached the courtyard. They lined across the front of the castle and waited. The bell did not ring. It could be heard from miles away, and they did not want to let their enemy know they were ready for battle.

The lanterns were all snuffed out and other than the light from the sky, which wasn't much yet, the castle remained dark. The triggerman was locked and loaded on the large bow at the top of the castle and ready for the dragon to make an appearance. The city guard and able-bodied civilians gathered in formation around the front gates of the courtyard and stood with their weapons at the ready.

They waited just like that for what seemed like an eternity. Akiri was almost relieved and thought that maybe Nohan would decide that it wasn't worth it to pursue her after all, but the relief was short-lived because, at that same moment, an ear-piercing screech echoed through the sky. Akiri kept watch in the direction the sound came from and soon realized that it was not an echo after all, but a battle cry from multiple dragons. They flew in formation across Ash and breathed fire onto every wooden house in the kingdom. Akiri knew that would happen and was glad that they evacuated the city, but the dragons circled the area, she knew they were expecting screams of fear and panic.

The black dragon roared a guttural, angry-sounding roar and flew straight for the castle, leading the others in an angular formation. An enormous arrow flew through the sky toward Nohan, he performed a barrel roll out of the way, and the bolt struck one of the dragons behind him. It screamed in pain as it spiraled and fell from the sky. Akiri heard it land with a crash on what sounded like the stables. Lucky for the horses they had been moved behind the castle earlier that day.

Akiri let out a roar, letting the others know that it was time to attack. They took flight, Bastian flew straight for the gray dragon, and surprised it by swinging his tail like a club. He hit the gray dragon right in the chest which hurt, but it seemed to only make him angry. The gray dragon flew at Bastian and breathed a dark cloud of smoke at him. Bastian dipped below it, quickly flew behind the gray dragon, and sank his teeth deep into his scale-covered tail. The dragon wailed in pain and flicked his tail toward his front claw and hooked Bastian's cheek.

Akiri rushed straight for Nohan and shot her dark green acidic sludge at him. He dodged it easily and seemed to laugh as he circled to face her again. He rushed her and slammed his body into hers. He tried to wrap his tail around hers and tried to lift it. She roared in anger and disgust, even now, he was trying to mate with her. She slapped her tail across his face and turned around as quickly as she could. She bit his neck, but her teeth barely punctured his scales. He pushed her off of him, and she heard him laugh again. *Impossible, how?* Akiri thought.

"I don't want to hurt you, I just want you to fulfill your duty to our kind, to dragonkind." She wasn't crazy, she heard him speak in her mind.

"Then come down and talk to me, face to face." Akiri thought about the words she wanted to say to him, she didn't know if the technique would work, but she had to try.

"Maybe, in a minute." Nohan did a nose dive and then lifted just before hitting the ground, he barreled through the armored men with swords in the front line of the formation surrounding the courtyard. A few brave members of the city guard stabbed him with their swords, barely breaking through the dragon's thick skin. He knew these men, and they knew him, or they thought they had.

Some of the men in the back rows witnessed the front row get taken out like ants and a few of them dropped their weapons and were now cowering at the castle doors, trying to get back inside. Akiri had to get him back into the sky so that the triggerman could have another shot at him. Akiri flew just over the top of him and let out a roar as she passed. He looked up at her and started chasing her. She circled the tower, trying to get Nohan in a position that revealed his less armored underbelly to the bolt.

She heard the weapon fire and listened as it whistled through the wind. It found its mark and embedded deep into the soft tissue of Nohan's underarm. He howled, but not in pain, in frustration. The bolt seemed to be no more than a thorn in his very large side. He tried to pull it out, but the barbs on the tip of the arrow were made to open. What he didn't notice until it was too late, was the chain attached to the end of the bolt. It jerked him toward the tower as they began rolling the chain in with a hand crank.

Nohan tried to resist, but the more he tried to fight against it, the more the barb ripped into the fleshy un-armored part of his body. He had no other choice, he shifted. His body released the bolt and he began to fall from the sky at an alarming rate, his first attempt to shift back failed and the ground grew closer by the second. Humans have one major flaw; they're squishy. Nohan gave one more desperate attempt to shift and his wings lifted him back into the sky just before he hit the ground. He drew in a deep breath as arrows flew at him from every direction.

He blasted half of the archers out of the forma-tion with one breath and then flew toward Akiri with a screech, but before he could reach her, Dominic crashed into his body and sent him rolling backward. Kamara tried to attack Nohan from behind, but a cone of fiery breath shot between them. Kamara pulled back, drew in a deep breath, and unleashed an icy cold that dropped the dragon to the ground, she watched as he transformed back into the shape of a human. His skin was a light blue as he lay shivering on the ground, unable to feel the warmth. Kamara landed and shifted so that she could get a closer look, she didn't want to kill anyone if she could help it. When she saw that he was starting to regain mobility in his hands and feet Kamara called to the remaining soldiers waiting on the front line.

"Seize him," Kamara commanded, and two of the city guards took the shivering man into custody and carried him by the arms to the dungeon. Two gray dragons, a red, and another brown, and Nohan, a dark green, remained, although, Kamara could only see two of them. The sound of a horn blasted from every direction but south where the castle stood and in moments, the castle gates were surrounded. The dragons weren't alone, they brought an army with them. Kamara looked up, she couldn't see anyone. If they didn't knock back some of the ground forces, the battle would be lost.

Kamara shifted and flew straight up into the sky and let out a wail that would fill a banshee with envy. The soldiers on the ground dropped their weapons, and the other dragons started to fall from the sky to escape the sound, she held the high-pitched note until she spotted Dominic, Akiri, and Bastian. She rushed to them in her human form and waited for them to shift as well.

"Kamara, what was *that?*" Dominic asked.

"I'm not sure, I was just trying to get your attention." She pointed to the heavily armored forces that stood ominously, waiting for the command of their officer. There must have been five hundred in all. Ash's Army was puny in comparison. They all looked at each other in defeat. Gabe emerged from the formation behind them.

"I've taken all of the injured to the kitchen, there's no room in the infirmary, Nadine is working as fast as she can to keep them all alive, but we have lost a lot of men." Akiri ran to him and hugged him.

"I'm so sorry, I should have stayed, I should have stayed in the lair and given Nohan what he wanted and none of this would be happening." Her face was streaked with tears.

"I only wanted what was mine." Nohan appeared in front of his troops.

"What do you mean?" Gabe asked.

"My children, of course. Didn't your wife tell you?"

"Tell me what? Akiri, what happened?"

"I-" Akiri choked on her words and couldn't bring herself to break Gabe's heart. Nohan walked closer, but Gabe's eyes were fixed on Akiri.

"She didn't tell you, because the truth is; she knows I'm right, she is only wasting her time with you. We are mated, and the eggs that she will lay will be dragons, not some half-human-dragon outcast with no chance in this world."

"What are you talking about, *mated?*" Gabe asked clenching his fists. He was staring directly at Nohan, but it was Akiri who spoke.

"When they captured me, he told me if I produced a clutch of eggs with him, they would allow me to come home, but I couldn't wait that long so I escaped."

"But not before we made love in our dragon forms, you should have heard her roar for me, Gabe, it was like... well, nothing like you will ever experience, ohh it makes me hard just thinking about it." Nohan reached out his hand and fondled Akiri's breast. She slapped his hand away and covered herself as she stepped behind Gabe for cover.

"Shut your mouth, I swear to the Gods, I will end you right here if you touch her again." Gabe pointed his sword at Nohan.

Nohan held out his hand to the soldiers behind him and without a word, they passed him a sword. "Let's see what you got, loverboy," Nohan said with a sick grin. "If anyone interferes, I will give the command to my troops to waste you all."

"And If I win?" Gabe asked.

"Unlikely, but sure, if I die, my troops and the other dragons will return to Choddrath and leave what's left of this dump to its Queen. It has to be a fair fight though, lose the armor, and the clothes." Nohan pointed to Gabe and moved the tip of his sword up and down, gesturing for Gabe to remove everything. When Gabe was naked and armed with his sword, they rushed into battle. The clanking and scraping of metal against metal rang in everyone's ears as they watched the two men block strike after strike. They whirled, and ducked, then parried, like they were performing a choreographed dance with swords. Gabe ducked low and swung his foot behind Nohan's and hooked him by the ankle. The move swept him off his feet and his back hit the ground with a smack. Gabe pointed his sword at him and cheers erupted from the people and friends of Ash, but Nohan was far from finished, he flicked his wrist and hooked Gabe's sword by the hilt. He pulled back with a quick flourish and sent Gabe's sword flying from his hand. Gabe backed away, then ducked and rolled toward his weapon. He slashed his sword just as Nohan rushed him, opening a shallow gash across Nohan's stomach. Bright red blood started to bead up inside the cut and in a rage, Nohan rushed forward, grabbed Gabe by the back of the head, and drove his sword through his middle.

"I told you it was unlikely," Nohan whispered as he pulled up sharply on his sword.

"You're still going to die, I poisoned my blade." Gabe laughed and then started coughing as blood started splattering out of his mouth. Nohan's vision started to blur and he felt dizzy. He felt his blood grow thicker as it congealed and bubbled. The beads of blood in the gash on his abdomen turned black and festered as the same black fluid began leaking from his eyes, nose, and ears. He fell to his knees as he coughed up the black sludge.

When the gurgling stopped, Nohan collapsed in front of Gabe who still had Nohan's sword through his abdomen. Akiri ran to Gabe's side to support him.

"You heard him, He's dead! Leave my Kingdom, and never return." Akiri shouted. The sound of heavy armor retreating was all Gabe heard before his vision tunneled and he felt his body collapse in Akiri's arms.

"Help me please!" She screamed as Gabe's light faded away. Kamara and Dominic cradled his shoulders, as Bastian supported his legs. They carried him inside and straight to the kitchen.

"Nadine, help him, please." Akiri pleaded. Nadine rushed over to them and saw the sword in Gabe's middle. She looked at Gabe, and then Akiri with tears in her eyes.

"I am sorry, Your Grace, his wounds are too great. I told you that I am not a cleric, I can't heal his severed organs." Nadine's face streamed with tears as Akiri's scream of anguish filled the room. They laid Gabe on an empty bedroll, his breaths were shallow and his heartbeat had slowed. There was a trail of blood droplets from the front door to the bedroll where he now rested. Akiri curled up beside him with her head on the bedroll next to his. She kissed his face as she sobbed and he reached for her hand. His grip was weak, but she held onto it firmly.

"My love for you will never die." Gabe's raspy voice whispered in Akiri's ear.

"I will love you forever. I am so sorry, Gabe." She held him even after his breathing stopped, and his heart was still, she lay beside her husband until his body went cold and Dominic finally helped her to her feet.

"My Queen, would you like something for the pain?" Nadine asked. Akiri didn't know if there was anything that could take away the pain of a broken heart, but she was willing to try anything.

"Would you please get her cleaned up and settled in bed? I will bring her some tea." Nadine asked. The two chambermaids that had been helping her nodded and helped Akiri to her room. It wasn't her room- it was Gabe's room. Her cries of sorrow returned as the chamber maids scrubbed Akiri's body clean of the blood and dirt from battle. They dressed her in a loose-fitting gown and helped her to bed. One of them grabbed a warming pan and slid in under the covers at Akiri's feet, and the other girl knelt at Akiri's bedside and stroked her hair as she mourned her husband.

"Here you go, this will help you get some sleep." Nadine came in carrying a cup of tea. Akiri sat up and took the cup from her.

"Uggh, this smells like sweaty stockings, what is this?" Akiri asked with a look of disgust.

"It's tea made from the root of valerian, a wonderful flower with powerful medicinal properties," Nadine explained. "It has honey in it too, so I promise it won't taste as bad as it smells."

Akiri held her breath and drank it down. Nadine was right about the honey making it palatable. She handed the cup back to Nadine with her thanks and then snuggled back down into her comforter. Nadine left the room quietly, but one of the chambermaids stayed behind to keep watch over The Queen.

39

KAMARA

The entire castle was in mourning. The damages from the battle had been catastrophic, not only to Akiri, who lost her husband but to every citizen of Ash who lost their homes and their livelihoods. The city had been burned to the ground, and not a single structure stood unscathed, not even the castle. The Western tower was crumbling, and the dragon-sized crossbow had been ripped from the East tower and now lay on the ground beneath it like a pile of old junk, broken and beyond repair. The men who survived the battle cradled their sons, friends, fathers, or neighbors that didn't make it through the battle alive.

Sorrow hung like a heavy cloud over all of them. Kamara, Dominic, and Bastian all sat in the council chamber at the long table. They were silent for a long time, contemplating their next move. "I checked on Her Grace this morning, she was still sleeping. She didn't touch her breakfast." I'm worried about her," Kamara said.

"Me too, but we still have to tell Sophie." Dominic looked at Kamara, who looked at Bastian.

"I know, he was her best friend, she loved him. I knew the first night we met when he asked to cut in during our dance. The way she looked at him... I'd be lying if I said I wasn't a little jealous." Bastian looked away from them with shame in his eyes.

"What are we going to do about all these people and Akiri? I mean, they can't stay here, this place is nothing but...*ash*." Kamara asked. They all realized how ironic it was, like the name of the Kingdom had been prophesied from the start.

"We could offer to take her back to Temple Ophay. We will leave there one day to rule Ledora anyway, and it will be good for Akiri to have friends in her court." Dominic suggested.

"Do you think she will go for it? I mean, leaving your home after you've lost everything else seems like a kick while you're down."

"Why don't you talk to her about it, I will fly to Ledora and break the news to Sophie, Bastian, do you want to come with me?" Dominic asked. Bastian agreed but thought the news would be easier to hear coming from someone who knew them well.

"I'll let you do the talking, and I will be the shoulder," he said.

When Dominic and Bastian left, Kamara went to Akiri's chamber. Kamara looked at the tray on the night-stand, Akiri's breakfast was still untouched. She hadn't even sipped her water.

"Honey, come on, you have to take care of yourself." Kamara was nervous as she approached the Queen. Her eyes were open, but they were glossed over like she was somewhere else. Kamara was afraid that something bad had happened. She sat on the bed next to Akiri and put her finger under her nose. Akiri's warm breath warmed Kamara's finger and she sighed in relief that Akiri was responsive.

"You want me to make you something different to eat?" She asked.

"More tea." Akiri's mouth was muffled against the pillow and she made no effort to move.

"I think you should wake up, maybe take a bath, or get some air maybe?" Kamara urged.

"When I sleep, I dream of Gabe, when I wake up, he's dead. I don't want to wake up. It's all my fault." Akiri turned over, but her shoulders heaved and shook. Kamara knew she was crying.

"I know, it's hard, but you have to get up or the grief will swallow you whole. Come on, one step at a time, let's try sitting up." Kamara tried to help Akiri sit up, but she groaned and rolled herself into her comforter. "Akiri, please."

"Just leave me alone," Akiri groaned.

"Okay, well, I have something I want to talk to you about and it's pretty important. You are the Queen, so I can't make this decision for you."

"It doesn't matter, there's nothing left for me to rule, my people are gone, their homes are destroyed, and we lost so many good people. That's all on me. It's my fault."

"It's not your fault at all, Nohan was a terrible person and his actions are on him, not you," Kamara argued. Akiri sat up and looked Kamara in the eye.

"You don't understand, when I was captured, he told me that all he wanted was half a clutch of pure dragon eggs. He said that if I complied, then I could take half our eggs and come back to Ash with future dragons to protect the Kingdom." Akiri wiped tears from her face. "He coerced me into copulating with him by dangling my Kingdom and my husband in front of me like some prize I had to earn. I finally figured out a way to escape and I had only ever seen two of them, Nohan, and the one in the dragon mask. I didn't think he had that much support, so I risked it to come home, I put all of you in danger and now Gabe is dead. I've lost him forever now because I was selfish, and only thought about getting home." Akiri leaned her head against Kamara's shoulder.

"I know you feel like you can't forgive yourself, but believe me when I tell you that Gabe was ready to go to war to find you, if you hadn't come home, we would have taken the fight to Choddrath. There's no telling if it would have turned out differently, but we can't let the past beat us down, we can only move forward and worry about the future, and right now, there are a lot of people that are depending on you to lead them. Now, I know there is nothing left here, but Dominic and I have been thinking that you could move your people to Ophay. Dominic and I will have to rule Ledora someday, and we can't possibly be in two places at once, maybe it's time for a fresh start for you and your people and it will be good for you to have friends nearby." Kamara said. Akiri nodded and smiled. This was the first time anyone in her life had called her a friend. She wrapped her arms around Kamara and hugged her tightly.

"I will think about it," Akiri said.

"Okay. There's one other thing, Dominic is going to have your people shipped back here for the funeral of those we lost during the battle. Gabe's body has been prepared, but with the future location of the kingdom in question, we were wondering if you would like for us to prepare a pyre so that we might collect Gabe's ashes in an urn so that you can take him with you?"

"I do think that is best, but we will need three urns, one for Gabe's mother, one for me, and one for Sophie. She will be mourning too, and I think she should carry a piece of him with her too." She started to cry again, and Kamara just held her in her arms and rubbed a comforting hand on her back. Kamara couldn't imagine the pain Akiri was feeling, she didn't want to think about ever losing Dominic. Her heart broke for Akiri, there were no words that would comfort her or lessen the pain, so they sat in silent despair well into the afternoon. When lunch was delivered to them, Kamara was able to coax Akiri to eat a little. She thought of Sophie, and knew that the grief she felt being here with Akiri, would be doubled when Sophie returned.

40

SOPHIE

T he beach on the Western shore of Ledora was a little rockier than the beach on the Eastern side. Sophie had not gone to the castle or the Golden City. She stayed on the beach all night, waiting for Bastian to come and tell her that the battle was won. He promised that he would come back to her. She felt so helpless. She could still cast, and she could have helped, but Bastian insisted that she go to Ledora.

Sophie spent two days on the ship to get to Ledora, and she now had spent the night on the beach, waiting for news, so when she finally saw two dragons soaring her way in the early afternoon, she was overcome with joy. She watched Dominic and Bastian land on the beach and ran over to greet them, but stopped short when she saw their sullen faces.

"What happened?" Sophie asked.

"Maybe you should sit down," Dominic suggested.

"Just tell me, please," she said. Dominic tried to gather himself, to find the right words. No amount of delicacy was going to soften this blow and he knew it was going to be hard news to hear.

"It's Gabe, Sophie…" Dominic's voice cracked as he choked back tears. "He didn't make it out of the battle." he finished.

Sophie stepped away from them with her mouth open and her hands clasped tightly over it. She shook her head in disbelief.

"No, no, please tell me it isn't true." Her hands shook as she spoke.

"I'm sorry, Sophie, I know how much he meant to you." Bastian moved forward to hold her and she collapsed into his arms and cried.

"I'm going to go get dressed and then gather Akiri's people and have them go to the ships, are you okay here with Sophie?" Dominic asked as he handed Bastian a change of clothes from the bag he brought with them.

"We'll be okay, we will meet you back at the castle," Bastian said.

Bastian put his trousers on so that at least he wasn't completely nude, and then sat down beside Sophie in one of the very few patches of soft sand on the rocky beach. He put his arm around her as she tried to stifle her tears. He didn't speak, and Sophie wasn't ready to talk about it, so they listened only to the ocean waves lapping onto the shore, and the sound of the seagulls overhead. Sophie laid down and rested her head on Bastian's thigh.

He stroked her hair, and let her tears dampen his trouser leg.

"Hey, maybe we should go eat something before we go back," Bastian suggested. Sophie agreed and stood up. She had cried out all the tears she had left and now there was a painful throbbing at her temples and behind her eyes which she was sure were puffy and as red as her hair.

Bastian and Sophie walked into the Western gate of The Golden City and found a tavern that was still serving lunch. The smell of seafood chowder greeted them as they walked through the tavern door and Sophie's stomach grumbled. She hadn't even realized how hungry she was. They each ordered a bowl of chowder and a basket of fresh rolls.

Even though she was hungry, Sophie ate a roll, then took one bite of chowder and instantly felt ill. Her skin paled from its normal rosy complexion and she had to push the bowl away so that the smell wouldn't be as strong.

"Are you okay?" Bastian asked.

"I'm- nope!" Sophie clutched her mouth as she shot up from her seat and ran to the privy, which was in the garden outside the back door of the tavern. Sophie never ran so fast in her life and barely got her face over the chamber pot before the bread she had eaten made a reappearance, accompanied by an acidic fluid that she didn't remember ever ingesting. Sophie drew some water from the well to wash out the chamber pot and she cupped her hands and brought the fresh water to her mouth to rinse out the taste. She had almost finished when Bastian came out to check on her.

"How are you feeling?" He asked.

"Not great, but better than I was a minute ago."

"I already paid so we can go back to the castle and rest before we fly back to Ash." Bastian put his arm around her and she leaned into him as they left the tavern.

Dominic was directing groups of people to the caravan of wagons when they arrived at the castle. He carried bags for elderly citizens and helped others who could not walk long distances into the wagon.

"Hi, glad you made it back, we have one more group after this, they're finishing up lunch in the banquet hall right now. Feel free to freshen up or get some rest, I will have Hannah come wake you for dinner and we can fly out just after sunset." Dominic said.

"Okay, we will see you at dinner." Bastian smiled and patted Dominic on the shoulder. This side of Dominic was not one that Bastian had ever been here to witness before. He admired Dominic's helpful nature and thought about what a great king he was going to make someday.

Sophie's room was just as she had left it the last time she was in Ledora. The dress she had worn to the ball the night she found out that Gabe was engaged to Akiri caught her eye as they walked in. It had been freshly laundered and hung on the hook beside the wardrobe. Sophie had purchased many dresses since she started participating in court life, the wardrobe was full of them.

She opened the door to the old armoire and slid the dresses one at a time from the right to the left until she found a black one. It was made of lace and tulle. Sophie rubbed the material between her fingers as she pulled it from the cabinet and held it up.

"What are you doing?" Bastian asked.

"I need something to wear for the funeral, I should pack it," Sophie said, the sadness on her face was apparent and Bastian wished he could take it away, and carry it for her somehow, but he knew that it was not possible.

"Kamara told Dominic that we would hold the funeral as soon as we got back, maybe instead of packing it, you should wear it." Bastian walked up behind Sophie and wrapped his arms around her. He kissed the top of her head as she continued to examine the dress.

"I think I will wear it, that's a good idea." Sophie yawned, and Bastian took the freshly laundered dress off the hook, hung it inside the wardrobe, and then hung Sophie's funeral dress in its place. He led Sophie to the bed and pulled down the comforter, blanket, and sheet for her to crawl into it.

"Are you going to lay with me?" Sophie asked.

"If you want me to, but if you need space, I can sleep in the chair," he replied.

"No, I need you to hold me, I feel so lonely, and if you were not here... I don't even want to think about that." Sophie said.

Sophie was laying on her left side and Bastian crawled into bed behind her and held her close. He felt her body heaving as she started to cry again, but he continued to hold her and softly kiss her hair now and again until she fell asleep. He knew that he should get some rest too, but he couldn't. He was worried about Sophie and wanted to be awake if she needed him.

When Hannah came to tell them that it was time for dinner, Bastian got up first and heated some water for the wash basin so that Sophie could wash up. He brought her a warm, wet, face towel so that she could wash the sleep from her eyes. She stood up and stretched, bending forward to touch her toes, and then to each side to loosen the muscles that had tensed up from crying.

Sophie was wearing trousers and a blue tunic and a brown leather belt which she thought was good enough for dinner. "I'll change after dinner," Sophie said as Bastian began laying out her dress to make getting into it easier.

"Okay, It will be ready for you," he said with all the smile he could muster. He could feel her pain, like a blacksmith's vise crushing his chest and he knew that her pain must be a thousand times worse than that.

"I'm ready, let's get this over with," Sophie said.

"We don't have to go, I can ask Hannah to bring our dinner up here if you're not ready."

"No, I need to face this." Sophie took in a deep breath and looked at the door.

"I'll be right beside you."

The table was set when they arrived in the banquet hall. King Haki, Prince Dominic, and Princess Kamara were already seated at one end of the table. Hannah led

Sophie and Bastian to the chairs across from them and as soon as they were seated a server filled their drinking cups with water.

"I am truly sorry for your loss, Queen Sophie, I know that King Gabriel was a very close childhood friend of yours. We don't need to speak anymore on the matter because I know how much it must pain you, but I would like to toast to you, may the Goddess give you strength and safe travels, and I would also like to toast to King Gabriel. From what I hear, his sacrifice, and quick thinking saved Queen Akiri and the people of Ash. To Sophie, and Gabriel." The king raised his cup.

"To Sophie and Gabe," they all repeated.

"Now, on to happy news, Prince Dominic and his lovely bride-to-be, have chosen to wed, here in Ledora on the Summer Solstice, at which time, they will assume the throne as King and Queen, and I will be Dominic's advisor until my end of days."

Sophie was happy for them, but it was difficult to outwardly show it. She congratulated them and went through the motions as everyone toasted. She ate a bite or two of each course, not wanting to re-live the seafood chowder incident. Sophie wasn't listening to the rest of the conversations; she only thought of returning to Ash. She had never been to a funeral or been through the grief of losing someone so important to her. Sophie looked at Kamara, who was smiling and talking to King Haki, ready to get married and become Queen of Ledora. It gave Sophie hope that the grief she felt would not consume the rest life and that one day, she too would be happy again.

41

KAMARA

T he royal families and the staff of Castle Ash gathered at dawn on the Northern beach after a procession through the ruins of Ash. White remnants of the
wooden houses still floated softly on the breeze and a
light fog hung in the distance, waiting for them just off
the shore.

Gabe's body was unwrapped and placed on a stone
slab. Nadine's assistant rubbed oil all over his body to
prepare him for the fire. Everyone was dressed in black,
and Akiri wore a veil of mourning as per the tradition of
a widowed Queen. Akiri also had a veil made for Sophie.
She knew that Sophie loved Gabe just as much and that
she deserved to receive condolences as much, if not,
more than she did.

Sophie and Akiri stood side by side with their arms
linked. Since Sophie couldn't shift, Akiri asked Dominic
to breathe fire over the altar. He stood at the head of the

altar and looked down at Gabe. Even in dragon form, the sadness showed on his face. Kamara linked her arm through Akiri's and Bastian held his out for Sophie. The four of them watched as Dominic drew in a deep breath and exhaled a cone of fire across Gabe's body. The oil fueled the flames and released a fragrant scent that covered the smell of the burned flesh. Everyone stood on either side of the altar and watched the fire burn until there was nothing left but ashes. Nadine scooped the ashes into three identical urns. She sealed the lids with wax and then gave one to Akiri, and two to Sophie.

"This one is for King Gabriel's mother, will you please deliver it to her?" Nadine asked. Sophie nodded. Bastian took one of the urns from Sophie to help her as she prepared her bag. Sophie couldn't remember where she had left her father's leather backpack that she always carried, so she packed the urns into a cloth messenger bag from Ledora and wrapped the urns in her spare clothing to protect them.

"I'm ready when you are." Sophie turned to Bastian. He offered to fly her home to Blackwater to see her family, and Gabe's. Sophie hugged Akiri and promised to see her soon. She said goodbye to everyone else and then she and Bastian walked down the beach away from the funeral site. Akiri watched as Bastian flew away with Sophie on his back.

"Come, Your Grace, we will warm you a bath while the builders prepare the funeral rafts." Mister Koffery led Akiri away from the beach. Kamara waited for Dominic to shift and dress, which he waited to do until the beach was deserted.

That night, Akiri, Dominic, and Kamara sat together in a small sitting room, offering company to one another and sharing their memories of Gabe. Kamara did not doubt that all of their memories together could not compare to the memories that Sophie held of him and she wished that Sophie was there to share some memories with them. It had been a strange couple of years, but in this time, they all had managed to become friends; a year before, Kamara never would have thought that they would be friends with Akiri and she was glad for it but wished that their friendship had come because of happier circumstances.

"Can you guys keep a secret?" Akiri asked.

"Sure," Dominic said, and Kamara nodded excitedly.

"Follow me." Akiri led them out the back doors and to her lair. They walked down the stairs and into an empty lair.

"What's the secret?" Kamara asked. Akiri cast light on a stone in the back of the lair and it illuminated from the back wall, toward them in a soft glow. She waved her hand to drop the illusion on the lair. A nest appeared against the wall to the right and Kamara walked forward to look at the eggs inside of it. Six eggs, all dark bluish-green in color.

"Feel this," Akiri walked to the nest and placed her hand on the floor, Kamara and Dominic did the same. The floor was hot, like a fire burned beneath it, but the floor was made of stone and therefore protected the eggs from harm.

"How did you manage to get all of this done?" Kamara asked.

"I asked the builder's guild to make some upgrades before I left to go to Ophay. The morning before the battle, I felt a hard knot in my stomach, it hurt, like I was going to explode. I didn't tell anyone, not even Gabe because I didn't want anyone to know until after the battle. I knew I couldn't handle the pain in my human form, but my dragon form could. I went to the lair and to my surprise, I began laying eggs. I knew they would be safe if no one knew they were here.

"Are these... Gabe's?" Kamara asked.

"No," Akiri said. Her face fell and she looked pained by this.

"I have already decided, raising six baby dragons will be too difficult, there are six eggs, which means two for Ophay, two for Ledora, and two for Lapis Highland."

"Akiri, you don't have to..." Dominic started.

"I know, but I *want* to." Akiri waved her hand and the illusion appeared again, the nest faded away and they were once again standing in a dingy old stone lair.

Kamara hugged Akiri, "I am so happy for you." She said, but Akiri heard the sadness in her voice.

"What's wrong?" Akiri asked.

"I just long to be a mother, Sophie is with child, you have baby dragons on the way, but we have decided to wait until we are married and take the throne, any children we have before that will not be considered eligible for the throne of Ledora.

"As King and Queen couldn't you change that law?" Akiri asked.

"It's not a law, it is a belief of the Ledoran people that the throne must be passed to a legitimate child of the King and Queen only after they assume the throne. A child born before that is not viewed as royal and therefore could not rule after us," Dominic explained, "but it's okay, we will be wed this summer, and we will have as many children as you want," Dominic promised.

"I should get some sleep, there's a lot to do before tomorrow night when the ships arrive," Akiri said as they walked back into the castle. She gave Kamara a quick sly smile as she walked toward her room. Kamara looked at Dominic, he didn't seem to catch it."

When Kamara and Dominic got to their room, they undressed for bed. Kamara approached Dominic just as he pulled his tunic off and stood on her toes to press her lips to his.

"Just because we can't have children right now, doesn't mean we can't *practice*," Kamara said as she dropped to her knees and took him in her mouth. He moaned in surprise but did not push her away, it felt good, and he wanted more. She felt him harden in her mouth and caressed him with her tongue. She put her arms around him and placed her hands on his backside. She pulled his hips forward as she took him deeper. He looked up at the ceiling and groaned, hungry with need. He bent down and picked her up off of her knees. He turned her around and bent her over the bed. He would not wait a moment longer to give her what she wanted. He inserted himself into her wet, tight sex slowly, at first, working his erection deeper inside her. She screamed with excitement and begged him for more as he pulled her hips back and thrust his own forward. He had to stop, he felt himself getting close and he knew that if they had a child out of wedlock it would never be accepted as their heir. He pulled out of her and waited a moment for the feeling to pass, which was just long enough for Kamara to turn around and lay down in front of him. She opened her legs and looked up at him as he bent down to kiss her lips. His braids fell loose around their faces like a curtain. He didn't even need a hand to guide himself back inside of her. He gazed into her silver eyes as he slid in and out of her slowly, drawing out the duration of pleasure and delaying their climax. They made love for hours, and when he did finally allow them to reach climax, he made sure she went first multiple times, then he pulled out of her and spilled his seed on her stomach so he would not impregnate her.

"I love you," he said as he gazed down at her beautiful dark brown skin and her silver eyes which reminded him of diamonds. Her skin glistened with sweat and her cheeks had a slight golden shimmer.

"I love you too. I can't wait until we are married." Kamara reached her hand to the back of his neck and pulled his lips to hers. He felt the hardening of her nipples against his chest and his body responded similarly. They made love again and when they finished a few hours later they were both satisfied and exhausted. They slept better than they had in weeks and when they woke up, it was lunchtime.

After the funeral for the fallen citizens of Ash, the people loaded back onto the ships to head for Black-water Bay. They would port one at a time in Torzana and then walk through the forest to their new home, The Kingdom of Ophay. Dominic and Kamara flew back that night to begin the town's construction before people started arriving.

The next morning, Laughlin brought the entire builders sect of the guild and they got to work. Kamara made them all fresh apple cider and cooked a feast for the builders.

"Where is Juniper?" Kamara asked.

"She's at the cabin with Dusk and Opal, our daughter," Laughlin replied.

"Oh, that's right! We have been gone for so long it seems, I forgot that she was with child the last time we were here. I feel like such a terrible friend now." Kamara said.

"Nonsense, you were dealing with very important things, like rescuing an entire country and defeating an evil dragon. When we finish building here, Juniper and I would love to have you come and visit us," Laughlin said.

"We would be honored," Kamara told him.

42

SOPHIE

S ophie dug a hole under the willow tree and poured some of Gabe's ashes into it. She took the remaining ashes and emptied the urn into the creek where he used to wade and throw rocks. She sat under the willow tree and felt the breeze on her face. Sophie closed her eyes and cried, there was so much she wanted to say to him.

"Gabe, I miss you so much. I'm so sorry that we never had a chance to explore the feelings between us and I know it was my fault. I left for the Highland, and you joined the guild, got married, and now here we are. I thought that we would have so much more time, I always thought there would be more time. When I left for the wizard tower right after we got back from Choddrath, I thought when I finished training that I would come home and we would be together. I wonder if the reason nothing ever worked out for us was that you were destined for something greater. I know that it was you that softened Akiri's heart, we heard about some of the awful things she did, but you... you could always see the good in people, and you brought it out in her. She has become a friend to me now and I know she grieves for you the same way I do. It seems strange, talking to you here in our spot like I can see you laying in the moss with your hands behind your head listening as I rattle on about this or that. You were always a good listener. Bastian and I are going to have a baby by winter solstice this year, I suppose I ought to introduce him to my dad and mom. Do you think that my dad will like him?" The wind kicked up and blew a few leaves from the nearby oak tree into Sophie's hair.

"You're right, he will never think anyone is good enough for me, but he will at least be civil, I hope. I suppose at some point we will get married, or not, we haven't really talked about it." Sophie smiled, happy that she could feel Gabe's spirit there with her.

"I delivered an urn of your ashes to your mother, that was the second hardest thing I have ever gone through, the first of course, being your funeral. She cried, I cried, it was a whole thing. She's doing okay though, all things considered. I checked on the deed to her house, in the event of your death, ownership was transferred to the guild, that's smart. They're taking good care of her, she even started dating again. Her boyfriend seems nice, he is a lot like you, I think you'd like him. He's good to your mom too and that's what matters most. Anyway, I should be getting back. Bastian is waiting for me at Blackwater Tavern and we're going to go break the news to my family. Wish me luck." She stood up and when the wind blew again, she felt a warm tingle on her cheek, like someone's hand gently caressed it. She knew it was Gabe and it made her feel like everything was going to be okay.

Blackwater Tavern was a hole-in-the-wall tavern that only locals knew about, so when strangers wandered in, it wasn't hard to spot them in the crowd of regulars. Bastian was sitting at a big round table, drinking and playing cards with Old Man Brenner and his normal round of poker players. They were betting coppers and silver pieces. Brenner rarely played for gold, he liked to keep his game friendly, and he found that when people lose something as precious as gold, they were the opposite of friendly.

"Hiya Sophie! Your boyfriend was just telling us all about your terrible poker-playing skills, care to lose a few coppers?" Brenner teased. Sophie smiled.

"Boyfriend? Where? I don't remember anyone asking to be my boyfriend." Sophie looked all around and turned in a circle scanning the tavern with her hand on her eyebrows like she was shielding them from the sun." The guys at the table all laughed and nudged Bastian.

"Well, I uh- I thought it was just an unspoken agreement." Bastian winked at her and smiled.

Sophie blushed, Bastian's smile was adorable. He had dimples that she had never noticed before and his blue eyes sparkled.

"If you don't speak it, how do you know if you agree?" Sophie sat down next to Old Man Brenner.

"That's a good point there, Sophie," Brenner said. She looked at Bastian who smiled like a kid who got caught with their hand in the cookie jar.

"Forgive me, please, for my grave error in social etiquette." Bastian got up and walked over to Sophie. He dropped to one knee in front of her and reached for her hand.

"My darling, Sophie, will you make me the happiest man in the world and make our courtship official, here in front of these witnesses?" Bastian kissed her hand. His lips were warm and gentle against her skin.

"Well when you put it like that, how could I refuse?" Sophie leaned forward and kissed him. "Now are you ready to lose at poker? I've been practicing, Mr. Brenner, you sure you want me to play?" Sophie joked.

"Deal her in, Lenny," Brenner said. The man with the cards shuffled and then dealt them all two cards, except for himself, He wasn't playing, just dealing. Sophie looked at her cards, she had been dealt pocket aces. She placed her cards face down in front of her and slid two coppers into the pot to match the big blind. Play circled the table and when the pot was good, the dealer turned three cards face up in the middle of the table; a three of hearts, a Jack of spades, and a three of clubs. Brenner was next to the dealer, Lenny, and he bet a silver on the flop. Sophie matched, Bastian matched, the guy next to Bastian folded, and the guy on the other side of Lenny matched.

"Pot's good," Lenny said and he flipped the next card; ten of diamonds. Brenner threw in two silver, Sophie thought about her hand, two pair was pretty good, but if Brenner had another three though, she was out. *Ah, what the hell* Sophie threw in her two silver to match the pot and looked at Bastian who slid his cards toward the dealer.

"Awe, folding? Bastian... tsk tsk," Sophie scolded, jokingly. The guy next to Lenny also folded.

"Okie dokie, pot's good. Lenny said, and laid the river on the table; ace of hearts. It was Brenner's bet. Sophie saw him glance at her, but her face was stone, she wasn't giving anything away. Brenner threw in a silver piece just to bet something, and Sophie raised. She put in three silver pieces. Everyone let out an "ooooooh" in unison as they looked at Brenner for his next move.

Brenner thought about the cards on the table, looked at the cards in his hand one more time, and then threw in his two silver to match Sophie's bet.

"I'm only doing this 'cause I wanna see whachu got in your hand there, Soph," he said as he tossed the coins to the center of the table. Brenner turned his cards first, Sophie was right, he did have another three.

"I got three of a kind," he said proudly.

"That's pretty good, but I got a full house," Sophie said as she laid down her aces. "Three aces and two threes."

"Yep, ya beat me fair n' square, Sophie Rend. Your father will hear about this, young lady." Brenner teased. Sophie laughed as she scooped up the coins in the center of the table.

"In this small town Mr. Brenner, I would be surprised if he hadn't already."

"Ha ha! You got that right!" Brenner laughed heartily. "You playing another hand, Miss Sophie?"

"I would, but Daddy hasn't met my boyfriend yet, and I was hoping we could share the news over supper, we better get going so I can let them know we plan to join them," Sophie said.

"Okay, well, young man, it was nice to meet you, make sure you take good care of this girl right here, I wouldn't want to make an enemy of her father," Brenner joked.

"Yes, Sir," Bastian said as he shook the man's hand.

"That was a good hand back there, I didn't know you knew how to play poker, not many people do, I have only seen a game played twice in my life, once here, just now, and then once on Immernacht," Bastian said as they walked down the cobblestone street toward Sophie's parents' house.

"I imagine there are a lot of things about me that you don't know yet, and no one knows how much time we have, so you better start asking some questions." Sophie smiled but kept looking forward.

"Okay, what is your favorite color?"

"Really? All the questions you could ask and you're going with that?" Sophie asked.

"What am I supposed to ask?"

I don't know, things like what I want to do for a living, or how many kids I want, you know, things that will help you get to know me," she said.

"Oh, okay, who is the-" Bastian began, but Sophie cut him off.

"No, you already asked your question, my favorite color is emerald green. It's my turn now. What is your mom like?" Sophie asked.

"Well, my birth mother passed during childbirth, so I don't remember her. I was adopted by the Delacroix, the royal family of Immernacht."

"Is your mother the Queen, are you Prince of Immernacht?" Sophie asked in surprise.

"Sort of. The King and Queen have two children of their own, His Royal Highness, Louis Delacroix, and his sister, Her Royal Highness, Serena Delacroix. My official title is Duke, and I am addressed as 'Your Grace' or 'Your Highness,' but never *Royal Highness*, because I am not in line for the throne, I can only serve the sovereign." Bastian said.

"We're here," Sophie said as she stepped up to the front door of a modest house made of stone.

"I think I need a kiss for luck first, I'm worried your parents won't like me." Bastian gave her a charming smile and leaned down to meet her lips. He pulled her closer, resting one hand on the back of her neck and his other on the small of her back. They broke apart quickly when they heard someone clear their throat behind them.

"Father, I want you to meet Bastian Delacroix, Bastian, this is my father, Leon," Sophie said.

"It is a pleasure to meet you, Sir." Bastian extended his hand to Leon. It seemed like a long and awkward amount of time before Leon spoke, or took Bastian's hand, but in the end, he did both.

"Welcome to our home, Bastian. Please, come in." Leon led them through the front door and then sat down to take off his boots. Sophie breathed in the sweet smell of home. Her mother had been baking, it smelled of cinnamon and vanilla. Sophie took Bastian's hand and led him into the kitchen where her mother, Samantha was just taking cinnamon sweet rolls out of the wood fire oven.

"Sophie! Oh, I missed you so much!" Samantha exclaimed. She crossed the kitchen, wiped her hands on her apron, and then wrapped Sophie in her arms. "Who is this handsome gentleman you've brought to meet us today?" Samantha studied Bastian's face as she reached out to greet him.

"I'm Bastian, Ma'am, it's lovely to meet you," he said. Sophie could tell he was nervous because little beads of sweat started appearing on his forehead and he wiped his hands on his trousers more than once before taking Samantha's hand.

"Relax," Sophie whispered.

"Bastian and I would like to join you for dinner tonight if that's okay?"

"You know there's always room at our table for you and guests," Samantha said.

"Hey, uh, Bastian is it?" Leon walked into the kitchen.

"Yes, sir."

"I was wondering if you would give me a hand with something? I could use some more muscle."

"Happy to help, Mr. Rend," Bastian told him as he followed Leon out of the room.

Samantha watched them walk outside and waited until Bastian closed the door behind them before asking Sophie what she really to ask her.

"How are you, honey? I was so sorry to hear about what happened to Gabe, he was such a nice boy." Sophie nodded.

"This whole year has been a whirlwind, first, Ryul left for Ravenhall, and then I found out that Gabe was engaged, I met Bastian, and then what happened with Gabe, It's been hard," she replied.

"You know I am always here for you, any time." Samantha held her daughter in a soft embrace and Sophie loved the way her mother always smelled like the sweet shop. "You look happy, though. Something is different about you, I can't quite put my finger on it." Samantha looked at her daughter suspiciously.

"My hair got longer," Sophie joked.

"That must be it. Now, why don't you go wash up and help me chop some vegetables for dinner?"

Sophie grabbed a pail and walked outside to the well. She could hear her father talking to Bastian on the back side of the house. She knew that it was wrong to eavesdrop, but she couldn't help it. She wanted her parents to like him.

"Why are you here?" Leon asked.

"Because Sophie asked me to come."

"Your father didn't send you?"

"No, Sir. Why would my father send me?" Bastian sounded confused.

"To procure a bargaining chip, perhaps?"

"What do you mean? What would he need a bargaining chip for?"

"I want you to leave. Make something up, and go back to Immernacht. Remind your father that the magical protections that shroud your city were part of an agreement, and I've held up my end." Leon said.

"NO!" Sophie screamed. She threw the bucket down on the ground and it clattered as it rolled to Leon's feet. "You don't get to decide the details of MY life anymore. Every time you're afraid someone might love me, you send them away, you did it with Gabe, and now you're doing it with Bastian. I am not your prisoner." Sophie shook with anger.

"Sophie, you don't understand about his family, you don't know what they are, I'm only trying to protect you." Leon pleaded.

"We're leaving, come on, Bastian." Sophie grabbed his hand and began pulling Bastian away from her father. "And to think, we came here to tell you that you were going to be a grandfather, but I guess you don't have to worry about that now." Sophie spat.

Oh no... She's pregnant. Leon's heart sank. He wasn't certain if it was a trick of the light or his imagination, but he could have sworn he saw a smirk of triumph on Bastian's face as he put his arm around Sophie's waist and led her away.

ACKNOWLEDGMENTS

I would like to thank my editor, Mina, for talking with me about the characters and plots in my book like it's a show we are watching together on HBO or Netflix. (HINT HINT) I would also like to thank my husband for being the ever-constant support for me and my writing goals! I would like to thank my Grandmother, Charlotte, for giving me all of her books after she read them. I also need to say thank you to the booktok community for endless recommendations, writing sprints, and publishing advice, and also for being a source of my procrastination when my brain and the blank page did not want to connect. Thank you to my Alpha team, and Beta team for your insight and feedback! You helped make this book the best that it could be!

I can't forget about the most important person, YOU! Yes, you, the reader. Thank you for reading my book and supporting my lifelong dream of being an author!

ABOUT AUTHOR

C.L. Carner is a U.S. Army veteran and former teacher. She is also the author of My Fair Verona and The Orb of Dragonkind. Due to her wandering spirit, she has lived in many states, including Alaska, Georgia, and Ohio. Mrs. Carner currently resides in Texas with her husband, two children, and her golden retriever.

CPSIA information can be obtained
at www.ICGtesting.com
Printed in the USA
BVHW032034100323
660178BV00002B/651